THE ONE THAT GOT AWAY

OLIVIA SPRING

Boldwood

First published in Great Britain in 2024 by Boldwood Books Ltd.

Cover Design by Rachel Lawston

Cover Illustration: Rachel Lawston

A CIP catalogue record for this book is available from the British Library.

Paperback ISBN 978-1-83617-992-4

Large Print ISBN 978-1-83617-993-1

Hardback ISBN 978-1-83617-991-7

Ebook ISBN 978-1-83617-994-8

Kindle ISBN 978-1-83617-995-5

Audio CD ISBN 978-1-83617-986-3

MP3 CD ISBN 978-1-83617-987-0

Digital audio download ISBN 978-1-83617-988-7

Boldwood Books Ltd
23 Bowerdean Street
London SW6 3TN
www.boldwoodbooks.com

To Loz: my amazing niece.

1

STELLA

'Yes, yes, *yes!*' I cried out, lifting my hips off the bed as the waves of pleasure rippled through me.

But just as I was on the verge of seeing stars, the sweet buzzing sensation stopped and my vibrator died.

'No, no, no!' I pleaded, pressing the on/off button repeatedly, hoping I could bring it back to life. *Wishful thinking.* 'Aaarghhh!' I groaned in frustration as my bum crashed onto the mattress.

Talk about bad timing.

I was *so* close.

Life could be really cruel sometimes.

I should've known not to read that steamy romance novel before bed. If I hadn't got so worked up about the unthinkable things the hot hockey player was doing to the female main character in the shower, I wouldn't have needed *emergency assistance*.

All wasn't lost though. I just had to get some new batteries and I'd be good to go.

After placing the neon-pink silicone rod beside me, I pulled on my dressing gown, washed my hands in the bathroom, tossed my thick curly brown hair into a messy bun, then raced downstairs. The sooner I returned to finish the job, the sooner I could go to sleep.

The light was on in the kitchen. Shit. I didn't realise she was back already.

'Hi, Mum.' I breezed through the door, trying to act natural. 'How was your date?'

Mum was sitting at the table with a pair of lace knickers in one hand and a needle and thread in the other. She was still dressed in the sparkly lilac dress she'd left in two hours ago, but had tied her freshly dyed black hair up.

Her light brown skin was a similar shade to mine, except tonight Mum was wearing her favourite rose-coloured blusher, which made her cheekbones pop.

'Fine, I suppose,' Mum replied. 'Thought I'd come home early and get a head start on those new orders. Thanks for saving me the last few slices of pizza. I'll have that for breakfast.'

'You're welcome,' I said, striding towards the drawer.

'What you looking for?' Mum said, as I started rooting through the disorganised pile of light bulbs and unused gadgets.

'Just some, erm, triple A batteries. Do we have any?'

'What do you need them for?'

'Just…' I paused, thinking of a plausible response. '*Stuff.*'

Mum and I were close, but some things, like what I chose to do in my bedroom during the rare evenings I was home alone, were best kept to myself.

'For your vibrator?' she said casually.

'What?' My cheeks flamed with embarrassment. Thank goodness I had my back to her. 'No, it's for my… er… I…'

'Oh, *come on*, Stella! I didn't raise you to be a prude! Nothing wrong with a bit of *self-care*. I was listening to an interview with that TV presenter Davina McCall the other day who said that every woman should have some lube and a toy in her bedside drawer. And she's right. Women have been pleasing themselves for centuries. Did you know that Cleopatra invented the first vibrator?'

'Er, no...'

'Apparently she filled a container with bees and all their angry buzzing made it vibrate. Then she put it on her...'

'Mum!' I turned to face her, horror written all over my face. 'I don't need specifics! I get the idea.'

'I think it's *genius!*' She threw her head back, laughing. 'But you wouldn't need buzzing bees or batteries if you found yourself a decent man...'

'Give me a break!' I sighed, sensing another lecture was coming.

'What? I'd love grandkids whilst I'm still young enough to enjoy them! And as advanced as your Waterfall Turbo 3,000 is, I'm pretty sure it doesn't have the ability to impregnate you!' She laughed again.

'Not funny.'

I didn't even want to know how Mum knew the name of my one and only adult toy. It was at times like these that I regretted moving back home. If I had my own place, I wouldn't have to suffer through discussions like this.

'I'm only joking. Well, sort of. It's not just about grandchildren. I know things are different these days. I just worry about you, that's all.'

'I'm fine. Don't worry. I'll meet someone one day.'

'How? You deleted all the apps and you spend all your time here, at home working. I'm grateful for your help, you know I am, but since you've moved back home you've got stuck in a bit of a rut. Apart from seeing Samantha, you never go out. You're not going to find a man sitting on the sofa every night. Unless of course you fancy the pizza delivery guy!'

Kevin was sweet and always made sure my Meat Feast arrived nice and hot, but he wasn't the man for me.

And I definitely wasn't using the apps again. Not after what happened before.

'I haven't had time! We've been rushed off our feet with orders and I had to create the new website and...'

'The website's been done for months! It's been over a year since you've dated. You're thirty-one. I'm sixty and even *I'm* getting more action than you. It's not right! You used to love going out. And you used to tell me you wanted to travel the world. But apart from the time you came to visit my family in Jamaica two years ago, I can't remember the last time you ventured further than the high street!'

'I'm saving up for a mortgage! I can't fritter money away on holidays,' I protested. Property in London these days wasn't cheap.

'You can't put your life on hold whilst you do that though, sweetheart. Life's for living, *now*. I want you to get out there and enjoy yourself. Travel to somewhere hot, feel the sun on your skin, meet new people, have new experiences. Be happy.'

'I'm fine!' I repeated, not sure whether I was trying to convince Mum or myself. 'I'm going back to bed.' I closed the drawer and strode towards the door.

'Wait!' She grabbed my arm. 'There's something I need to show you.' She plucked a glossy magazine off the table, flicked through it and thrust a double-page spread under my nose. 'Look. It's another feature on that hotel I was telling you about before. There's three case studies of women in their thirties who were unlucky in love like you. Then they all went to The Love Hotel and found the men of their dreams!'

'Not this again,' I huffed. 'I told you months ago, it's not for people like me.'

The Love Hotel was an exclusive luxury resort near Marbella in Spain, which claimed to help people find their perfect match.

'It's for *anyone* who wants to meet someone special. People arrive single and leave madly in love. It's magical!'

'It's super fancy and expensive. Never mind saving up for a mortgage to buy a flat, the price of staying there for two weeks is a mortgage on its own.'

'Yes, it's pricey, but you get what you pay for. It's five-star, all-inclusive accommodation and they hire the world's best match-making experts to find the perfect partner for all their guests – that can't come cheap.'

'Exactly! Even if I thought it was a good idea, which I don't, unless I win the lottery, there's no way I'd be able to afford to go. You have to pay a massive deposit without any guarantee that you'll even go to the hotel, never mind finding your *knight in shining armour*.'

'They ask for money upfront so their experts can search for a match on their high-tech database. You can't expect them to do that for free. I really think it's worth a try. Read the article. See for yourself.'

My gaze dropped to the pages. There was a couple kissing on the beach with a backdrop of an admittedly gorgeous, sun-drenched hotel.

'It's all very nice, but like I said, it's out of my price range. My holiday budget is more Margate than Marbella. Night, Mum.' I left the room.

Forget about the batteries. Thanks to that conversation, any desire I had ten minutes ago had evaporated.

I slipped back under the duvet, squeezed my eyes shut and willed the sleep to come, but it resisted. My mind was still racing.

Of course I'd love to travel more. And find the man of my

dreams. Who wouldn't? But I wasn't ready. I didn't want to be pressured into dating again.

When I moved back home a year and a half ago, after breaking up with Tom, Mum went on and on, saying I needed to 'get out there' again.

Eventually she wore me down. I joined different apps, went on several dates and they all ended badly.

So, no. This time I was standing my ground. There'd be no apps and I definitely wouldn't be applying for that posh hotel.

By next year hopefully I'd be able to scrape together enough for a deposit and could finally get a mortgage and buy a proper place of my own.

Once I'd got settled, I could think about dating again.

But until then, I was just fine being single.

All I needed was romance novels and my buzz buddy.

And maybe a spare set of batteries.

2

MAX

'Damn. This is adorable.' As I looked at the colourful painting my best friend Colton put on my desk, my heart squeezed.

'What can I say?' he beamed. 'My daughter is talented.'

'And she really painted this for me?'

'She did.'

Well, fuck. What was it about children? They knew how to get you right in the feels.

Colton took off his dark grey suit jacket then sat down. His short Afro hair looked like it'd been shaved at the sides since I last saw him. Wouldn't surprise me. He always looked sharp.

'So, obviously I can see this is the sky.' I pointed to the blue brushstrokes at the top which had a ginormous yellow circle that I knew must be the sun. 'And I'm guessing I'm the white guy with the dark brown hair and big muscles.'

'*Obviously,*' he chuckled.

'Nice to know someone recognises all the hard work I put in at the gym!' I laughed. 'But why am I with your wife and kid? Where are you? Did you send Betty to bed with no ice cream or do something to piss her off so she deliberately left you out?'

'No. That's not Natalie and Betty standing in the photo. That's *your* wife and kid.'

'Wow. You and Natalie got your sweet, innocent daughter to draw a fake family painting just to convince me to join some dating apps? Wasn't using her to make me sign up to that other stupid thing bad enough? That's low, man. Even for you!'

'Nope. She did that all by herself. When you didn't come round for breakfast on Sunday, she asked why. And when we told her you were away, she asked if she could make a painting for you and voilà – here it is.'

'Well, tell her I said thanks. Here.' I reached beside my desk and handed him a large bag. 'Got these for you guys.'

Colton took the bag and when he opened it a big smile spread across his face.

'Olive oil, Ibérico ham and two bottles of our favourite Rioja? You should visit our factory in Spain more often if you're going to bring back gifts like this! Thanks!'

'You're welcome. It was worth the trip. I think the new olive oil body cream will be a big hit.'

I was the Managing Director of Olibella, a natural skincare company. It was the polar opposite of the career I'd always imagined I'd have, but as Colton always said, I had to make the most of the cards life had dealt me.

'Sounds like it'll give a nice boost to Q4 profits when it launches.'

'Should do,' I nodded. As well as being my best friend, Colton was our Financial Director, so success for him was always measured in numbers and the bottom line. 'Oh and there's some souvenirs in the bag for Betty too. Couldn't forget my goddaughter.'

'She'll be so happy when she sees this!' He pulled out the

pink T-shirt. 'You could be happy too if you stopped being such a workaholic.'

'I'm not a workaholic!'

'What time did you leave the office last night?'

'Can't remember,' I lied.

'Bet it wasn't before ten.'

I definitely wasn't gonna tell him it was just before midnight.

'I had stuff to catch up on. That's what happens when I'm away from the office. The work piles up and it's not gonna get done by itself.'

'That's why you have staff. Like I keep saying, you need to delegate more. Then you'd have time to get a hobby. And a life. All this working isn't healthy.'

'I am healthy. And I already have a hobby: I go to the gym.'

'Yeah, the one you had built here in this office building. I'm talking about a hobby *outside* of these four walls. Apart from coming to my place, I can't remember you going somewhere that wasn't work-related. When was the last time you had fun, took a holiday or *dated*?'

'Not this again,' I sighed and undid the top button of my crisp white shirt. It had suddenly got hot in here. 'I don't have time.'

'You do and you know it.'

'I'm running a business. I owe it to Mum to make it a success.'

'It already is. She would've been so proud of what you've achieved. Everything's running well here. You don't have to work twenty-four seven any more. Take a break. You haven't had a proper holiday in years.'

'Er, *hello*! I was in Spain just last week! That's how I brought you the stuff you're holding right now.'

'That was for *business*. I'm talking about a holiday for *pleasure*. Remember that word?'

'Course I do.'

I didn't. He was right. It'd been a while.

'Come on! Just one dating app. That's all I'm suggesting. Or I can ask Natalie to set you up with one of her single friends. Just do *something!*'

'I already signed up to that stupid hotel thing after you blackmailed me. And look how that turned out. Waste of money.'

'It's only been two months. There's still time.'

'*Yeah, right.*' I rolled my eyes. 'Anyway, it doesn't matter. Not everyone wants the whole marriage and kids thing. I'm happy that works for you, but that life isn't for me.'

Colton and I had been friends since we were teenagers and for as long as I remembered, he'd always wanted that lifestyle. It suited him too.

One Sunday morning he'd invited me around to his place for breakfast. When I arrived, he was sitting around the table with Natalie and Betty, laughing and joking. They looked like they were starring in a TV commercial advertising the perfect family life. And I told them so.

He'd wrongly assumed that my comment meant I wanted the same thing and before I knew it, Natalie had whipped out an article from one of the Sunday newspaper supplements, gushing about some place called The Love Hotel. Minutes later, the website was on their iPad and they were signing me up.

There was still a chance I could've backed out, but then they used the ultimate low blow tactic: their adorable six-year-old daughter, Betty.

They asked her if she thought I'd make a good dad and she said in her cute voice, 'Uncle Max would be the *best* daddy!'

'So do you think he should go to the lovely hotel in the sunshine and find a nice lady to marry so he can be happy and make babies?' they'd asked her.

I immediately wanted to object and remind them that this wasn't the dark ages and people didn't have to get married and have kids to be happy. I wanted to say that joy came in many forms and that I was just fine with my bachelor life, but I didn't get the chance.

'Yes!' Betty had cheered, flashing her toothy grin then throwing her arms around me.

I was only human. How was I supposed to say no to that?

Less than thirty seconds later, I was handing over my credit card and it was too late to go back.

But that was months ago and we hadn't heard a bean. Other than the automated email to say they'd got my details and would be in touch.

If it meant I got Colton off my back about finding a girlfriend, it almost would've been worth paying the hefty one thousand pounds deposit, but that was wishful thinking because here we were again, having the same conversation about my non-existent love life.

'It's still early days. They keep your details on file indefinitely until they find you a match that they know you'll be perfect for.'

'*Sure,*' I said, my voice dripping with sarcasm.

'I think it's good that they do it that way instead of taking the full amount, inviting you to the hotel, pairing you up with someone incompatible, and then when it doesn't work, just shrugging their shoulders and sending you home. At least you know that when you hear back from them, it's going to be worth making the trip.'

'If you say so.'

'Just picture it: two weeks away from the office, switching off completely from work. Relaxing in paradise. Enjoying some sun, sea, sangria... and if you just happened to meet your perfect match there too, that'd be the cherry on top.'

'Anyway,' I said, eager to change the subject, 'has the new shipment of body oils come in yet?'

'Yep. Arrived last night. The warehouse are going through the delivery right now.'

'Great. I've got a meeting now with marketing about the beauty show in Dubai and the branding for the new range.'

'I know marketing isn't my forte, but I didn't like those designs that company sent over.'

'Me neither. Too dated. They've got complacent. Maybe it's time to switch things up a bit. Start looking for someone else to do our branding.'

'Yeah. What you got planned for the weekend? A few of us are going to the Liverpool vs Arsenal game. I've got a spare ticket if you...'

'Can't,' I jumped in. 'Got plans.'

'Really? What?'

'Doesn't matter.'

'Come on. I know it's not easy, but I really think if you try, it'll be good for you.'

'Drop it, okay?' I snapped. 'Sorry, I didn't mean to...'

'No worries. I know it's still a sensitive subject. Even after all these years. I'm just trying to help.'

'I know.'

'Same goes for the whole travelling and dating thing. Maybe I'll call The Love Hotel people to see if there's any news. You're my best mate. I want you to be happy. There's more to life than just work. If you just...'

'Bye, Colton!' I picked up my phone and headed towards the door. I loved him like a brother, but I couldn't listen to him repeat the same *you need to get a life* spiel again.

'See you at lunch?' he called out.

'Okay.'

All through the meeting I was distracted. That conversation with Colton had stirred up a whole hornets' nest of thoughts I didn't want to discuss. He'd picked my least favourite topics of conversation. Dating and football. Even now, I hated talking about them.

Don't get me wrong. It wasn't like I hadn't been with a woman in years. When I needed to let off steam and the gym wasn't cutting it, I'd hook up. It'd only ever last one night though. Usually I preferred to do it when I was travelling, because there was an understanding that it was temporary. I was just passing through town on business, so it could only ever be a one-off. And that was how I liked it.

After the way my one and only serious relationship ended, it was clear I wasn't cut out to have them. I didn't deserve to. I always screwed things up. I couldn't hurt anyone else.

And like I said, I was busy running a business. I had big plans to expand overseas, which would take up more of my time.

A lot of people depended on me for their salaries. If I was off my game and the company failed, my employees wouldn't be able to pay their rent or take care of their families, which was something I took seriously.

And as for the whole football thing, I couldn't even think about that. Football used to be my whole world. My everything. But not any more.

When I returned to my office, Colton was sitting on my black leather sofa with a smile the size of Asia across his face.

'Someone's happy!' I said. 'Did we get a big order?'

'Nope. I've got great news!'

'Come on – spit it out!'

'You know I said I was going to call The Love Hotel, to follow up?'

'Yeah,' I groaned.

'I didn't need to. Because look at this!' He jumped up and flashed his phone in my face. 'Natalie just forwarded it to me!'

I grabbed the phone and looked at the screen.

Congratulations! We've found your perfect match!

You are cordially invited to join us at The Love Hotel to meet the woman of your dreams…

'Wait, what?'

'They've found your soulmate! *It's on, baby*! You're going to The Love Hotel. Next week! It's finally happening.'

Shit.

3

STELLA

'Are these ready to package up?' I asked Mum, pointing to the two lacy thongs.

'Yep! All good to go.'

I put on a fresh pair of plastic gloves and plucked them from Mum's workbench.

We ran a small business called Pretty Little Kitty, which provided personalised handmade underwear. Some of it was standard frilly knickers, but our biggest earners were the custom lace thongs which could be personalised with a name or short phrase in crystal letters.

I glanced down at the items to see what the customer had chosen.

Along the back of the black thong was the word *Daddy*. And on the red thong it simply read *Mine*.

Okay then...

I'd worked with Mum for eighteen months so I was used to the different requests that came through. Some just had the name of the recipient or their partner, but others like this order were a little naughtier.

'I'll get started on these now so they're ready to take to the post office later. By the way, your laptop's been pinging. Want me to check your emails?'

I knew it couldn't be more orders because they always came straight through to my computer.

As the business started to grow, Mum struggled to manage it all. So when I got laid off from my graphic design job, I'd offered to come and help. With the market being more competitive than ever, finding a new role was hard. So moving back home with Mum and working alongside her seemed like the logical solution.

So far, I'd given her website and marketing materials a complete overhaul which I'd enjoyed and I'd set up some new systems for managing orders so that everything ran more smoothly.

'Don't worry. I'll go. I need a break.'

'Tea?' I asked.

'Love one!'

Mum left the workshop, which used to be her dining room, and headed to the living room where her laptop was resting on the sofa.

Just as I was about to fill the kettle with water in the kitchen, I heard Mum scream.

I dropped the kettle on the counter and raced to find out what was wrong.

'What happened?' I rushed over to her. 'Are you okay?'

Mum started jumping up and down on the spot.

'Yes! I'm more than okay! I'm *amazing*!'

'What's amazing? Did Ann Summers get back to you about stocking some of our thongs?'

'Nope!' She continued jumping.

'Have you heard back from Lovehoney? Are *they* interested?'

'It's much better news than that!'

Now she was doing the dance Carlton from *The Fresh Prince of Bel Air* used to do. *Very badly.*

'Are you going to keep jumping up and down like a lunatic or are you actually going to tell me what this amazing news is sometime this century?'

'Don't get upset with me,' she paused, 'but I did something that you might not be happy with right now, but I'm sure it'll all work out in the end. You just have to trust me.'

'What are you going on about?'

'Do you promise not to shout or get angry if I tell you?'

'I'd need to know what you've done first before I do that!'

'Okay...' She sat down and patted the space beside her. 'Sit.' I did as she asked, my heart racing. 'So you remember I was telling you about The Love Hotel...'

'Mum!' I blew out an exasperated breath. 'I've told you a million times, I'm not interested!'

'Well, I kind of, maybe, *might* have applied already on your behalf a few weeks ago. Just on a whim. To see what would happen...'

'But the deposit's a thousand pounds! We need a new sewing machine and computer. You can't throw away that kind of money!'

'My one and only child's happiness is priceless! And I'm a grown woman. I can do what I want with my savings. So anyway, I applied and *look*!' She turned the laptop to face me. 'They've accepted you! They've found your perfect match! Isn't that *brilliant*!' She danced around in her seat.

'What?' I blinked rapidly, trying to register what was on the screen.

'You've got a place at The Love Hotel! They've found you a hot sexy man who's your Mr Right. Isn't it amazing?'

I froze and swallowed the concrete lump in my throat.

As the reality of what Mum said started to dawn on me, my heart thundered in my chest and my pulse raced so fast that if I wasn't already sitting down I would've passed out.

Despite me telling her repeatedly that I wasn't interested, Mum had gone behind my back and applied. Wasting valuable money she didn't have on the deposit.

And now *apparently* they'd found my perfect match.

Yeah, right.

'It's not amazing! It's a disaster!'

'Don't be so dramatic!' She turned the laptop back to face her. 'It's an *opportunity*. You haven't had a holiday in ages and you need a good man in your life. This is perfect!'

'It really isn't! Anyway, I can't go. The trip's for two weeks, right?'

'Correct.'

'So who'll help you whilst I'm gone?'

'Despite what you think, you're not indispensable, sweetheart. I'll get someone in to take care of the orders.'

'Like who?'

'I'll ask Marjorie.'

'The vicar's wife?'

'That's the one.'

'Somehow I don't think she'd be happy wrapping thongs with "Kiss My Arse" on them!'

Only our closest friends and family knew the full nature of our business and it was better that way.

'She might like it! You know what they say about the quiet ones!' Mum chuckled.

'I'm not going! And I'm really angry with you. I know your heart was in the right place, but you've put me in an awkward position because I'll have to pay you back for the deposit.'

I really needed to get my own place and reimbursing Mum's one-thousand-pound payment would throw me off target for my mortgage savings and take me months to recover.

Mum didn't reply. Her gaze was fixed to the screen whilst she moved her fingers around on the laptop track pad.

'Are you even listening to me?' I blew out a frustrated breath.

'Mmm, hmm,' she nodded, keeping her eyes firmly on her laptop. 'There!' she looked up, grinning from ear to ear. 'All done.'

'Sorry, what? What's all done? Have you cancelled it?'

'Of course not! I've just confirmed the booking and paid the balance! Forget about posting those orders. You'd better go shopping for some clothes and a new suitcase. You're off to sunny Spain!'

4

MAX

'Have you arrived yet?' Colton's voice sounded down the phone.

'Almost,' I said, glancing out of the window at the clear blue skies. 'The driver said we're ten minutes away.'

I took in the sight of the pretty pink flowers in the centre of the motorway. It didn't matter how many times I visited Spain, I never tired of seeing them. In the UK, motorways were just grey and depressing. But here, the central reservations on the motorway that took you to Marbella had a beautiful floral strip. It was like it was part of the welcome.

'How you feeling?'

'Apart from being pissed off about wasting two weeks of my life on this stupid holiday?'

I shouldn't even be going. I was already scheduled to go to Dubai in a fortnight for a big beauty exhibition. Now I'd have to fly out the day after I got back from this trip, which was stressful.

'No need to worry about that, bro,' Colton laughed. 'You never had a life to begin with! All you did was work, sleep, eat and repeat. You should be happy you'll be doing something fun for a change.'

'There's nothing *fun* about being forced to spend two weeks with a complete stranger. What if we don't get on? What if I don't fancy her? And what if *she* doesn't fancy *me*? This is gonna be so fucking awkward.'

I'd barely slept last night worrying about this damn trip. I hadn't dated seriously in years, but even I knew finding that connection wasn't easy.

'First up, I don't think we have to worry about her not finding you attractive. Annoyingly, I don't think there's a woman on the planet that doesn't think you're hot, including my wife and every female who works for us. And a handful of the guys too. It's sickening that God gave you good looks *and* a decent personality.'

'Cheers,' I laughed. 'Cheque's in the post.'

'Second, this company are experts in matching people so *of course* you're gonna get on.'

'Just because an algorithm says we match on paper, doesn't mean we'll have chemistry in person.'

'Maybe. But let's focus on the positive. Trust the process. You're almost there now, so just make the most of it. What time's your dinner date?'

'Nine.'

'Cool. So you'll have loads of time to chill and get ready.'

'I'd rather just meet her straight away, get the silly date over and done with, then get on the next plane to London.'

'No! You agreed. Hold on one sec.' The phone went silent for a few seconds before a request to switch to a video call popped up. I tapped the screen to accept.

'Hello, Uncle Maxey!' Betty's cute face filled the screen.

That clever son of a bitch had drafted in my goddaughter again. And he'd switched to FaceTime. The man had no shame.

'Hello, Betty-Boo!' I smiled. 'What you up to?'

'Just painting. Daddy said you've gone to the sunny hotel to meet your new girlfriend. Are you getting married?'

'No, sweetheart,' I said, trying not to show my frustration. I'd be having words with him later for filling her head with this nonsense. 'I'm just going there as an experiment. It's like a little test.'

'Like a spelling test?'

'Sort of, but it's more like a speaking test. I have to talk to someone about different things and if we both pass, we'll meet again and do another test.'

'Oh,' she said. I wasn't sure she understood but it was the best way I could think to describe it to a child. 'I hope you do well. Sometimes tests are hard, but my teacher said you have to keep trying and don't give up until you get to the end. That's what I did for my spelling test and I got eight out of ten!'

'That's brilliant! I'm so proud of you!'

'Thank you! Are you going to do your best, Uncle Maxey?'

'I will.'

'Do you pinky promise?'

'I do,' I agreed before I could stop myself. I was putty in her hands.

'Yay! Daddy wants to talk to you again. And can you bring me back some sweets, *please*?'

'If Mummy and Daddy say it's okay, I will. See you soon.'

'Well, that's settled then.' Colton came back on the phone.

'What, bringing your adorable daughter back some sweets?' I joked.

'You can bring her a lollipop, but that wasn't what I was talking about and you know it. You've just promised Betty you'll see it through until the end, so there's no going back now.'

'So manipulative.' I rolled my eyes.

'Mr Moore,' the driver called out in his thick Spanish accent. 'We have arrived.'

'*Gracias*,' I replied. 'Better go, Col. We're here.'

'Okay. Think positive and enjoy. This is going to be so great for you.'

'Talk soon,' I replied, beads of sweat trickling down my back.

As the driver pulled up outside a striking white building and a smartly dressed porter opened the door, the enormity of everything dawned on me.

This was it.

I was here at The Love Hotel in Spain.

This was really happening.

5

STELLA

'Ready to go?' Mum asked as I zipped up my suitcase.

'Think so. I've got my passport, ticket, phone...'

'I almost forgot!' Mum rushed into her workshop, then returned to the hallway clutching a gift bag. 'I got you a few *extras...*'

'Thanks!' I smiled. I'd almost made my peace with Mum about forcing me on this trip. It clearly meant a lot to her, so I'd agreed to go. Reluctantly.

I'd changed my perspective about the whole thing. Whilst Mum thought I was going to find the love of my life, I'd decided to see it as a holiday. After all, it wasn't like I was being shipped off to hell for two weeks. I was going to an all-inclusive luxury resort near sunny Marbella. I'd always wanted to visit Spain and now I had the chance.

The hotel was right by the beach and there was a gorgeous pool, so I'd be able to sit in the sun and relax. My Kindle was stacked with a load of eBooks and I'd bought a couple of new paperbacks, so I could finally make a dent in my TBR list. Maybe the trip wouldn't be so bad after all.

'Oh my God!' I gasped as I unwrapped the tissue paper from the first gift in the bag. Mum had given me a whole set of thongs with different messages including: 'Touch Me', 'Kiss Me' and 'Call Me Baby'.

'What?' she smirked. 'If this was one of your steamy romance novels, it'd have something racier like "Spank Me!"'

She wasn't wrong.

'Thank you,' I said, deciding it was easier to accept the gesture.

'I got you some condoms as well!' she beamed as I groaned inwardly. *Reason number two hundred and one not to move back home with your mum as an adult.* 'There's so much variety these days so I wasn't sure what to choose. I got some fruity ones, ribbed ones and a jumbo-sized three pack too. Just in case he's hung like a horse. Or is it a donkey? I forget the saying now!'

I shook my head, speechless. Did I really say I *didn't* want to go on this holiday? The sooner I got out of here, the better.

* * *

Thankfully the flight went smoothly and I was now in a fancy chauffeur-driven car the hotel had arranged, minutes away from arriving at the resort.

My heart raced and a million questions flooded my brain as the reality of what was happening hit me.

In just a few hours I'd be meeting a man. Going on a date, for the first time in what felt like thirteen years rather than just thirteen months.

Once it was clear that I couldn't back out of the holiday, I'd decided that if I had to go, I'd be more comfortable if I was prepared.

So I'd gone to the salon and been waxed within an inch of

my life, had a new haircut and even had a mani-pedi. Something I hadn't done since, well, probably never.

And I'd got a gorgeous new bikini and a few summery dresses. If I was going to meet the supposed love of my life, I had to be prepared.

I'll admit. I was a teeny bit excited. I'd spent the last two weeks reading every review and case study for The Love Hotel that I could find online and they had a fantastic reputation.

The magazine articles had featured the impossibly good-looking couples that had found success there. But there were also more average-looking people like me who'd found partners too.

It was weird to think that after years of wondering if I'd ever find love again, now I had a real chance of discovering that needle in a haystack: a man that I wouldn't otherwise have found if I hadn't been put in touch with a team of dating and relationship experts.

Plus, my match would've been vetted. So there wouldn't be any horrible surprises like the last guy I dated who conveniently 'forgot' to tell me he was married until our fourth date. Apparently his wife was aware he was on the apps and they'd both agreed bringing a third person into their marriage would help to 'spice it up'. I politely declined.

There was no guarantee that The Lovel Hotel's professional matchmaking skills could prevent me from meeting a man who would break my heart beyond repair like my first love did years ago. But if I was going to try this whole relationship thing again, maybe this was a good way to dip my toe back in the dating waters.

Mum was right. This was a big opportunity. So many people dreamed of securing a place at this hotel and here I was on my way to spend two weeks there. I was basically Charlie Bucket with a golden ticket to enter Willy Wonka's Chocolate Factory.

As the driver pulled up outside the resort, my jaw dropped. Wow.

The photos didn't do it justice. This place was stunning.

The two-storey building had whitewashed walls, bright terracotta roof tiles and lush manicured gardens including pretty palm trees of all shapes and sizes.

The car door opened and as I stepped outside the intoxicating fresh sea air flooded my nostrils and the heat from the blazing sun hit my skin.

When I left London it was overcast, dark and gloomy. This was the total opposite. There wasn't a single cloud in the picture-perfect blue sky. I'd been here for less than a minute and it already felt like I was in paradise.

'Hello, Stella!' A tall, smiley woman shook my hand. 'I'm Jasmine, your Love Alchemist. Welcome to The Love Hotel!'

'Thanks!' I said, trying not to laugh at her job title. *Love Alchemist*? How did she even say that with a straight face?

Jasmine had brown skin and shiny jet-black shoulder-length hair. She reminded me of the actress Kerry Washington when she played Olivia Pope in the TV show *Scandal*.

Even though I'd known her two seconds, Jasmine came across as organised and confident: the kind of woman who was good at getting shit done.

She was pretty and immaculately dressed in a white blouse with a fitted electric-blue skirt, which matched the colour of the plant pots decorating the walls. I assumed it was a uniform because the other staff members I saw milling around were dressed in the same colours.

'Simón here is our Suitcase Superintendent. He will ensure

your luggage is taken to your room. Follow me and we'll get you checked in.'

Jasmine led me through the door to the elegant reception area. The white marble floor was immaculately polished and striking white marble columns surrounded the matching check-in desk.

Once I'd given my details and the receptionist did all the usual check-in admin stuff, Jasmine said she'd show me to my room.

As we were about to leave, a lady in a colourful kaftan breezed through the automatic double doors at the back of the hotel and I caught a glimpse of the swimming pool.

'Wow!' I gasped. 'The pool looks amazing!'

'Glad you like it,' she smiled. 'I'll take you on a tour of the resort once you're settled in, but you're welcome to take a look now if you like?'

'I'll just take a quick peek,' I said. 'I'm not dressed for the pool and if dinner's at nine, I should really start to get ready soon.'

It was almost six now and considering it had been so long since I'd been on a date and got all dressed up, I needed all the time I could get.

'Of course. You go ahead and I'll join you in a moment.'

I strolled over to the window to get a closer look. The turquoise pool was surrounded by immaculate white sun loungers and a few couples were relaxing on comfy Balinese daybeds under the shade of the tall palm trees.

Although there were scheduled activities every day, I was sure they'd give us some downtime. I couldn't wait to sit out there and read.

Just as I was about to leave, a man slowly exited the pool and as I took in the sight of him I swallowed hard.

I called him a man but 'god' would've been a more accurate description. He had his back to me and it was probably the most exquisite back I'd ever seen. Smooth, tanned skin, broad shoulders and incredible triceps. No need to ask if he worked out.

He raked his hand through his short dark damp hair, causing his bicep to bulge, like a tennis ball was lodged under his skin.

As my gaze dropped to his arse, I swear some dribble rolled down my chin. I quickly wiped my mouth with the back of my hand, just in case.

His wet swimming trunks clung to his buns and desire pulsed through me.

Please, universe, let him be my date.

I might not have been out with anyone for a while, but I still knew a hot guy when I saw one. And as shallow as it sounded, I'd love to get the chance to run my hands over a toned, muscular body like that.

The only exercise the last two guys I dated did was lifting their beer glass from the table to their mouths. Such a stark contrast to my first boyfriend.

He was a professional football player, so he was always in good shape. Not as muscular as the Pool God in front of me, but I used to worship his body. I worshipped everything about him. Until he broke my heart.

'So, what do you think?' Jasmine appeared beside me. 'Gorgeous views, right?'

'Ye-yeah! Definitely!' I stuttered. 'Very impressive,' I said, before realising she was referring to the views of the hotel's surroundings, not Hot Pool Guy who was now strutting over to the beach bar.

'The pool's great, but I definitely recommend heading down to the sea too. The water is amazing.'

Sea?

I snapped myself out of my thoughts. What the hell was wrong with me? I was standing here, ogling a complete stranger as he got out of the pool. Rather than acting like a pervert, I should be appreciating the beauty of the hotel grounds.

Tearing my gaze from him, I focused on what I was supposed to be looking at and gasped. Jasmine was right. The views really were stunning.

Just metres away from the pool area was a gorgeous sandy beach and the sparkling blue sea stretched as far as the eye could see.

'I can't wait to check it out,' I said, turning away from the window.

'Let me show you to your room.'

Jasmine led me along a white stone tree-lined pathway, tapped the key card on a white door, then pushed it open for me.

'This is your room. I'll leave you to settle in. If you need anything, press the love heart symbol on the phone and it'll connect you straight to me. Remember, dinner with your Mr Right is at nine sharp at Aphrodisiac, our romantic restaurant, which is signposted from your room, but if you need me to escort you there, let me know.'

'Okay, great, thanks.'

As soon as Jasmine left, I let out a loud squeal and starfished on the plush four-poster bed. I'd always wanted to do that. This room was a dream. Terracotta tiled floors, wooden beams across the ceilings and pretty paintings of Spanish scenery on the white walls. I couldn't believe I was here and that it was even better than I'd imagined.

I should start getting ready, but there was something I had to do first. I reached in my bag and pulled out my phone.

'Hey, Mum, I've arrived safely at the hotel.'

'Hi, darling! How is it?'

'It's... it's *a-mazing*! Thank you for arranging everything. This place is like paradise on earth. I'm so sorry I argued with you about coming. I'll pay you back every penny.'

'No, you won't. Just enjoy yourself. That's payment enough.'

'Thanks, Mum. I better start getting ready.'

'Okay, darling. Send me a selfie, when you're dressed. Have you decided what to wear yet?'

'No, but I've narrowed it down to the orange maxi dress or the pink mid-length dress.'

'Good luck.'

'Thanks!'

Once I'd been in the gorgeous walk-in shower, I unzipped my suitcase and pulled out my dress options. I still couldn't decide, but I knew just the person who could help me.

I dialled the number of Samantha, my best friend.

'Hey.' Her face appeared on the screen. 'Are you there? How is it? Have you met him yet? Is he fit?'

'Whoa there! So many questions! Yes, it's amazing and no, I haven't met him yet. But I did see a fit guy at the pool, so if my date looks anything like him, I'll be very happy.'

'Oooh! I'm so excited for you! I haven't heard you this enthusiastic about a man in real life since, well, ages. Normally you're gushing about your fictional book boyfriends.'

'Yeah, you're right. But this guy would give a book hero a run for their money. I didn't see his face, but I can just tell it'll be as gorgeous as his body.'

'Sounds like a wet dream!' she laughed. 'Well, if they've set you up with someone dull and his date doesn't work out either, maybe you could accidentally drop your sunglasses in front of him or something and hope he picks them up.'

'That's so lame!'

'No, it's a proper meet cute! Or you could pretend to drown in front of him and he could do a Zac Efron in *Baywatch* and dive in to save you!'

'Knowing me, though, I probably would drown!'

'Anyway, what you wearing?'

'Can't decide. What d'you think? This one?' I held up the orange dress. 'Or this?' I put the pink one against me.

'Which one shows the most boob and arse?' she laughed.

'Neither!' I rolled my eyes. 'I'm trying to find someone who will be interested in my mind and sparkling personality, not just the size of my tits!'

'You do have a great rack, though. If I had your chest, I'd definitely be flaunting my assets on the first date.'

'That settles it. I'm definitely going for the loose-fitting maxi dress. Then I can be sure he likes me for me.'

'Spoilsport! What time's the date?'

'In exactly forty-nine minutes and I still need to do my hair, make-up and get dressed so I better go.'

'Okay! And let me know how it all goes! If this all works out, maybe I'll apply too!'

'I'll keep you posted. Bye.'

Forty minutes later, I was picking up my key card and heading to the door. I took one final glance at myself in the full-length mirror. I hadn't scrubbed up too badly. I'd sent a selfie to Mum and Samantha (or Sammie as I usually liked to call her) ten minutes ago and they'd both replied with lots of love heart eyes, fire and thumbs up emojis which was a good sign.

As I closed the door and set off down the path towards the restaurant, my heart thundered through my chest.

I'd barely been outside for two minutes and I could already feel sweat pooling on my hairline. I quickly reached into my handbag and dabbed my forehead, taking care not to smudge my make-up.

When I arrived at the restaurant, I took a deep breath then opened the door.

The handsome maître d' greeted me with a warm smile.

'Stella?' he asked.

'That's me!'

'Welcome to Aphrodisiac. My name is Manuel and I will be your Dining Director this evening.'

'Lovely to meet you, Manuel,' I said, thinking how funny it was that everyone had weird job titles.

'Your date has not arrived yet. Perhaps you would like a drink at the bar while you wait?'

'Sounds lovely.'

I took a seat at the bar and went for the barman's, oops, sorry, *Chief Mixologist's* sangria recommendation which slipped down very nicely. Perhaps a little too well, because before I knew it, my glass was half empty.

I glanced at my watch. It was ten past nine. He was late. That wasn't a good sign. *So much for being my Mr Right.* If the match-makers really knew me, they'd understand that I hated being late and I hated when other people were too. Sometimes it couldn't be avoided, but I doubted that was the case today.

Everyone had to arrive at the hotel at least three hours before their scheduled date. So he couldn't blame his lateness on the traffic or getting lost.

Then I felt guilty for being too harsh. Maybe he was nervous. Or...

Oh, God. I hoped he hadn't stood me up. Wouldn't be the first time that'd happened. I downed the rest of my drink as I thought about how mortifying that would be.

I felt a tap on my shoulder and I instantly relaxed. I hadn't been stood up. I put on my best smile then spun around ready to greet him.

But it wasn't my date. It was Manuel.

'I'm so sorry, Miss Stella,' he said. My stomach instantly tightened. 'But your date is running late. He will, however, be here shortly.'

'Oh, okay. Thanks for letting me know. Where are the ladies', please?' After finishing my drink, I was sure my lipstick needed touching up and I didn't want to do it in public. Knowing me, he'd walk in just as I was applying it and I'd get flustered and swipe it all over my teeth.

'Just down there on the left,' he pointed.

'Thanks.' I slid off the barstool. 'I'll be right back.'

Once I'd touched up my make-up, I headed out of the bathroom door. As I took a few steps into the main restaurant area, Manuel rushed over to greet me.

'Good news, *Señora*. Your date has arrived. He is waiting for you at the bar. He is a very handsome man. I am sure you will be very happy.'

Delighted butterflies fluttered in my stomach and as we got closer to the bar, they went into overdrive.

The guy sitting at the bar had his back to us and was wearing a white shirt with his sleeves rolled up to his elbows, which was already a big green flag. And he had a muscular back and arms like Hot Pool Guy. His hair was short and dark, just like his too.

Oh my God! My date was the man I saw earlier. I couldn't believe my luck. This was brilliant!

I sent a silent prayer to God, the universe, my mum and everyone involved in making this wonderful miracle happen.

'*Señora*,' Manuel said to me as he tapped my dream man on his shoulder. 'It gives me great pleasure to introduce you to your date.'

My heart fluttered and I smiled so wide I thought my face was going to crack.

That was until my date spun around and I saw his face.

Then my heart crashed through the ground.

I couldn't believe it.

It may have been years, but I'd recognise that face anywhere.

The small scar just beneath his right eye that I used to kiss.

Those thick brows.

The square jaw.

Those sparkly, deep brown eyes I used to get lost in.

The ridiculously long eyelashes.

His full pink lips that I used to love roaming all over my body.

'Stella?' His eyes bulged.

'Max,' I spat.

'You two know each other?' Manuel frowned. *Yeah, I recognised him all right.* 'Did you meet earlier at the hotel?'

'No.' I folded my arms angrily. 'Max is my ex. The arsehole who broke my heart.'

6

MAX

'Fuck.' I dragged my hand down my face.

I couldn't believe I'd flown all the way to Spain to meet my perfect woman and they'd matched me with my ex.

This was a nightmare.

I should've worn a stab-proof vest instead of this shirt, because Stella was looking at me like she wanted to plunge a knife into my chest.

And I couldn't blame her. The way things ended between us was... *messy*.

'I need to see a manager!' Stella shouted. 'Or My Love Alchemist lady, Jasmine. I'm not going on a date with *him*. No way!'

The restaurant fell silent and the other guests' heads whipped in our direction.

'I... um, of course. *Señora, por favor*, please follow me.'

As the maître d' led Stella away she gave me a look so dirty, a million gallons of bleach couldn't wash it away.

Yep, she hated me.

Looked like I'd be getting my wish to go home early. But they at least owed me a refund.

This hotel was supposed to be run by a reputable company who employed the world's best matchmaking experts. But I was starting to question their skills. Who set two exes up together? I'd say it was a joke, but it wasn't remotely funny.

I needed air. I strode towards the door and stepped outside. The hot, sticky heat seared my skin. Even though it was past nine, it was still thirty degrees.

I crashed onto the outdoor sofa and put my head in my hands. My mind raced. What a shit show.

I'd thought about Stella a lot over the years, wondering how she was, whether she'd met someone and if she looked the same.

Tonight two questions were answered: she was single and I didn't think it was possible, but Stella was even hotter now than when we dated.

Although she was wearing a long dress with just her arms, shoulders and neckline on show, she looked sexy as hell. Her light brown skin glowed, her pretty dark brown eyes sparkled and her hair was shorter than before, but she still had those gorgeous curls that I loved.

And even though she'd scowled at me the whole time, I found my gaze fixed to her lips for longer than was appropriate. I'd always loved kissing that mouth.

On the way here, I'd worried whether I'd find my date attractive. Now I knew that wasn't an issue. But if someone asked Stella whether she was attracted to me, I could guarantee that the feeling would *not* be mutual.

Thoughts of how things ended between us flooded into my mind.

Shit, shit, shit.

If all the stuff that happened in the past wasn't bad enough, I was late for our date. And I knew Stella hated when people weren't on time. But I had to help that lady. I hoped reception had passed on the message explaining why. That was the least of my worries right now, though.

I reached into my pocket for my phone and dialled Colton.

'Hey! You on your way to your date now? Wait.' He paused. 'No. It's past nine over there and your date was at nine, so... what's up? Did something happen?'

'It's a fucking disaster.'

'I'm sure you're exaggerating. Did she have two heads? Even if she did, it's no bad thing. That means two sets of lips and double the kisses, right?' He laughed. I didn't.

'You know earlier you joked about every woman liking me?'

'Yeah. It's true.'

'I knew it wasn't true before, but now it's confirmed. My date definitely *doesn't* fancy me. I'd bet my life on it.'

'Impossible! Who is this anomaly?'

'They matched me with Stella.'

'Who's Stella?'

'Stella *Matthews*.'

The phone went silent.

'Babe,' he called out to Natalie. 'I need to take this call upstairs.'

The sound of his footsteps echoed through the phone. I heard a door open then close again.

'You still there?'

'Yeah, I'm just... trying to take it all in. They matched you with *Stella*? Shit, man. This is *bad*.'

'I know.'

'*Very, very bad*. You were not good to her towards the end.'

'I know. I wasn't nice to anyone back then.'

'Yeah. Even *I* hated you. But you had your reasons. And eventually, I understood. Maybe Stella will too.'

'Doubtful. It took me months to win back your friendship. This holiday is only for two weeks. And she won't even talk to me.'

'I'm not gonna lie. I wouldn't blame her. You've got your work cut out to bring her round. And I don't rate your chances...' Wow. If Mr Optimistic, glass half full didn't think I had any hope, then it was even worse than I thought. 'But there's still a chance. Even if it's one in a billion, it's still a chance, so you have to try.'

'I don't know, man.'

'Remember, you promised Betty that you'd see this challenge through 'til the end.'

'But this *is* the end. There's nothing I can do if she won't talk to me.'

'*Try*. Until you've attempted multiple times and Stella has categorically refused and left the resort, it's not the end. Find her and try to talk to her. Even if she doesn't want to date you, you at least owe her an explanation. Give her a better ending than you did before.'

He was right.

And that was all that I could ask for.

One conversation.

My chest tightened. I was dreading it, but it had to be done.

If only I had some body armour.

Something told me I was gonna need it.

7

STELLA

As I sat in an office at the back of the restaurant, anger bubbled in my chest.

I knew from the moment Mum mentioned this hotel that it was a bad idea, but I let her talk me into it. I even started to believe coming here could be a good thing. I'd even called Mum just hours ago to thank her and stupidly hoped that I was about to meet my Mr Right.

How wrong could I be?

Maxwell Moore couldn't be further away from being my Mr Right if he lived on the moon.

I didn't know how this happened, but there was no way I was going through with this. I couldn't. It took me ages to get over him and I had no desire to drag myself back to hell again.

Why was I even waiting for Jasmine? There was nothing to talk about. I was going back to my room to pack. Then first thing in the morning I'd catch a flight to London.

Just as I got up to leave, Jasmine came in.

'Stella, hi,' she said softly. 'Manuel explained what happened and I just saw Max outside too, I...'

'I'm sorry, but I've got to go.'

'Wait. Please. Just give me two minutes.'

I paused and sat back down.

'I'm listening.'

'Now I understand that obviously it's a shock to arrive here expecting to meet someone new then discover that you've been matched with your ex. Believe me, I understand. I recently got divorced and if my ex turned up, I'd freak out too. But the algorithms don't lie. And neither do our experts. We work with the best matchmakers and relationship gurus in the business. The track record for matching couples successfully at this hotel is flawless. So as uncomfortable as it may seem right now, please try and trust the process. You've come all this way. Taken time off work. Invested a lot of money coming here. Don't throw it all away without even giving it a go.'

'Can't you just give me a refund?'

'I'm going to ask you some questions and I need you to answer truthfully, please.'

'Okay.' I shuffled in my seat.

'Was Max ever violent or abusive towards you in any way?'

'No, never.' I shook my head.

'Did he cheat?'

'No. That's not why we broke up.'

'Well, then, I'm sorry, but I'm afraid a refund won't be possible. It's in the terms and conditions. All bookings are final.'

I hadn't read the small print but Jasmine seemed genuine. If Max had been abusive then it seemed like they'd reconsider, but I wasn't about to lie about something as serious as that.

He'd still hurt me though and right now, I'd rather spend two weeks in the dentist's chair than suffer through a single minute with him. But this trip had cost Mum a lot of money and she'd already warned me not to try and pay her back. If I left now, her hard-earned savings would go to waste and just thinking about that made me sick to the stomach.

'It's just... things ended badly between us.'

'I get that. I really do. How long ago did you date?'

'Twelve years ago. We broke up when I was nineteen.'

'So you're probably completely different people now. I know it won't be easy, but try and see this as an opportunity to clear the air. At least have dinner together. The new chef here is *gorgeous*, I mean, his *food* is delicious,' she blushed. Sounded like someone had a little crush. 'So you'll enjoy the food, even if at first the company isn't to your taste.'

'Okay.' I exhaled loudly. 'I'll try. Do you have a dry cleaners nearby?'

'We can arrange for clothes to be cleaned, why?'

'Because I noticed Max is wearing a white shirt and if he upsets me, which I can guarantee will happen, I can't promise that I won't throw my sangria all over him.'

Jasmine's mouth turned up into a smile.

'Don't worry. I'll have our dry cleaners on standby. Shall we go?'

'I suppose.'

I stood up and walked to the door, my heart thundering against my ribcage.

After years of wondering why Max acted the way he did towards me, it looked like I was finally going to get an explanation.

But whether I was ready to hear it was a different story.

8

MAX

'Max?'

I looked up from my phone screen and saw Jasmine, my, what did she say she was called? My *Love Alchemist*? I assumed that was just a strange word for some sort of client relations manager.

'Hi,' I said.

'So, Stella's agreed to speak to you...'

'What?' My eyes popped from their sockets. 'How did you manage that?'

'We're called *Love Alchemists* for a reason,' she smiled. 'Don't tell anyone, but when I first heard the job title I thought it sounded silly.' I fought the urge to say I agreed. 'But now it actually makes sense. Anyway, I don't know what happened between you, but she's really hurt. So it's important that you tread carefully. Go at her pace. If you want this to even stand a chance of working, you'll need to work hard to win her back.'

The thing was, although I agreed that I owed Stella an explanation, trying to *win her back* wasn't what I wanted. I had enough going on in my life. I didn't see the point in wasting time trying to chase someone who wasn't interested, especially when I didn't even want a serious relationship.

'I understand,' I said diplomatically.

I'd speak to Stella and stay here for the two weeks as planned. Like I'd agreed. I wasn't a quitter. Whether Stella lasted that long was up to her.

One thing was clear, though. Even though I admit I found her attractive, there wouldn't be any romance. I'd try and make the most of my time here doing whatever activities they had planned, but after that, Stella would go her way and I'd go mine – hopefully with a clearer conscience and with less bad blood between us.

That was all that I could ask for. And I was fine with that.

'Great! I'll bring her through!' Jasmine beamed.

When I looked up and saw Stella walking towards me, I swallowed hard. She was breathtaking. Then she scowled and my heart thundered in my chest. I was actually nervous.

Stella was always the one that got away. I'd lost count of all the times I'd wished I could turn back the clock and do things differently. Have a chance to talk to her again. Although I couldn't change the past, at least I now had the opportunity to try and make her understand my actions.

That was if I could find the right words.

Stella pulled out the chair, sat down, crossed her arms across her chest and glared at me.

'So...' I started, desperate to fill the silence. 'This is a surprise, right?'

Nothing.

Not even a grunt of acknowledgement.

'Look, about what happened between us,' I tried again. 'I'm sorry, I didn't mean to hurt you, I just had a lot going on and...'

'Don't make excuses,' she snapped.

At least she'd spoken. A few words were better than nothing, right?

More silence.

'Would you prefer to talk about the weather? It's pretty nice here. The hotel is too. I went for a swim earlier and the water was...'

'I can't do this.' Stella got up.

'Wait.' I put my hand on hers. Making contact with her skin sent a jolt of electricity through me. I quickly pulled away. 'Just give me a minute. *Please*.'

'Fine.' She sat back down.

'Look, I know I fucked up. I can't change that. Whenever you're ready, I'll explain. But until then, we're here, in this amazing hotel. I know it won't be easy for you, but can we try and make the most of it? I'm not asking you to like me – just to *tolerate* me for a bit. Let's try doing a few activities. And if you still hate me by the end of the week, we can talk to Jasmine again. As screwed up as it seems right now, they've matched us for a reason. So shall we give it a go? Even if it's to prove them wrong? What do you say?'

I stopped talking, fixed my gaze on Stella and waited for her response.

That actually came out better than I hoped. With any luck I'd won her over. Not to liking me, but to at least seeing my way of thinking.

Stella looked at me with a blank expression, pushed her chair back again then stood up.

'I'm going to my room.'

And then she was gone.

I had no idea whether she was gonna consider my suggestion or leave for good.

I guessed I'd have to wait until tomorrow to find out.

9

STELLA

'That's crazy!' Sammie gasped as I relayed the story of what had just happened with Max.

As soon as I saw him at the table, I knew I wouldn't be able to stay. The second his hypnotic eyes met mine, my brain turned to mush. How was it possible that he looked even more attractive than when we were together?

My gaze had dropped from his mouth to his muscular chest before I'd caught myself and came to my senses. I could *not* be attracted to him. He hurt me.

Max was an arsehole.

When he started to try and explain himself, part of me wanted to hear what he had to say, especially after waiting so long. But the other part wanted to keep the past buried away, because I knew dredging everything up again would be painful.

So I left.

Then the minute I'd shut my room door and crashed on the bed, I'd called Sammie.

'Tell me about it.' I shook my head in disbelief.

'So have you decided what you're gonna do?'

'I want to leave. If I could, I'd go to the airport right now and get on the first plane out of here. But I can't. They won't give Mum a refund and I can't waste her money. So I've got no choice. I have to stay.'

I'd texted Mum to say I'd call to update her tomorrow. I had too many emotions swimming around me to speak to her tonight.

I knew that I didn't want to let Mum down. I was her only child and ever since my so-called 'dad' walked out on us when I was just ten months old, Mum had raised me single-handedly. She'd made a lot of sacrifices for me so although this was going to be a nightmare, the least I could do was try to see this through and make Mum happy.

'You're doing the right thing. Don't get me wrong, I'm not condoning the way he treated you back then, I was there. You were heartbroken.'

'That's an understatement.'

Sammie and I had been friends since we met at secondary school when we were eleven and she was one of the people who helped me get through the break-up.

'But people can change. Try sticking it out for a bit and if by the end of the week you feel like you're in danger of committing murder then you can re-evaluate. What's on the agenda for tomorrow?'

'Not sure. There's an induction after breakfast so they're going to let us know then.'

'Cool. Hopefully it'll be something less intense than a candlelit dinner so you don't have to sit there and stare into each other's eyes. By the way, you didn't tell me, how did Max look? Does he have a beer gut and moobs? Has he lost all his hair? Not that he couldn't still look hot if he was bald, I mean, *hello*, Jason Statham. Ooh and Dwayne Johnson... *Yes, please*! What I wouldn't do to shine his head between my thighs!'

'Stop!' I laughed.

'Come on then, how has Max aged? Like a fine wine or a shrivelled prune?'

'I wish I could say he looked shit, but annoyingly he didn't. So much for karma,' I sighed.

'On a scale of one to ten, how did Max compare to the Hot Pool Guy you saw when you arrived?'

Then I remembered. I'd been so focused on venting about him turning up at the date that I hadn't told Sammie about that part.

'You're not going to believe this, but turns out that *Max* was the guy I saw at the pool.'

'*No way!*' she gasped.

'*Yes, way.*'

'How did you not recognise him?'

'I didn't see his face, remember? And even though Max always had a great body because of all the training he did, it wasn't like it is now. *Now* he has *muscles. Everywhere.*' As I replayed the images of him getting out of the pool, seeing him at the bar and at the table, my pulse raced. 'Anyway. It doesn't matter.'

'Holy crap!' Sammie gasped. 'You fancy him!'

'No, I don't!'

'You were gushing about how fit Hot Pool Guy was earlier and Max is him so, *doh*, of course you do!'

Dammit.

'There's more to attraction than just looks,' I said quickly. 'Yes, Max is physically attractive, but that's it. I'm not staying for him. I'm doing it for Mum. Nothing's going to happen between us.'

'If you say so...'

'I'm tired,' I said, fighting the temptation to roll my eyes at Sammie's ridiculous statement.

I was single, but I wasn't desperate. I wasn't some sad pathetic woman who just ran back to her ex because he said sorry a few times.

I'd take part in the activities with him, try to be civil and that was it. There'd be no romantic reunion.

'Okay, hon. I'll let you get your beauty sleep. Let me know how it goes tomorrow.'

'Will do. Night.'

'Night, night.'

10

STELLA

I was on my way to the induction. I'd already eaten breakfast at lightning speed because I was terrified that Max would turn up. Thankfully there was no sign of him and I hoped it was because he'd decided to go back to London. Assuming of course that was where he still lived.

For the first few years after we broke up I looked him up from time to time, but I never really found anything. Then I realised it wasn't healthy and stopped.

It was so annoying that I'd successfully avoided him for years and now we'd be stuck in the same hotel together for *two bloody weeks.*

The induction was taking place by the pool. Just as I was about to take the corner that led me there, I spotted Max walking towards me. He was dressed in a dark blue vest, which of course showed off his incredible biceps and khaki shorts.

'You stayed!' He took off his sunglasses and as he looked at me, it was like his eyes were lasers, boring into my skin.

'Ten out of ten for observation,' I snapped.

'You going to the induction?'

'Yes.'

'See you there.'

'It starts in ten minutes. Try not to be late. *Again*.'

'Yeah, about last night, I didn't get to apologise for not being on time. I would've been early, but there was this woman and she...'

'Doesn't matter,' I replied, pushing my sunglasses further up my nose then striding off to the pool. I didn't want to hear about Max chatting up another woman when he was supposed to be meeting me.

Pairs of chairs had been arranged near the pool in a semicircle. Soft music played in the background and a gentle sea breeze tickled my bare legs.

A few couples were already seated. I headed to the back row. If we sat at the front and Max was late, it'd disrupt the presentation. I readjusted my white kaftan and sat down.

We'd been told to wear swimwear, so I'd picked the new bikini I'd bought just for this trip. It was bright orange with a pretty green palm tree pattern. As soon as I saw it, I loved it.

It was the last one the shop had and although the top was a little tight, I'd reasoned that wasn't a bad thing because it squished my boobs together, giving me extra cleavage. But if I'd known Max would be here, I would've brought a swimsuit that covered everything. He didn't deserve to see my body.

Two more couples filtered in and took their seats. The sound of chatter vibrated in the air. Everyone seemed to be conversing happily. I was glad their matches were more successful than mine.

Jasmine headed to the front of the section of chairs and waved when she spotted me. I waved back then started to wonder what our first activity would be.

A delicious woody scent flooded my nostrils. I turned to see

Max had sat next to me. *Ugh.* I moved my chair away to create some distance.

'Hello, everyone! Welcome!' Jasmine raised her voice, causing all the chatter to die down. 'I'm Jasmine – one of the Love Alchemists here. Are you enjoying your stay at The Love Hotel so far?'

'Yes!' everyone cheered, except me and Max who kept our mouths firmly shut.

'Great!' Jasmine responded. 'Now you've had a chance to meet your match, I'm going to explain how things will work. During your first week, usually there'll be one organised couple's activity each day in a group setting. Then in the second week, although we'll be here to help and support you with whatever you need, you'll organise your own one-to-one activities, based on what you think your Mr or Mrs Right will love. Sound good?'

'Yes!' everyone but us replied enthusiastically again.

I was glad that at least this week Max and I wouldn't be stuck alone. With other people around that I could chat to, hopefully it'd be less awkward.

As for week two, I didn't need to worry about that because I doubted we'd make it that far.

'Wonderful!' Jasmine smiled. 'Loving your enthusiasm! As well as the scheduled daily activity, you'll also have Love Tasks to complete in your own time. One of those tasks will be compiling a memory book.'

'What's that?' a guy at the front asked.

'I was just about to explain,' Jasmine smiled.

'Sorry!' he said. 'I'm too eager!'

'No worries! So the memory book is like a photo album. You can of course use your phone to take pictures, but each of you will also be provided with a digital camera to take photos of the activities you do together. During group activities, our Love Alchemists will take photos for you. Each night, they'll be uploaded and printed. Then the next day, we'd like you to spend time as a couple going through the pics from the previous day. You'll then each pick one of your favourites to be put in your book. So by the end of your stay, you'll have an album filled with happy memories!'

'Awww,' the woman in front of me gushed. 'That's a lovely idea!'

I could see how it would be romantic: if you *hadn't* been set up with your ex. Spending time with Max was bad enough. The last thing I wanted was photographic evidence to remind me of the ordeal.

'Your second daily Love Task will be creating a playlist for your match.'

'What?' I called out, my brows shooting to the sky. Everyone looked at me. *Oops.* I hadn't meant to say that out loud. Preparing a playlist was so romantic and intimate, so in our case it wouldn't be appropriate. Hopefully Jasmine would understand and let Max and me skip it.

'A playlist,' Jasmine repeated. 'You've all been set up with Spotify so we'd like you to select at least five songs each day, to reflect your feelings about your partner, so that by the end of the experience, you'll have a soundtrack of how you both fell in love!'

I resisted the temptation to laugh. There was no way I'd fall in love with Max again.

Speaking of the devil himself, I wondered how he felt about all of this. Considering he was the one who dumped me, he couldn't be happy about cosying up for photos together and making me a lovey-dovey playlist.

When I tried to steal a look at him from the corner of my eye, his face seemed expressionless. As he played with the hem of his shorts, I tried not to look at his muscular thighs which had a sprinkling of dark hair.

As my eyes roamed downwards, I noticed a scar on his right leg. I knew exactly how he'd got it, but it was the first time I'd seen it in the flesh.

'What songs do we include today seeing as we've just met?' someone asked. I wasn't sure who, because I was distracted. I quickly tore my eyes from Max's legs hoping he hadn't noticed. Thank goodness I was wearing sunglasses.

'Great question!' Jasmine replied. 'You can choose songs that reflect your first impressions of each other. So for example it could be "You're Beautiful" by James Blunt or "Happy" by Pharell Williams. You don't have to think too deeply about every lyric. As long as it means something to you about how they made you feel for example during dinner last night or today's activity, that's the important thing. It's a good way to document your journey together. And hopefully you'll play this playlist for many years to come!'

Actually, now that Jasmine had explained, choosing songs for the first part of the playlist wouldn't be difficult. 'Caught Out There' by Kelis sprang to mind. Max didn't cheat, but I related to the part in the song where she screamed about how much she hated her ex *right now*.

That angry Alanis Morissette break-up anthem 'You Oughta Know' would be perfect too. This exercise could be quite therapeutic.

'And do we wait until the end of the trip to share them?' a guy with short locks asked.

'No. We think it's nice to share them as you make them.

There'll be instructions on how to do it on The Love Hotel manual which will be in your rooms when you return.'

Jasmine explained that they'd chosen to use a hard copy manual rather than a phone app because they wanted to encourage us to disconnect from our phones as much as possible during our stay.

'Any other questions?' Jasmine scanned the group. 'No? Great! As you can see, it's a glorious day.' She pointed to the clear blue sky. 'So today's activity will be a Pool Volleyball Tournament! You and your match will work as a team to compete against the other seven couples here. The winning team from each round will go through to the next stage and so on until the finals and the winners will receive a prize.'

'Oooh!' a lady two rows in front called out. 'What's the prize?'

'It's a secret, but I'm sure you'll love it! First, I need you to work with your match to think of a team name. You've got ten minutes, starting... now!'

Everyone turned to face their partners. Max got up and moved his seat opposite me.

'Any ideas?' he smiled and his dimples appeared.

Damn those dimples. My stomach flipped and I reminded myself that when it came to Max, stomach flipping was not allowed.

'How about *Nemesis*?' I suggested.

'Erm,' he sighed. 'I can see why you might think that's valid...'

'Or *Team Mismatch*?' I tilted my head. 'Actually, no. How about *Calamity*, *Worst Nightmare* or just *Misery*?'

'Okay, I get it. You'd rather pull off your toenails with a pair of hot, rusty tweezers than spend time with me. But like I said last night, we're here, so let's try and make the most of it. How about

something a bit more positive like *Destiny*, *Fortune* or...
Serendipity?'

'The problem with those names is that they imply that us being reunited is a good thing. But we aren't *destined* to be together. This situation *isn't* good fortune and it isn't remotely lucky that we've both ended up here.'

We sat in silence. I hated the anger simmering inside me. Normally I was fairly easy going, but it was hard to feel calm right now. Even though we broke up years ago, Max really hurt me and I could remember the pain like it happened recently. Seeing him just brought those emotions flooding back.

'What about *Team Chance*?' Max said. 'Or *Team Unexpected*? No, I've got it: *Thunderbolt*. It's a strong name and shows our shock at seeing each other again.'

I paused, considering his suggestion. As much as I wanted to get as far away from him as possible, I'd committed to stay and we'd been given a task, so I had to try my best to put my feelings aside and get on with it. We only had a few minutes left until Jasmine asked for our team names and I didn't want us to be the only ones who hadn't come up with something.

'That could work,' I replied. 'No one likes when thunder strikes. It's sudden and unpleasant. Just like the shitty situation we're in right now.'

'Yeah...' His voice trailed off. 'How are your volleyball skills these days?'

'About as good as your communication skills.'

'That bad?' he grimaced. 'You were pretty good that time we played volleyball on Brighton beach. We made a great team.'

I was surprised that he remembered. A group of us from college had driven there one weekend. Pretty sure we'd won too. Max was always good at sport so it wasn't a big surprise.

'Has everyone got their names?' Jasmine called out.

She wrote them on a white board then announced that Max and I would be in the first round.

Once two hotel workers had set up the net in the pool and dropped the ball inside, Jasmine asked us to take our positions.

I walked over to one of the sun loungers at the opposite end of the pool so that I was as far away from Max as possible. I cautiously removed my kaftan and sunglasses, adjusted my bikini top which felt tighter than I remembered, then hurried down the steps and into the pool.

As I sank into the cool water, I exhaled. It felt so good. The other team were already in the water, which only left Max. I turned around to see where he was and immediately regretted it.

Just as I spotted him standing beside a daybed on the opposite side, Max peeled off his vest, revealing a torso that wouldn't look out of place on the cover of a men's fitness magazine.

His body looked like it'd been sculpted from marble. His pecs were toned and of course he couldn't just settle for a six-pack. He had to go one step further with an eight-pack. No, wait. Maybe it was ten? Was that even possible?

Two, four, six...

I caught myself counting then quickly averted my gaze to his face.

'Are you getting in?' I called out.

'Yep.' He dropped his vest on the daybed then sauntered to the pool.

I tried really hard not to look but it was difficult. To get a body like that he must live in the gym. Maybe he was a personal trainer. He was always passionate about football, so I wouldn't be surprised if he ended up doing something sports related.

'Finally!' I huffed as he got in the pool and stood beside me on our side of the net. 'Was it really necessary for you to show off your muscular chest? We've got a game to play.'

'I wasn't *showing off*,' he replied. 'I was taking off my vest, which is the normal thing to do before you get in a pool. Nice to know you think my chest is muscular, though.' He smirked.

'I... I was...' I stuttered as my cheeks burned. There was no point in denying it. 'Anyway, let's just focus on winning this game.'

Once Jasmine explained the rules, the game started. We returned the other team's shots consistently, securing almost every point. The fact that Max's six foot three frame towered over our opponents worked in our favour.

The games were short and it wasn't long before we won the first round.

After taking a break by the side of the pool whilst the other two couples played their round, we got back inside.

Turned out my volleyball skills weren't so bad after all. And of course, Max played brilliantly. Now we were just a few points away from winning our second round and securing a spot in the semi-finals.

As the other team hit the ball over the net, Max rushed forward and whacked it back so hard it sped past them, crashing onto the water.

'Yes!' he cheered and my stomach flipped. Annoyingly, there was something attractive about his competence.

Max raised his hand in the air for me to high five him. Although I wanted to ignore him, I couldn't leave his hand hanging, so I slapped his palm triumphantly, trying not to look at his sculpted bicep.

As my hand made contact with his, a shot of electricity raced through me. I quickly pulled away.

'Next one's mine,' I shouted, trying to bring my thoughts back to the game.

'Okay,' he nodded.

The man from the other team launched the ball over the net. Determined not to miss it, I jumped up and whacked it with all my strength. Max wasn't the only one who could hit well.

As the ball flew past them, our opponents' eyes widened. They must have been impressed with my shot. A warm feeling of pride filled my belly.

I turned to face Max and was just about to lift my hand to high five him again when he grabbed my head and pushed it under the water.

'What the hell!' I screamed, water rushing in my mouth and up my nose.

Max joined me underwater and before I could register what was happening, he yanked my arms up to my chest and pressed them against my boobs.

'Look down,' he commanded. I frowned, gasping for breath.

When I glanced at my chest, my soul left my body.

My bikini top wasn't there. It'd flown off.

Shit.

I'd just flashed my boobs to Max.

And the entire hotel.

My heart raced and my stomach churned. I was mortified.

Yes, Max had seen my breasts before, but that was years ago. My body had changed since then and I had no intention of exposing myself to him or to a group of strangers.

I was tempted to stay under the water indefinitely, but I needed air so quickly pushed my head above the surface, just as Max did the same.

'Wait there,' he said. 'Don't move!'

That wasn't likely. There was no way I could get out of the pool like this. I'd need my hands to hold on to the stairs and it was impossible to do that and cover my chest at the same time.

Max dived back below the water as I clutched my boobs

tighter and looked around me. The couple we were playing against were still staring.

Seconds later, Max appeared.

'I've got your bikini top, but it's probably too complicated to put on in the pool, so hold on.' He jumped out, raced to his daybed, grabbed his vest then dived back in again. 'Put this on. Because it's dark, it won't be see-through when it's wet. I'll put my back to you to act as a shield so no one will see, okay?'

'Okay,' I nodded, my heart rate stabilising.

'I'm gonna count and when I get to three, let's go back under the water. Ready?'

I nodded again.

'One, two, *three*.'

We both ducked beneath the surface and Max put his back to me, just like he'd promised. I quickly slid his vest over my head. Although it was now sodden, I could still smell Max's woody scent.

As I pulled the fabric down over my breasts, I exhaled then tapped him on his shoulder. It was just as firm as I'd imagined.

Max turned his head slowly, keeping his eyes firmly fixed to my face. I pointed upwards, signalling that I was about to go up for air.

We both pushed our heads above water and then stood up.

Jasmine was now at the edge of the pool.

'Are you okay?' Her face creased with concern.

'Yeah. I am now. Sorry, I didn't mean to put on an X-rated show!' I squeezed my eyes shut with embarrassment, wishing I could escape down the pool drain and never resurface.

'Maybe we could take a break?' Max said. 'Give Stella a chance to get changed into something more comfortable?'

My heart swelled a little. It was sweet of Max to suggest that.

'Of course!' Jasmine confirmed.

Now I wished I'd had the foresight to bring a towel. Even though my bikini bottoms were still firmly intact, knowing everyone was still staring made me feel self-conscious so I wanted to cover up as much as possible.

'Let me get you a towel.' Max climbed out of the pool.

The man was a mind reader.

He strode over to a little wooden hut I hadn't noticed before. After speaking to the hotel worker standing inside it, Max walked away with a towel and returned to the pool.

'Come over by the stairs,' he commanded. I did what he asked and Max stood at the top holding open the towel for me to step into.

As he wrapped the soft, fluffy fabric around my body, relief washed over me.

I never thought I'd say this, but I was grateful that Max was here.

Who knows how long I would've flashed everyone if he hadn't pushed me under the water when he did.

And if he hadn't got his vest, I would've had to get out of the pool topless. My hands weren't big enough to cover my boobs completely, so it would've been so humiliating.

'What a hero!' A grin spread across Jasmine's face. 'I bet you're glad Max was there to help.'

'Yeah,' I said, quickly stepping back from him. It wasn't a good idea for us to stand too close, especially given how my body had reacted when our palms touched earlier. 'Thanks.' I looked up at him.

'It was nothing.' He waved his hand dismissively. As his gaze met mine, butterflies fluttered in my stomach and I chastised myself.

Max had done a kind thing and I was grateful. I truly was. But that didn't mean I'd forgiven him. And it definitely didn't mean my feelings had changed. One nice gesture didn't mean I was about to fall for him. I was too smart for that.

But then he smiled at me and the butterflies started dancing again.

Shit.

My mind might have decided not to be affected by Max's presence, but unfortunately my body hadn't quite got the message.

11

MAX

If some sadistic force was trying to test my willpower, they'd succeeded.

When Stella's bikini top had flown off, my first thought was *wow*. She'd always had a hot body and the most amazing tits, but now? They were incredible. I wasn't proud of the indecent scenarios that flicked through my head at that point of what I'd like to do with them, but I was only human. Even though things between us were strained, you'd have to not have a pulse not to be affected by the sight of her.

Stella was *all woman*.

Luckily, I'd quickly dragged my thoughts from the gutter and my second thought was *shit: she doesn't realise that she's standing there topless*. And that's when I knew I had to do something.

Pushing her under water wasn't ideal, but every second counted. Telling her to put her hands over her chest would've added another ten seconds of embarrassment, so I thought it was better to do that below the surface where no one else could see.

In the end I think she appreciated my intervention. When she thanked me, a weird warm feeling filled my chest.

I was under no illusion, though. Just because I helped out didn't mean I was off the hook. Even if I did something nice every day for a decade, it wouldn't change the fact that she hated me.

Doing an activity with Stella every day was going to be challenging enough. And when they mentioned that shit about choosing photos together and doing playlists, I was tempted to throw in the towel. That was gonna be awkward as fuck.

But I'd made a commitment to stay. So I had to see it through. Starting with winning this first task.

Stella returned in a different bikini and as she walked to the pool with her head down, I tried my best not to look, but it was difficult.

I got up from the sun lounger and went over to her.

'You good?' I asked.

'Yeah,' she said softly. Even though she was wearing sunglasses, I could tell from her body language that she was still embarrassed.

'Come on. Let's go and win this thing!'

A small smile touched her lips and I felt that weird fluttery feeling again in my chest.

At least we still had one thing in common. We both liked to succeed. Stella wanted to win this tournament just as much as I did.

We won the rest of our games and now we were only one point away from being declared champions.

As the ball hurtled over the net, we both raced forward.

'Go for it!' I said to Stella. Even though I didn't think she had anything to be ashamed of, I knew that if she got the winning point it'd boost her confidence.

Stella hit the ball at full force and it flew past them before our opponents got the chance to return it.

Jasmine blew the whistle.

'The winners are: Thunderbolt!' she cheered.

'Yes!' I held my palm up for Stella to high five.

As our hands connected, something shot through me. Our team name felt appropriate because it was like a bolt of lightning had struck me.

'We did it!' Stella smiled.

'Yeah,' I grinned before realising our fingers were intertwined. I pulled my hand away quickly to avoid upsetting Stella. Not even sure how or why that'd happened, but I knew she'd want as little contact with me as possible.

'Come up!' Jasmine said excitedly.

Stella got out of the pool and I averted my eyes to the other guests, then to the sky. Anywhere but looking at her arse.

'Team Thunderbolt: it gives me great pleasure to present your prize.' She whipped out a gold envelope. 'Who'd like to do the honours?'

'Ladies first,' I gestured to Stella. It was probably something crappy like a bottle of wine so I wasn't bothered. Knowing that we'd won was enough.

Stella beamed as she took the envelope. She made quick work of opening it. But when she pulled out the paper, her face fell and she glared at me. You didn't need to be a detective to tell that Stella wasn't happy.

'No way,' she scowled.

'What is it?' I asked.

When Stella handed me the paper, I winced.

Most couples would be thrilled with this prize, but not us. Never mind a bottle of wine. I think we'd both have been happier with a bottle of stagnant seawater.

This was the worst activity you could give a pair of exes who'd been forced together.

I was worried before about things getting awkward and I was right.

There was no way either of us would be going through with *this*.

12

STELLA

'Th-thank you...' I plastered on a fake grin.

I didn't want to sound ungrateful, but there was no way I was accepting this prize.

Once Jasmine had congratulated us again and the guests had dispersed, I turned to face her.

'Um, Jasmine, this is really kind of you, but I'm not having a couple's massage with *him*.'

'Maybe Stella can just use the voucher for two separate massage treatments or something?' Max said.

That was decent of him to suggest. But he'd won the tournament too, so as much as I'd prefer to avoid him, it wouldn't be fair for me to get all the benefits.

'Or I could take one massage by myself and Max could take the other?'

'Awww, I'm really sorry,' Jasmine winced. 'But this is a couple's activity. It's not a traditional massage. It's a masterclass where you'll learn how to massage your partner, so it won't work as a solo activity. It's not like you can massage your own back!' She laughed as the blood drained from my face.

'But... but... is it even *appropriate*? I mean, strictly speaking all of the couples have only just met, so I doubt anyone who won this would feel comfortable taking their clothes off in front of a stranger.'

'I understand you may have some concerns, but most massages are done by strangers,' Jasmine said. 'The focus will be on your back and shoulders and Olga, our *Relaxation Facilitator*, will be there the whole time. If it makes you feel better, we can arrange it for later in the trip so you have time to get more comfortable with one another?'

Even if she arranged it next century it wouldn't be long enough.

'Maybe we'll let you know?' Max said.

'I'll leave you both to celebrate,' Jasmine smiled. 'Today's group activity is done. Feel free to dine together in the restaurant for dinner, oh, and don't forget to submit your playlists. Enjoy!' She walked off.

I'd forgotten about those stupid playlists.

'I'm going to my room.' I strode away quickly before Max had a chance to say anything.

Once I got inside, I jumped on the bed and screamed into the pillow. I was trying, but this was so difficult.

I couldn't sit through a dinner with Max tonight. And I definitely couldn't go to a couple's massage lesson with him. Imagine a whole hour of him running his hands all over my back.

An image of his bare chest, incredible arms and his toned arse in those swimming trunks flashed through my head.

Then I thought about the way he'd looked out for me when my bikini top flew off. And the tingles that'd raced through me when our fingers intertwined after we'd high-fived. We used to always hold hands.

Then I remembered the way he'd yanked his hand away

from me in the pool when he realised he was still holding mine. Like he was repulsed. My stomach twisted.

This was too much. I just wanted to go home.

I reached for my phone. I'd already had two missed calls from Mum. I had to call her back. She'd probably be worried.

'Hi, Mum.' I flipped myself over on the bed and stared up at the ceiling.

'Hi! How's it going over there? You having fun?'

'It's... the hotel's lovely and the weather's great here. Much better than in London,' I said, trying to focus on the positive.

'That's all lovely, but tell me about your date! Is he handsome? Where's he from? Tell me everything!'

'It's Max.'

'What's *Max*?'

'My date. They've set me up with Max. My ex.'

'No!' she gasped. 'Oh. Wow. That's... a surprise.'

'Tell me about it!'

'And I'm guessing you're not thrilled?'

'Nope. Mum, it's so hard.'

'I can imagine. But you were just kids back then. This doesn't have to be a bad thing. He was always a sweetheart, well until, y'know, all that terrible stuff happened. What's he like now?'

'He's... he's aged well. We haven't spoken much because it was such a shock. We played a volleyball tournament today. We won, but something embarrassing happened.'

I filled Mum in on the bikini mishap, which she laughed about, and told her how Max had stepped in. I also explained everything about the daily activities and our silly Love Tasks.

'It all sounds great, sweetie. I know it's difficult, but you're doing really well. Despite your differences, you and Max worked together today and you won a whole tournament. That's brilliant. People change. Just give it a few more days and then reassess, okay?'

'Okay.' My shoulders relaxed a little. 'I'll try.'

'I'll leave you to get on with your Love Task. Do you know what songs you're going to choose yet for your playlist?'

'I have an idea...'

'Great! Have fun and speak soon.'

'Love you.'

'Love you too.'

I hung up feeling a little better.

There was a manual on the table so I got up to get it. Inside were instructions for the playlist. Although I was exhausted and wanted to have a nap before dinner, I decided it was best to get this out of the way first.

I'll admit: Max did a kind thing today and I was grateful for his help. But that didn't mean I forgave him. And Jasmine said that the first playlist was about our first impressions yesterday, right? Just like that a flurry of song ideas flew into my head.

As I launched Spotify and clicked on my first choice, I turned up the volume and danced around the room.

I couldn't wait to see Max's face when he heard what I'd picked.

13

MAX

As I stepped into the restaurant for breakfast, I scanned the room. There was no sign of Stella and as bad as it sounded, I was kind of relieved.

She hadn't shown up for dinner last night either. Or maybe she did, but managed to avoid me. The last thing I needed was to sit with someone who hated my guts.

If I had any doubts about her feelings towards me before, they were definitely confirmed when I listened to her playlist.

The opening track was 'Dickhead' by Kate Nash. That was followed by 'We Are Never Ever Getting Back Together' by Taylor Swift, 'Walk Away' by Kelly Clarkson, 'Silly Boy' by Rihanna with Lady Gaga, and that angry 'You Oughta Know' Alanis Morissette song.

Even though Jasmine said we only had to include five songs, Stella clearly thought I deserved three bonus tracks so she'd added OneRepublic's 'Apologize', Dua Lipa's 'IDGAF' and finished with 'Bye, Bye, Bye' from *NSYNC.

It could've been worse, I supposed. At least she hadn't included 'Eat Shit and Die' by Paloma Faith.

But she'd succeeded in communicating her feelings. She didn't like me. Message received loud and clear.

My playlist was more apologetic, but I doubted she'd even listened to it.

I sat at the table and ordered an egg-white omelette and a coffee. As the waiter walked away, I glanced at the door again.

Speak of the devil.

Stella breezed into the room and I swallowed hard.

Fuck. She looked good.

Her hair was tied up into a ponytail and she was wearing a white sleeveless top that showed off her incredible shoulders and clung to her chest. And that bright yellow skirt accentuated her toned thighs and perfect legs.

I was trying really hard not to let her affect me, but it was difficult. Despite the bad blood between us, I was attracted to her. I had to find a way to get that under control.

I dropped my gaze to the table and pretended to scroll on my phone. I hoped she wouldn't see me. Or if she did, that she'd have the sense to ignore me and find her own table.

Those hopes went out the window when I heard the sound of the chair opposite me being scraped across the floor.

'Before you get any ideas that I'm sitting with you by choice, the restaurant's fully booked this morning. That's the only reason I'm here.'

'Don't worry.' I looked up at her, instantly wishing I hadn't when I saw that she looked even prettier up close. 'I know you wouldn't choose to live on the same continent as me, never mind eat with me. You made that clear by not coming to dinner last night. Oh and of course with your *lovely* playlist.'

'Last night I fell asleep, so I didn't have dinner.' Skipping meals, even though it wasn't intentional, wasn't good, but I wasn't about to lecture her. 'Glad you enjoyed the playlist, though.'

She flashed a mischievous grin, before turning to the waiter who'd just arrived and placing her breakfast order.

'I got the photos.' I slid the envelope I'd collected from reception earlier.

'What photos?'

'The photos from yesterday. For the Love Task book thing. I haven't looked at them yet because we're supposed to go through them together.'

'Let's get this over and done with.' She pulled out the selection and placed them in the centre of the table.

As Stella flicked through the photos, she frowned.

'What's wrong?'

'These can't be right.' She went through the selection again. 'These are...'

'Nice?' I replied.

'Yeah.' Her face creased. 'They're all happy and smiley and... this is fake.'

I picked them up to have a closer look. There were photos of each of us hitting the ball across the net, one with us smiling as we high-fived after winning a game and Stella wrapped in the towel I gave her after the *incident* looking up at me with what a stranger might wrongly assume was awe.

The next shot was a photo I'd prefer wasn't taken. It was me looking at Stella like she was a snack I wanted to devour. The last picture showed us outside the pool grinning as Jasmine handed over the gold envelope containing our nightmare prize.

'I see what you're saying. How many do we have to choose again?'

'One each.' I put them back down in the middle of the table.

If I was being honest, I'd choose the one where she was in the towel, looking up at me.

She looked happy. Grateful. Relieved. Like she actually liked me. I used to love the way Stella looked at me. It was a million miles away from the death glares she'd given me since we were paired up.

I also liked the triumphant high-five photo. A flashback of the bolt of electricity I'd felt when our hands connected jumped into my brain and I pushed it out again.

Nope. I couldn't choose that photo either.

'I like the one of us hitting the ball over the net,' I said.

'Only because *you're* the one hitting it.'

'No, that's not why I...'

'Fine,' she snapped. 'Choose whatever you want.'

'What about you?' I asked. 'Which one do *you* like?'

'If I was forced to choose, then maybe the envelope one. Even though the smiles are fake and we won't get to use the prize, it shows that we won the competition, so it's like an achievement, which is good.'

'Great,' I said, relieved when the waiter returned with our breakfast.

At least our first set of Love Tasks were complete.

After breakfast we'd be heading to the pool to find out what today's activity would be.

I'd like to say I was looking forward to it, but seeing as it meant spending more time with Stella, the chances were slim.

14

STELLA

It was now Tuesday morning and Max and I were outside waiting for the coach the hotel had hired to take us to today's activity.

I still had no idea where we were going. When we'd arrived for the daily debrief at the pool, I'd asked Jasmine, but she'd said it was a surprise.

Whilst all the other guests around us were chatting with their partners, I was standing here with Max in silence. We'd only been here for a few minutes but the awkwardness made it feel like hours.

Thankfully yesterday's sandcastle-building competition was less eventful than the pool volleyball activity on Sunday. We were given two hours to create a beach masterpiece. Even though Max and I argued about whether or not to include windows, how many flags to have and how big the towers should be, we managed to make something half decent.

I wasn't too bothered that we didn't win. Especially if the first prize we won at volleyball was anything to go by.

For the rest of the day I'd avoided talking to Max by eating by the pool instead of the restaurant and burying my head in a book.

Sadly, I didn't think I'd be lucky enough to escape spending time with him today though.

Just as I was about to pull out my phone as a distraction, a woman with white shoulder-length hair and an elegant summer dress came over.

'Hello, young Max!' she smiled.

'Dorothy! Hey! How's it going?'

'Good, thank you. They matched me with a very lovely young man.'

'How young we talking?' Max cocked his head.

'He's sixty-five, so a whole seven years younger than me!'

'Brilliant! You sound chuffed!'

'I am! I've always wanted a toy boy!' She winked.

'You saucy little minx!' Max teased. 'Go easy on him!'

'Not a chance! Anyway, I wanted to say thanks again for your help.'

'No probs,' Max said. I frowned, wondering what she was talking about. I hadn't seen her before so she must be in a separate group.

I was happy at least that she'd been set up with someone she was interested in. And I liked that the hotel had guests of all ages too.

'Did you find your other keycard?'

'Yes! It was on the bed!' Dorothy said. 'Under my handbag!'

'We've all been there!' Max laughed. 'Well, not the whole handbag thing, but I've left my keycard in my hotel room loads of times.'

'Forgive me.' Dorothy turned to face me. 'Is this your lovely match?'

'Dorothy, meet Stella. Stella, this is Dorothy.'

'Nice to meet you,' I smiled.

'I'm ever so sorry that I made Max late to your first date. I was on my way to the restaurant too, but realised I'd closed the door without my key which was in my handbag, which was also in my room and I couldn't get back in. My knees can be a bit temperamental, so I knew I wouldn't be able to get to reception and back again quickly enough, so Max offered to get a key for me. I don't know what I would've done without him!' she beamed.

Ohhhh. Now it made sense.

'You would've been fine.' Max waved his hand dismissively.

'You're far too modest!' Dorothy patted his arm. 'Anyway, I'll leave you two lovebirds to it. I'm off to meet my Lionel now.'

'Have fun. And tell him that if he doesn't take good care of you, he'll have *me* to answer to!' Max laughed and Dorothy blushed before waving goodbye and setting off towards reception.

'So...' I said, psyching myself up to apologise. 'Dorothy was the reason you were late?'

'Yep.'

'Sorry, I didn't realise.'

'I tried to explain.'

'I know, it's just that when you said you were with a woman...'

'You thought the worst.'

'Can you blame me?'

'Doesn't matter.'

I did kind of feel bad for judging him, but I'd apologised, so I didn't know what else he expected me to do.

'Coach is here!' Jasmine announced as it pulled in front of us.

Whoa. This was no ordinary coach. It wasn't like what we went on for school trips. This had a sleek, glossy black exterior like the ones they used to transport Premier League footballers or celebrities.

We joined the back of the queue and when we got inside, it was just as glam as the outside.

I walked along the spotless wooden flooring, taking in the sight of the tinted windows, plush grey and white reclining leather seats which had so much legroom even a basketball player could stretch out comfortably.

In front of the seats were large, shiny chrome tables that were a million miles away from the cheap plastic ones you got on trains and planes.

At the back of the coach there was even a kitchen with a coffee machine, fridge and microwave, plus loads of elegantly displayed drinks and snacks.

Wow. The Love Hotel really knew how to push the boat out. Now I understood why it was so pricey.

The coach was already full, so I had no choice but to sit next to Max. Thankfully, I'd come prepared. My phone was loaded with eBooks on the Kindle app, so I planned to read for the whole journey.

Although we'd survived breakfast together, I didn't want to chance it. Speaking of breakfast, yesterday I was surprised at how those photos from the volleyball tournament on Sunday came out.

In one of the pics it looked like Max was ogling me, but I knew that couldn't be right. All of the pictures were misleading. I mean I was smiling and looked happy which of course was ridiculous.

So was that snap they took where I was wrapped in the towel and looking up at Max like he'd just invented water. Yeah, I was grateful but that was all. I wasn't some stupid lovesick teenager any more. Now I knew better.

We didn't get a chance to pick up the sandcastle-building pictures yet. Maybe we'd do that when we got back.

I slid into a window seat and whipped out my phone. Max sat beside me and his scent flooded my nostrils. I hated how great he smelt.

He repositioned himself in the seat, his arms skimming mine. Goosebumps erupted over my skin and I warned my body to calm the hell down.

There was a reason I'd taken out my phone. What was it again?

Reading. That was it.

Good idea. I needed the distraction.

'Sorry.' Max moved around in the seat again, his bare arms pressing against mine.

I squeezed myself against the window to try and create some distance between us then launched my book app and tried to focus.

'What you reading?' Max said.

'Nothing you'd be interested in,' I replied, keeping my eyes firmly fixed to the screen.

'Is it a romance novel?'

'Yes,' I sighed. Why couldn't people understand that when someone was reading they didn't want interruptions?

'That's a shame.'

'What?' My head whipped up. 'There's nothing wrong with romance novels!'

'No, I know that. I wasn't dissing the genre. People should read whatever they want. And I love watching a good romcom, remember?'

I swallowed hard. He was right. Max always used to watch them with me. A lot of my friends' boyfriends only ever wanted to watch action films and they were jealous that Max was happy to binge romcoms with me.

'Yeah,' I replied, my gaze still fixed to my phone.

'When I said it's a shame, I meant it's a shame that you're reading. It's your first time in Spain, right? So I thought maybe you'd want to spend the journey looking at the scenery, that's all.'

Good point. I'd been so focused on trying to protect my emotions by ignoring him that I'd forgotten about enjoying the views.

I looked up and turned to the window. Colourful flowers lined the central reservation. I'd noticed them on the way here.

As we continued along the motorway I took in the clear blue skies and observed how the landscape changed. In some places the land was yellow where the grass had been dried out from the sun and in others there were fields upon fields of olive trees.

'It's so different to London,' I said before realising that I shouldn't be making conversation.

'Yeah. I love Spain. I always enjoy coming here.'

'Have you been here a lot?'

'I come a few times a year. I was here a couple of weeks ago.'

'On holiday?' I turned to face him. He must lead an extravagant lifestyle to be able to come twice in one month.

Although his career as a professional footballer hadn't worked out, I bet he was still doing something that raked in the cash. Maybe he was a personal trainer for celebrities who flew him over to their holiday homes in Ibiza and Marbella just to tell them how to do some sit ups.

'No,' he laughed. 'I don't really do holidays. This is my first one in ages. And I didn't even choose to go. I was blackmailed into coming by Colton.'

'Colton Brown?'

'The very one.'

'I didn't realise you two were still friends.'

'Yep. Although I questioned whether we should be when he signed me up for this and used his six-year-old daughter to coerce me.'

'Shameless!' I smiled. 'My mum signed me up for this, even though I told her I wasn't interested.'

'Looks like we were both lured here against our will.' Max looked at me and our eyes locked.

'Yeah,' I replied, trying to ignore the flutter in my stomach. 'So.' I looked out the window to avoid staring at him. He was annoyingly attractive. 'You came here for work then?'

'That's right.'

'And what do you do? If you don't mind me asking. You don't need to tell me if you don't want to,' I stuttered. Seeing as we were stuck here, I supposed it wouldn't hurt to make conversation. Hopefully the journey wouldn't be too long.

Okay and yeah, I'll admit. I was a little curious to know where he was working. That was normal. People always wanted to know where their old friends ended up.

'I run a beauty products company.'

'What?' I almost choked on my own saliva. 'Sorry, I... didn't mean... There's nothing wrong with that. It's just not what I was expecting.'

'Well, I couldn't play football any more, so y'know.' His gaze dropped to the floor. 'Why? What did you expect?'

'Um.' I felt bad for raising the question. I knew career choices was a bad topic of discussion for him given what happened. And although I shouldn't care about his feelings considering he never gave a shit about mine, I still didn't want to upset him.

'It's okay,' he shrugged. 'Don't feel bad.'

The way he could still read my mind was scary.

'Oh. Right. Okay. Well, I kind of thought you were still in the sports industry somehow. Like maybe a personal trainer.'

'What made you think that?'

'Just... y'know.' I gestured to his arms.

'No, I don't.' The corner of his mouth twitched.

'Now you're just fishing for compliments.' I rolled my eyes.

'Why? Were you about to give me one?'

'Of course not!' I became flustered.

'Then tell me. What made you think I was a personal trainer?'

'The... y'know.' Oh, God. Now I had to try and answer that without sounding like I'd been ogling him. 'Your big... muscles!' I sighed loudly.

'Right,' he smirked. 'I just like staying healthy, that's all.'

'Well, I know a lot of people who like to be healthy, but they don't have arms like *that*.'

My insides shrivelled like a prune when I realised what I'd just said. Now he was going to think I liked him.

Giving Max the silent treatment was a much better idea than this making conversation nonsense.

'Sounds like you've studied my arms a *lot*.'

'No!' I protested. 'No more than anyone else's here. I mean, they're hard to miss. And you've always got them out.'

'*Got them out*?' He laughed. 'You make it sound like I walk around flashing my balls! We're in Spain – y'know? Where it's hot. What do you suggest I wear? A woolly jumper? And just because I have a vest on, doesn't mean you have to look. Does that mean if you wear a low-cut top, I should stare at your tits?'

'That's different!'

'Why?'

'Because...' I stuttered, struggling to think of an acceptable defence. 'Because breasts are more sexual than arms.'

'Really?' He cocked his head to one side. 'That's funny because I'm pretty sure I remember women swooning over men's muscles, including arms, in those romance novels you liked to read. Am I right?'

'That doesn't matter,' I said, knowing I was losing this battle. He was right, but there was no way I was telling him that. 'That's fiction.'

'If you say so. But anyway, thanks for the compliment. It's nice to know there's at least one thing you like about me.'

'I didn't say I...'

'Lovelies!' Jasmine's voice boomed around the coach. 'We've arrived at our destination!'

'Oh, shit!' a guy in front of us who sounded like he was from the US called out. 'We're going to the Caminito del Rey! That's fucking sick!'

'Yes!' Max cheered. 'I've always wanted to come here!'

'Same here, bro,' the guy said.

'What's the Camin... whatever you just said?' I asked him.

'It's this path that hangs from a cliff!' The guy jumped up like he'd just discovered he'd won the lottery and was rushing to collect his winnings. 'It's one of the world's most dangerous paths! It hangs from a cliff and they called it the *walk of death* because so many people fell off it and died! I love scary shit like this!'

'Sorry, *what*? We're going to walk on a path that hangs from a *cliff*? Where people *died*?'

The blood drained from my body.

As the coach pulled up and people started filing off and lining up with Jasmine outside, I stayed rooted to the spot.

I glared out the window, taking in the sight of the steep rocky cliffs. My heart raced. What kind of psycho believed coming *here* was a good idea?

I thought being paired up with Max was the worst thing that could happen on this trip.

I was wrong.

15

MAX

When I got off the coach, I looked behind and saw Stella walking towards me in a trance.

That was when I remembered. She was terrified of heights.

'Listen,' I said softly as I saw the fear in her eyes, 'I know what that guy said sounded terrifying, but...'

'What's wrong?' Jasmine joined me, concern written all over her face.

'I'm not really a fan of heights,' Stella said, her voice shaky.

'Really?' Jasmine pulled out her phone and tapped the screen. 'That's strange. I've got details of your preferences taken from your application form and it says that you love adventures and hiking...'

'I'm going to kill my mum!' Stella groaned.

'It's not as scary as it seems.' Jasmine rested her hand on Stella's shoulder. That was exactly what I was trying to explain before she came over. 'I'm not a fan of heights either, but I've done it a few times and it's been great. It's a really easy walk. I hate to rush you, but we need to get to the entrance or we'll miss our slot. Why don't you have a think and if you really don't feel like you can do it, we'll see what our options are, okay?'

Stella nodded. Yep. She was definitely shitting herself.

'Don't worry,' I said. 'I know that guy made it sound like a death trap but it's not like that any more. It used to have a reputation for being dangerous, but they've fixed all the paths since then and it's a really beautiful walk. It's been on my bucket list for years.'

'How did you hear about it?'

'It's known as one of the top things to do in Andalucía – maybe even in Spain. Millions of people have done it now. They wouldn't bring us here if it wasn't safe. If you want, I can walk on the outside so you won't be close to the edge. I'll make sure you're okay. Promise.'

Stella looked up and her eyes met mine. A jolt of electricity shot through my chest, just like it did when our arms touched on the coach.

It was interesting that she thought I was a personal trainer. And I wasn't gonna lie. Knowing that she'd been looking at my arms made me feel good.

'Okay,' she said softly, still looking at me. I was glad I'd reassured her. Stella acted tough on the outside, but I knew that she was soft and vulnerable on the inside. That was why I felt so bad about hurting her before.

I reminded myself for the millionth time that I couldn't do anything about the past, but whilst I was on the trip I'd try my best to show her I'd become a better man.

Once we'd arrived at the main entrance and gone to the toilet, we had a safety briefing. When the guide started handing out safety helmets, Stella's eyes bulged.

'It's just a precaution,' I whispered.

Once we'd put the radio we'd been given on a lanyard

around our necks and taken the earphones we'd use to listen to the tour guide, we set off.

As we stepped onto the first of the wooden slats, I positioned myself on the outside like I'd promised and held the handrail.

The wooden path had steel rods, which were pinned to the cliff. I wasn't bothered about heights, but even I had to admit that the drop below was pretty steep.

Beneath us was the narrow original pathway. I could see why it used to be dangerous. For starters there weren't any barriers. Thankfully the current walkway looked much more secure and had an iron mesh fence at the edge to stop us from falling.

I caught Stella glancing down and could tell she was freaking out, so I tried to distract her.

'It's beautiful, isn't it?' I pointed to the scenery and blue skies.

'Yeah… although it's difficult not to notice how steep that drop is.'

'Just keep your eyes straight ahead and you'll be good.'

'I'm trying.'

The tour guide talked us through some of the key sections of the walk and I kept an eye on Stella to check how she was coping. She wasn't.

A woman in front of us reached into her backpack and pulled out a bottle of water. As she guzzled it down, I noticed it'd trickled down onto the slats. But Stella had her gaze firmly fixed on the vultures that were flying overhead so she stepped right into a wet patch and slipped.

She shrieked and after quickly grabbing her arm, I helped her back upright.

'Shit!' she gasped, panic in her eyes. 'I-I…'

'Don't worry. It was just a bit of water. Nothing would've happened to you.'

'You don't know that,' she said. 'I'm trying to stay calm, but…'

'I know. It's okay. But like I said, I won't let anything happen to you. Maybe you could...'

'What?' She frowned.

'Forget it. I was just going to suggest something that might help, but I don't think you'll like it.'

'Tell me!'

'Well,' I exhaled, plucking up the courage to make a suggestion that could quite easily result in Stella throwing me over the edge of this pathway. 'I was gonna say you could... hold my hand. Just to make you feel better. Actually, *better* isn't the right word, because obviously you hate me. But more secure? Safer? So you know that if you slip again, which I'm sure you won't, you'll know you won't fall.'

Stella looked at me like she was weighing up my suggestion. Although I couldn't read her expression, the fact that she was taking a few seconds to consider it was more than I'd expected.

'But what if I fall and drag you down with me?'

'I'll take my chances. And anyway, I owe you, right?'

'True.'

'It's just until you feel comfortable. I promise I won't use superglue, so you'll be free to remove your hand whenever you want to. Okay?'

'Okay.'

My eyebrows hit the sky.

Stella had agreed to hold my hand. Shit.

To anyone else, it wouldn't seem like a big deal. It wasn't like we were kids in the playground about to hold hands with our crush for the first time. We were adults.

But I knew this was big for her. She must be *really* scared to agree.

I held out my palm and Stella wrapped her small hand in mine.

And as our skin connected and that same shot of electricity lit up inside of me I realised that I liked the feeling.

Which wasn't good.

At all...

16

STELLA

I couldn't believe I was holding Max's hand. *Voluntarily*.

That just showed how desperate I was.

I'd always been afraid of heights. I didn't even like anything remotely scary. Just the thought of watching a horror film made me break out in a cold sweat. So walking on what felt like a flimsy bridge hanging off a cliff with a steep drop beneath me was terrifying. And that was before you factored in this walk-way's reputation for being a death trap.

Yes, as the tour guide, Jasmine and Max had explained, it was safe now. But that didn't change the fact that it was over one hundred metres from the ground.

When the tour guide started talking about the pathway's history and how it was built to allow access for the workers at a power station and help them transport materials between the two power plants, I tried to focus. But instead my ears zeroed in on the sound of the walkway jingling up and down with every step we took.

Max had said not to look down and I'd tried. I really did. And I wished I'd listened because on more than one occasion I saw huge sections where there was nothing between the new walkway and the ground below. Which I assumed was where the old path had snapped and people had fallen to their deaths.

And when I looked up, it was hard to ignore the vultures circling – almost as if they were waiting for people to fall so they could swoop down and feast on them.

That was why when I slipped, I freaked out. Luckily Max had caught me, but that didn't stop my brain from spiralling and thinking what could've happened and what other fearful experiences were ahead of us.

I hadn't even realised that I was shaking when Max said it. But I did know I was scared. So when Max offered to hold my hand, as much as I didn't want to, I knew I had two choices: keep being stubborn and hostile and continue the walk feeling terrified. Or put my anger towards him aside for a couple of hours or however long this nightmare would last and feel safe.

So I accepted his offer. And as he wrapped his big, warm hand around mine, the effect was instant.

Butterflies erupted in my stomach and my heart raced. But this time, my pounding heartbeat wasn't caused by fear. It was something else. If it was any other man, I would've said it was excitement. That couldn't be true though. I didn't even like Max. Not any more.

That was what I kept telling myself anyway. But even I had to admit, it was getting harder and harder to continue this hatred towards him.

How he ended things between us was terrible. But I could see he was trying. He'd helped me at the pool on Sunday and he was being sweet to me now. And he was kind to that Dorothy woman.

That didn't mean I'd forgiven him. And it 100 per cent did *not* mean I wanted anything to happen between us. But maybe, just maybe I could think about trying to be more civil towards him.

Maybe.

'You good?' Max turned to face me.

'Yeah. Thanks.' Our eyes connected and my stomach flipped. He'd always had such lovely eyes and as much as I hated to say it, I could tell he was being sincere.

'No worries. I want you to enjoy this. Look at these views!' He pointed ahead.

Now I felt calmer I was able to appreciate the surroundings a bit more. The landscape was pretty stunning.

I took in the panoramic views of tall rocky mountains, rugged cliffs, valleys and canyons and lush greenery all set against the clear blue sky and warm sunshine which heated my skin. There was even a river flowing between two gorges.

'It *is* nice.'

'If you feel comfortable, we should take some photos. Y'know, for our memory photo album thing.'

'Oh. Yeah. I suppose.'

I'd seen people stopping to take pictures since the walk started, but I was too scared. Before I just wanted to get it over and done with as quickly as possible. But now, I was feeling more relaxed and could manage stopping for a few seconds.

As I paused on the walkway, Max pulled out his phone and held it up for a selfie.

'Ready?' he asked, still holding my hand.

'As I'll ever be!' I smiled.

After taking a few snaps, we continued the walk, the guide pointing out various things of interest including mountain goats and a bridge that was named after a king. I wasn't so keen to hear about the bat shelter though.

Throughout every step of the walk, Max kept hold of my hand and the strange thing was, it didn't feel weird.

If I closed my eyes (which of course given where we were, I

wouldn't dream of doing) and tried to clear my mind, it would be easy to believe that we were those two teenagers who used to always hold hands.

It felt like no time had passed. Which scared the shit out of me.

Well, that was until I saw what was ahead of us.

'Yes!' Max said enthusiastically. 'This is one of the best parts of the trail!'

It was a hanging bridge, connecting two sections of the walkway which like everything else was very, very high up from the ground and looked terrifying. Especially when the tour guide said that only ten people were allowed on the bridge at a time. That didn't exactly reassure me that it was stable.

'The *best*? I didn't think it could get any scarier, until I saw this.'

'Yeah, I know it's suspended midair, but that means there's nothing interrupting our view.'

'I'm sure it'll look amazing, but...' I paused, feeling embarrassed to say how I felt out loud. 'I'm scared.'

My gaze dropped to the floor which made me feel worse.

'Stella.' Max lifted my chin and looked me in the eyes so deeply it was like he was staring directly into my soul. My stomach did that silly flip-flop thing again. 'You're doing really well.' He let go of my hand and rubbed my back gently, causing goosebumps to erupt across my skin. 'If you really don't think you can do it, we can go back, but there isn't much more of the walk left, so I really think you'll be fine. Remember, I've got you.' He took my hand again and squeezed it tightly. 'Okay?'

'Okay.' My heart thundered against my chest.

If I was on my own, I would've considered giving up. But the way Max spoke in such soothing tones made me believe that I *could* do this. He'd be with me. I was going to be fine.

As the tour guide gave us the green light to walk across the bridge, I gripped Max's hand so tight I'm surprised I didn't break it.

With every step, the bridge swayed a little from left to right, but Max squeezed my hand, giving me the strength to continue.

When we reached the centre, he slowed down.

'We're halfway there. Look at the views. Aren't they incredible?'

'Yeah, they really are. Should we... take some photos, like really quickly? Before I lose my nerve.'

'It'd be a crime not to.'

Max made fast work of snapping some selfies.

And when he lifted my hand in the air in triumph for one of the poses, even though I was still really nervous and worried about the movement of the bridge caused by the other people walking across it, I tried to push my fear away and enjoy the moment.

'I reckon we've got some great shots! Come on,' he said, leading me further across the bridge.

Soon afterwards, we came to the end of the walk. And I was so relieved I almost kissed the ground.

Once we'd returned our helmets, stopped to use the toilet and got some snacks from the kiosks, we boarded our coach.

'How you feeling?' Max said as he slid into the seat next to me.

'Relieved.'

'You should also be proud of yourself. A lot of people with your fear of heights would've given up. But you kept going.'

'Thanks to you,' I said, trying to ignore the flipping again in my stomach as I thought about how he'd held my hand for ages. Sounded stupid but I kind of missed it now.

'No big deal.'

Hearing his words reminded me that I needed to get a grip. He'd held my hand just to help me. He would've done the same for anyone. It wasn't because he liked me. Not like *that* anyway.

During the walk I'd started to feel really comfortable around Max, but now I felt awkward again. I didn't think I could manage speaking to him for the whole journey back to the hotel. Every time he looked at me my stomach fizzed with excitement and I couldn't allow that to happen. I couldn't risk getting hurt again.

If we kept on chatting, I'd probably say something stupid and embarrass myself. I just needed to focus on speaking to Max during the tasks and then stay away from him when they were over. If I did that, hopefully I'd get through this week unscathed.

'I'm a bit tired,' I said. 'I'm going to have a quick nap.'

'Oh.' Max's eyes widened a little. 'Okay.'

I leant my head back on the seat and closed my eyes.

After what only seemed like ten minutes later, I heard my name being called.

'Stell. Stella. Wake up.'

I slowly opened my eyes and saw people in the rows in front getting up from their seats.

'We're here already?' I croaked.

'Yep. So if you maybe want to lift your head up...'

'My head?'

That was when I realised that it was resting on Max's shoulder.

'Oh, shit!' I bolted up. 'Sorry, I didn't mean to fall asleep on you.'

I glanced at Max, my eyes wide, and was horrified to see there was dribble all over his shoulder.

So much for not embarrassing myself.

17

MAX

'Don't worry about it,' I said. 'Once I'd stuffed some tissue in my ears, your snoring didn't seem so bad.'

'I was *snoring*?' Stella's eyes flew from their sockets.

'Just gently. Y'know, like an elephant that'd swallowed a trombone.' A smile tugged at my lips. 'A lot of people complained, but the driver turned up the music and after that it was fine.' When I saw the blood draining from Stella's face, I realised she believed me. 'I'm joking!'

'Oh, thank God!' She blew out a breath. 'You're so evil!'

'Sorry, I couldn't resist!'

'I'll let you off this time, only because of...' She paused, reached in her bag and pulled out a tissue. 'Sorry about... that.' Stella dabbed the tissue on my shoulder, wiping away the tiniest bit of dribble.

Stella always used to dribble on my chest when she slept over. Didn't bother me then and it didn't bother me now.

Sounded weird, but in some ways, I liked it. It meant she was comfortable.

When her head had dropped on my shoulder, I thought

about saying something, but she was sleeping so soundly, I didn't want to disturb her. Hearing her breathing so close to me was soothing. Just like when we held hands earlier.

I knew she was only doing it because she was desperate, but knowing that holding onto me was keeping her calm made me feel so damn good.

Seeing her complete the walk, especially the bit over the suspended bridge, warmed my chest. There were a few times when I'd glanced at her that she looked like she was seconds away from quitting, but she'd stuck it out and I loved that. She was so brave.

Once it was all over, Stella gave me that same look of gratitude that she'd shown after the whole bikini top thing. And this time I really felt like we'd turned a corner. She seemed more comfortable around me. We'd made decent conversation and I was looking forward to chatting more with her on the journey back to the hotel.

But as soon as we'd got on the coach, she'd shut down and said she was going to sleep.

Clearly I was still at the top of her shit list.

That was why when her head dropped on my shoulder, even though she didn't know it'd happened, it still felt nice. Comfortable. Familiar. Just like old times.

At one point, when a strand of hair fell onto her forehead, I caught myself wanting to move it away and stroke her hair. I resisted the temptation though. If she woke up and caught me, she'd think I was weird and I was already skating on thin ice.

So I'd sat there, alternating between taking in the views, closing my eyes and trying not to move too much in case I woke her up.

And now here we were. Back at the hotel.

'I suppose we should get off.' Stella stood up.

'Yeah.' I picked up my rucksack and walked down the aisle then down the steps into the hotel's forecourt. 'What are your plans now?' I asked when Stella appeared beside me.

'Er, I should probably go back to my room and shower.'

'And afterwards? I was thinking of having a swim in the pool or heading down to the beach before dinner. Wanna join me?'

Stella's mouth opened then closed again.

We both stood there in silence and I regretted saying anything. It sounded too much like a date and although this was The Love Hotel, we'd both agreed that we'd just be going through the motions. Doing whatever tasks we were set this week and that was it. I'd overstepped. It was clear that she wasn't interested in anything more.

And neither was I.

'Forget it.' I waved my hand and walked away.

Once I'd dumped my stuff in my room and replied to some emails, I had a quick shower, put on my trunks and headed down to the pool.

My mind was still racing, replaying everything that had happened today and I needed to clear it.

I hadn't been to the gym since I'd arrived and I wasn't used to not exercising. A few laps in the pool would do me good.

When I dragged myself out of the pool, I felt better. Once I'd dried off, I headed back to my room and checked my messages. Luckily there weren't as many emails as I thought, which was a relief.

I messaged Colton to check that everything had been okay at the office, then got changed for dinner and headed to the restaurant.

As always, I scanned the room for Stella, but there was no sign of her. After I placed my order, my gaze flicked back to the door where I saw Jasmine walking towards me.

'Hi!' she beamed. 'How are you? Did you enjoy the trip earlier?'

'Yeah, it was brilliant. It'd always been on my bucket list, so it was great to check it off.'

'And how are things with Stella? I saw you two holding hands earlier and spotted her asleep on your shoulder. That's a good sign, right?'

'She was just scared, that's all. And she fell asleep on my shoulder because she was exhausted.'

'Oh, that's a shame. I really hoped you two had turned a corner.' *Me too.* 'Give it time. I'm sure she'll come around.'

I wasn't so sure about that.

'Do you know if Stella's come for dinner already?' I asked.

Last night I'd eaten early, so I assumed that Stella had come to the restaurant after me. But tonight because of my swim, I'd come a lot later and I knew they'd be closing the kitchen in half an hour, so I doubted she'd come now.

'No.' Jasmine shook her head. 'She hasn't. I've been here since service started and haven't seen her.'

My chest tightened. I hated the fact that she kept skipping dinner. And knowing that it might be because she was trying to avoid me made me feel even worse.

'Do you think the kitchen could make something so I could bring it to her room?'

'Of course! That's a great idea. Do you know what she'd like?'

'I have an idea.' I immediately knew what to ask for. After telling Jasmine, she went to the kitchen to place the order and once it was ready she came back out.

'Do you want me to get one of the waiters, oops, I mean *Cuisine Champions* to deliver it?'

'Um, yeah. Actually.' I paused. 'Maybe I'll come with them. I'd kind of like to give this to her personally.'

'The personal touch,' Jasmine smiled. 'I like your thinking. How about I get José to wheel it along and then he can leave you to knock on the door?'

'Great idea.'

At least I thought it was.

I hoped that Stella agreed.

18

STELLA

I didn't know why it was taking me so long to do this bloody playlist. It was much easier before, but today I felt blocked.

After I'd showered and dressed, I'd texted Mum to let her know I was okay, then sifted through different songs, but I didn't know which ones accurately conveyed my feelings towards Max because I was confused.

On the one hand I was still angry about the past, but on the other I was grateful for the sweet things he'd done. And annoyingly, despite how afraid I was, I'd enjoyed spending time with Max today.

Every song I thought about sounded too mushy. I didn't want him to think I was pining for him, but I didn't want him to think I hated him either.

The songs he'd chosen for me so far had been apologetic. 'Sorry' by Justin Bieber, 'Heartbreaker' by will.i.am ft. Cheryl Cole, 'If I Could Turn Back Time' by Cher, 'Hello' by Adele and 'Purple Rain' by Prince and the Revolution.

It was actually a good selection. He'd managed to strike the balance between sincerity and entertainment. It'd be great if I could do the same.

I'd hoped to have a clearer idea once I'd taken a nap, but what was only supposed to be a short rest ended up with me sleeping for hours and now I'd missed dinner. Again.

Right on cue, my stomach rumbled loudly. I looked at my watch. It was too late to go to the restaurant now. I'd need to call reception and see if I could get room service.

Just as I was about to reach for the phone, there was a knock at the door.

'Coming!' I called out, wondering who it could be, then guessing it was Jasmine. I'd pissed Max off earlier so I knew it wouldn't be him.

When he'd invited me to the pool, I didn't know what to say. Part of me wanted to go, but I knew it wasn't a good idea. The last thing I wanted was to start liking him. That was why I hesitated. But he clearly took it to mean I wasn't interested and walked off. I supposed I couldn't blame him. Tomorrow was definitely going to be awkward.

As I opened the door, my jaw dropped.

It was Max.

'I thought you might be hungry,' he said.

Max was standing there with a trolley which had a silver cloche covering the plate and a bottle of wine in an ice bucket.

'Oh, I... wow,' I stuttered. 'Thanks.'

'You want me to wheel it in?' He gestured to the trolley.

'I can do it.' He'd already done enough.

'Okay. See you tomorrow.' He turned on his heels to leave.

'Wait!' I called out. 'Where are you... are you not joining me? I mean, do you want to come in?'

Inviting Max into my bedroom at almost eleven o'clock at

night wasn't the best idea, but he'd brought me food. It was the least I could do.

'Nah, I'm good. I've already eaten. Hope you like it.'

Before I had a chance to respond, Max was halfway down the pathway.

I wheeled the trolley in and closed the door. Whatever it was smelt amazing. When I lifted off the cloche, I gasped.

It was barbecue chicken and chips. My favourite.

A wave of happiness filled my heart. I couldn't believe he'd remembered.

As I sat down and slid the first forkful of food into my mouth, a flurry of ideas filled my head.

Now I knew exactly what songs to choose for Max.

And this time, it wasn't hatred I wanted to convey.

This time, I genuinely hoped he liked my selection.

19

MAX

As the playlist alert flashed up on my screen, I braced myself for Stella's selections.

After kicking off my shoes, I flopped down on the bed and pressed play.

Oh. I wasn't expecting that.

The first song was 'Thank You for Being a Friend'. It sounded familiar. I checked the screen and saw it was by someone called Andrew Gold.

That song was followed by 'Hold My Hand' by Jess Glynne and 'Lean on Me' by Bill Withers.

The last two songs were 'Torn' by Natalie Imbruglia and 'Don't Speak' by No Doubt which I'm pretty sure were both about break-ups or scumbag exes, but I wasn't gonna dwell on that. Three out of the five songs all seemed to convey that Stella was thankful which was a lot better than the angry songs from her previous playlists.

Maybe we'd made progress after all.

It didn't take me long to create my playlist. Once it was done,

I shared it then turned off the light. Something told me I was gonna sleep much better tonight.

* * *

'You're here.' I looked up from my breakfast as Stella slid onto the seat at my table.

'Yeah. Thought I'd try and catch you before the morning briefing.'

'What's up?' I frowned. She sounded serious.

'Nothing. I just... wanted to thank you. For last night. For bringing me dinner.'

'I know we're not exactly hitting it off, but despite what you think, I'm not a monster. And I didn't like the idea of you skipping another meal.'

'Thanks. I really appreciate it. Especially the fact that you'd bought me barbecue chicken and chips. They're my favourites.'

'I know.'

Our eyes connected. Stella looked so pretty today. Then again, she always did. The yellow sundress she was wearing suited her skin tone and even though she wasn't wearing any make-up, she was stunning.

I wished things were different so I could lean over and kiss her.

Shit. Where the hell did that come from?

I'd always loved kissing Stella. Sometimes we just used to kiss for hours. Okay. Maybe that was a slight exaggeration, but we used to kiss a lot. It was one of my favourite things to do.

For a split second, I wondered if her lips were as soft as they used to be. Then I remembered it was irrelevant. She wasn't interested in me romantically and the feeling was mutual. We were just being civil. That was all.

'So.' I broke the silence and looked down at the half-eaten omelette on my plate. 'The playlist you sent was cool. Thanks.'

'I hope the message of gratitude came across.' A small smile touched her lips.

'It did.'

'Your playlist was good too. Although it made me sound like I'd battled through some deep adversity rather than just walking for a few hours!' she laughed.

I'd picked: 'Eye of the Tiger' by Survivor, 'The Climb' by Miley Cyrus, 'Roar' by Katy Perry, 'FIYAH' by will.i.am and 'Brave' by Sara Bareilles.

'I disagree.' I shook my head. 'You faced a fear. Did something that was challenging, so those songs fitted perfectly. You were really brave.'

This time, Stella didn't argue. Instead she smiled.

'Thanks.'

I'd hoped that we'd made progress last night and it was feeling like we had. Stella had thanked me several times and that smile was the cherry on top. Today was off to a great start.

After breakfast, we headed to the briefing where Jasmine told us that we'd have free time all day, then there'd be a group barbecue and party in the evening. Sounded good.

'So what do you wanna do today?' I asked. Part of me regretted it as soon as the words flew out my mouth because when I suggested doing something together outside the compulsory tasks yesterday, Stella blanked me. But the other part said *fuck it*.

Like I said earlier, we were making progress.

Although it was kinda hard to admit, I wanted to spend time with her. And I might be misreading the signs, but Stella also seemed like she wanted to.

As well as being more civil, at breakfast I'd caught her staring at me for longer than normal a couple of times.

Anyway, *whatever*. The worst she could say was no.

'I don't know. Maybe we could hang out by the pool?' she asked.

'Cool. But we should get our photos first.'

'Good point. Meet back in reception in ten minutes? I just need to get changed.'

'Okay.'

Nine minutes later, Stella strolled towards me looking hotter than a jalapeño.

She was wearing some sort of crochet cover-up dress, but I could see that she had a pink bikini underneath.

I tried not to replay the memory of Stella's bare tits in my head. It was getting harder and harder not to be affected by her presence.

'Got them?' she asked.

'Yep.' I waved two envelopes in the air.

'Let's go and have a look!' she said enthusiastically.

As I followed behind her, I took in the sight of her firm arse and my dick twitched. Fuck. This was ridiculous.

'Wow. It's busy,' I said, trying to distract myself.

It was another hot day. The sky was clear blue and I could already feel the heat searing my skin. We stopped by the pool.

One couple were cosying up on an inflatable flamingo, another was reclined on two giant pizza slice floats and there were a handful of other couples in the pool just playing around and having fun.

'Um, there's no more sun loungers left,' Stella said.

'Looks like we're late to the party. Wait.' I paused as I scanned the area and caught sight of a fancy white cabana daybed with plush cushions, adjustable backrests and white curtains neatly tied to the sides. It looked so comfortable. 'There's an empty bed over there? Wanna share that?'

'You asking me to share a bed with you?' Stella tilted her head suggestively. I wished she wasn't wearing sunglasses so I could see her eyes.

'If I did, what would you say?' I replied cheekily.

'Sharing a bed with you in front of all of these people? That's a little risqué for me.'

'Good to know. Maybe next time I'll find something more private...' I licked my lips.

I knew my comment had pushed the boundaries so I waited for Stella's jaw to drop. For her to argue. For her to tell me that I didn't have a chance with her and that she'd rather eat a rotting cockroach than share a bed *in private* with me.

But her protests didn't come. Instead she smiled and started walking towards the daybed.

Well, shit.

Stella really was thawing.

I might be imagining things, but I was starting to think that maybe she didn't hate me after all...

20

STELLA

I blamed the heat.

That was the only logical explanation for why I had just flirted with Max.

On second thoughts, the fact that he was hotter than a plate of jerk chicken was probably a contributing factor too.

He was wearing a pair of navy swimming trunks and a white vest which of course showed off those muscles that I'd shamefully become obsessed with. God help me when he decided to peel off his top and expose his bare chest.

Especially considering we now had to cosy up together on the daybed. Oops. I meant *sit* on the daybed together and look at photos. There would be no *cosying up*. I needed to calm down.

I hurried over to the daybed before someone else came along and claimed it, then sat down, my feet still firmly on the ground.

Although I'd just flirted with Max, now I was actually on the bed I felt awkward about lying back on it.

Max clearly didn't feel the same though as he wasted no time in kicking off his flip-flops and reclining.

As I turned around and saw him with his hands behind his

head, I groaned inside. Why did he have to do *that*? Now his arms looked even more defined. I was really trying to keep my mind from straying into the gutter but he was making it difficult.

'So? You ready?'

'Ready?' I swallowed hard, before remembering what he was referring to. 'Oh, the photos!'

'Yeah. What did you think I was asking you if you were ready for?' He moved onto his side, propping himself up on his elbow.

That position wasn't any better for my libido.

'Um, nothing,' I said quickly. 'Come on then, let's do it.'

'The photos, right?' Max smirked.

'Of course the photos!'

He opened the first envelope and tipped them out on the bed.

'It's better if we go through them together. Come up here.' He patted the space beside him.

Shit.

It's fine. I'm just lying next to him. That's all. No big deal.

I kicked off my sandals and scooted up on the bed.

He moved closer and our thighs touched. A shot of electricity rocketed through me and as his scent surrounded me, I squeezed my eyes shut. Thank God I was wearing sunglasses so he couldn't see my reaction.

I wanted to pick up the photos, but I was worried that my hands might shake.

Max was so close to me right now and although my brain was trying to remind me of all the reasons being attracted to him was a bad idea, my traitorous body was aching to reach out and touch his arms. To slide my hands over his solid chest. To...

Jesus.

'Shall we start?' I said, desperate for a distraction.

'Yep.' He started sifting through the sandcastle competition photos and we quickly chose our favourites: one in front of the finished castle and another showing us both deep in concentration as we sculpted the towel.

Next he started going through the pics from yesterday.

There were the photos on the bridge that we'd paused to take which came out just as brilliantly as we'd both expected. But it wasn't just those ones that caught my eye. There was a shot, taken from behind, of the two us: holding hands.

Rather than going to the next photo straight away, Max paused.

'Cute,' he said.

If this was a couple of days ago, or maybe even yesterday, I would've added a smart comment or protested. But he was right. It actually was cute. If anyone else saw it, they'd think it was a photo of a couple in love.

Of course we weren't. It just looked that way.

Max moved to the next photo and my jaw dropped.

'Awww,' he said. 'We both look so peaceful.'

It was a picture of me with my head on his shoulder where I'd fallen asleep on the coach. Max's eyes were closed too.

'I'm guessing that Jasmine's responsible for these.' I suppressed a smile. 'At least you can't see me dribbling on your shoulder.' I laughed.

'It's a nice pic,' Max said.

'Yeah.'

'I think that one's my favourite,' he said and my eyes bulged beneath my sunglasses.

'Not the one on the walk?'

'Holding hands?' he asked.

'No. I mean I thought you'd like the posed one on the scary hanging bridge. That actually shows that we went there and did the walk.'

'I like that too. I like all of them. But the one on the coach is more symbolic. Maybe it's just me, but...' He paused.

'What?' I said, desperate to hear what he was about to say.

'I feel like, maybe we've... turned a corner? And before you think I'm being insensitive, I don't mean you've forgiven me and I don't expect you to. When I say we've turned a corner I mean because we can be in the same room without ripping each other's heads off. Before we were at war and now we're on the road to maybe making peace?'

'Maybe,' I said, not wanting to commit to anything. It sounded petty, but I didn't want to make it too easy for him. This was only our fifth day here. It seemed too early to declare that all was forgiven.

At the same time though, because we'd been forced to spend time together for hours every day, it felt like it had speeded up the process. Every task they'd given us was clearly designed to help deepen our bond and get to know each other better. And I hated to say it, but it was working.

I was also tired of being angry at him. It was exhausting.

Maybe the answer wasn't to either hate him or fall in love with him again, but just to find a middle ground. Some form of temporary friendship. Right now, that was the most I could commit to.

'So which photo are you choosing?' Max asked.

'I have to choose the one on the bridge.' The picture of us holding hands was the cutest option, but instead I went for the triumphant choice. It showed I'd pushed myself out of my comfort zone and done the walk.

'Cool.' Max slid the photos back in the envelope. 'I'm hot. I need to cool down.' *You and me both*, I thought to myself.

Max sat up then peeled off his vest.

Bloody hell.

The man really was a god.

I tried to look away, but it was like his chest was made of steel and my eyes were magnets that couldn't help but be drawn to him.

'Your shoulders look a bit red,' I said.

'I forgot to put sun lotion on this morning.'

'That's not good. Hold on.' I reached into my beach bag and handed him my bottle. 'Use this.'

'Lifesaver!' He took it, flipped the cap then squeezed lotion on his palm before rubbing his hands together and slathering it over his shoulders.

And his chest.

I bit my lip as tingles raced through me. What I wouldn't give to run my hands all over those pecs.

Max reached his hand behind him and attempted to apply lotion on his back.

'Want me to do it?' I offered before realising that was a bad idea.

'Please. That'd be great.'

Stay calm.

Don't get turned on.

Keep it together.

After squeezing a generous amount of lotion on my hands, I knelt on the bed, placed my palms on Max's back then started rubbing.

Oh. My. God.

His back felt so good.

Too good.

It was firm, muscular and hot. In every sense of the word.

'Damn,' Max groaned.

'Am I hurting you?' I quickly removed my hands.

'No.' He shook his head. 'I'd just forgotten how soft your hands are. Sorry. I hope that isn't inappropriate.'

Fireworks erupted inside me. Max was enjoying me touching him. Not in a sexual way obviously, just... he liked my hands.

I continued moving my palms over Max's back. Along the sides, down the middle and down to the base, skimming the tops of his swimming trunks, then back up across his shoulders.

The truth was, I could've finished the application of the sun lotion minutes ago, but I was enjoying this. Too much.

I continued running my hands over his back and was just about to squeeze more lotion onto my palms when I heard our names being called.

'Stella! Max!'

I whipped my head round to see Jasmine standing beside us.

'Oh, hey.' Max turned to face her.

'Nice to see you getting on so well. Are you practising for the couples massage, Stella?'

'No.' My cheeks flamed. 'I was just... Max forgot to put on sun lotion, so I was just helping him out because he couldn't reach his back.'

'*Mmm-hmmm,*' she said in a way that suggested she didn't believe me. 'I see. That's good. I hope you're going to return the favour, Max?' Jasmine tilted her head, waiting for his response.

'I, er, of course!' Max stuttered.

'Well, I'll leave you to it!' She turned on her heels and left.

'So...' Max said, his head still facing the pool. 'All good with my back?'

'Yeah. I think you're all covered now.'

'Want me to do you now?'

My lips parted and my horny vagina screamed *yes, please.*

'My back?' I clarified.

'Yeah, sorry. That came out wrong.'

I was about to tell him that I'd already slathered myself with sun lotion before I put on my bikini, but stopped myself. Another application wouldn't hurt. The more protection the better, right?

'Thanks. That'd be great. Should I lie down or sit up?'

'Up to you.'

If I lay down, at least I could bury my head in the towel and the bed and he wouldn't see my reaction.

After taking off my cover-up dress, I lay face down.

I heard the cap of the lotion pop and the sound of Max's palms rubbing together.

Even though I knew he was about to apply the lotion, when his hands made contact with my skin, I jumped.

'You okay?' His warm breath tickled the back of my neck. I wondered how close he was to me. 'Are my hands too hot?'

'No.' I attempted to steady my voice. 'They're perfect.'

I hadn't meant to gush, but they really were.

With every sweep of his big hands across my back, my body sparked. It'd been so long since I'd been touched by a man and I realised how much I'd missed it.

Any man I fancied could've affected me. But this was *Max*. The guy who used to know exactly how and where to touch me. He played my body like he was a world-class musician playing his favourite instrument.

And that was when we were in our late teens. Max had matured a lot physically since then. With a body like that, I'm sure he wasn't short of female attention. Women had swarmed around him back then. Especially when he got signed to play football professionally. He was hot before, but now he was pure fire.

As I thought about the bedroom skills he must've acquired

over the past twelve years, my nipples hardened and my clit pulsed.

'You should be good now.' Max lifted his hands away from me.

Already?

I'd massaged the lotion into his back for much longer than that. It wasn't fair that he'd decided to stop so soon.

'I'll see you in a bit.' I felt the bed move.

When I got up, Max was already at the pool and as he dived in, the water splashed up around him.

Wow. Touching me clearly repulsed him so much he couldn't wait to get away.

I on the other hand was lying here with erect nipples and damp bikini bottoms.

If that was the effect that Max had on me after just a few minutes of touching my back, imagine how my body would react if he kissed me.

Or touched my boobs.

Or fucked me.

Another shot of desire pulsed within me.

But that wasn't going to happen.

Not on this holiday.

Not ever.

And although, given our history, that was the sensible thing, there was still a part of me that thought that was a real shame.

21

MAX

I wondered how much longer I'd have to stay in this pool before my boner went down.

It was hard enough (excuse the pun) trying to keep my dick under control when Stella was putting sun lotion on my back. I'd closed my eyes and thought about my unanswered emails, but even that didn't work.

When Jasmine came over, Stella stopped, which gave me a few minutes to cool down. But when she'd suggested that I returned the favour I knew I was in deep shit.

Still, I'd agreed. I couldn't exactly say no.

As soon as my hands connected to Stella's skin, all the memories of how I used to touch her came flooding back.

I was so close I could smell her delicious, fruity scent and wanted to pepper kisses across Stella's shoulders and run my hands all over her.

When my palms skimmed her bikini bottoms, I knew I'd entered dangerous territory. I looked between my legs and I was hard. If anyone saw, they would've reported me for indecent exposure. And if Stella realised how aroused I was, she'd have been horrified. It would've poured cold water all over the progress we'd been making.

That was when I realised that *water* was the answer. Stella had her back to me. If I quickly got in the pool, I'd be able to calm the fuck down without her knowing. So when the coast was clear, I dived in.

Now the situation in my trunks was better, but it still wasn't completely under control.

I needed to remember to put sun lotion on myself before going to the pool or anywhere with Stella in future.

Just when I thought I was in the clear, she appeared at the edge of the pool looking like a fucking goddess.

'Decided to go in without me?'

'Yeah,' I replied, not being able to think of a feasible explanation. All of my brainpower was being used trying not to look at how good her tits looked in that bikini top.

'I'm getting a drink from the bar, want anything?'

'Nah, thanks. I'm good. I might go to my room in a bit. There's something I need to take care of.'

Literally.

At this point, it might be a good idea for me to get myself off. Either way, I needed a break from temptation.

'I'll be on the daybed reading.'

'Cool.'

As she walked away, my gaze dropped to her arse.

Yep.

I had it bad.

The more time I spent with Stella, the more I wanted to kiss her.

To touch her.

I had no idea how I'd get through the rest of the day, never mind another nine days.

After checking I was good, I climbed out of the pool, grabbed my towel and headed to my room. Once I'd showered and dressed, I pulled out my phone and called Colton.

'Hey,' he answered after two rings. 'How's it going in paradise?'

'Good.' Once I'd asked about work, I filled him in on what I'd been up to.

'Sounds like you're having a great time! And Stella? How are things with her?'

'Better. But...' I paused, wondering whether or not to come clean. 'There's a problem.'

'That's obvious. She's an angry ex.'

'That's the thing though. We're... I feel like there's been a shift. Although I'm under no illusion that I'm her favourite person, I think she's thawing a little.'

'That's a good thing, right?'

'Yes. And no. She's thawing but I'm on fire. I think I like her, man. Not the happily-ever-after serious like thing. Just the carnal *I wanna fuck her* thing.'

'Right. I see the problem. Let's face it, Stella's always been the one that got away. But you've already screwed with her once so casual fucking could get messy. If you hurt her again, you'd make things ten times worse.'

'Exactly.'

'Have you talked? Properly? Y'know, about what happened, yet?'

'No.'

'I think you should. And in terms of the whole attraction thing, I think you'll need to find a way to keep a lid on it. See how things go once you've had the conversation. You never know, she might be attracted to you too.'

'Doubt it.'

'Anything's possible. But either way, you have to leave the ball in her court.'

'Yeah. Okay. I'll talk to her.'

'Good luck.'

'Thanks. I'll need it.'

22

STELLA

This was bliss.

I'd spent the entire day curled up on the bed reading in the sunshine whilst sipping on cocktails and snacking on delicious bar food. I couldn't remember the last time I felt so relaxed.

After he'd left the pool, Max had disappeared for a couple of hours. When he came back, he'd moved a spare extra-large umbrella and placed it over the daybed because he said if I was going to stay outside reading, it was better I was in the shade, which was sweet.

I was starting to lose count of all the sweet things that he'd done for me, which was a problem. Combining the kind gestures with my growing attraction for him was a dangerous cocktail.

The last thing I wanted was to do something stupid like make a pass at him and get rejected.

He'd stayed for a few minutes but then started to act weird then said he was leaving. I wondered if he'd sensed that I liked him and thought it was better to create some distance. Either way, it was a good idea.

That was a few hours ago and I hadn't seen him since. I glanced up and saw that most of the sun loungers were empty. Most people had probably left to get ready for the barbecue. Which was what I should be doing.

I headed to my room, showered then texted Mum to check how everything was with her and let her know I'd had a lovely day.

After noticing the bottle of wine Max had delivered with my dinner the other day that I never got around to drinking, I opened it, poured myself a glass and took a few generous gulps.

Just as I was about to do my hair, my phone rang.

'Hi!'

'Ooh,' Sammie said, 'you sound much brighter! Did you and Max do the naked dance? Is that why you're in such a good mood?'

'No! A woman's happiness doesn't have to be defined by her attachment to a man's penis.'

'True. But it wouldn't hurt to have a go anyway!'

I wouldn't mind trying, but I wasn't going to tell her that.

'How are you?'

'I'm okay, just chugging along. You know how it is. Actually, you don't. I'm here in dreary London and you're relaxing in the sun with a hunky guy.'

'I can't lie. I spent a whole day reading by the pool, sipping Mojitos in the sunshine. It was heaven.' I took another large sip of wine.

'I know how much you love your books, but if I had a man like Max who'd come to my rescue after I flashed the entire hotel, I'd have my head buried between his legs instead of in a novel!' she laughed.

'So crude!' I stifled a giggle. 'That was only the start of the nice things he's done.'

As I poured myself some more wine, I told Sammie all about the walking trip, him bringing me dinner and how nice his playlists were.

When I also let slip how cute the photos were, she insisted I send some for her to look over immediately.

Earlier, Jasmine had sent a link to view the photos we'd chosen as our favourites so far, which were mainly taken on Max's mobile and digital camera and I may have downloaded them straight away on my phone.

I pulled them up on my screen then swooned. The one of me resting my head on Max's shoulder really was cute. I sent them to Sammie whilst she was still on the phone.

'Oh my God!' she screamed. 'You two are bloody adorable! And holy shit! Max is a fucking god! What the hell are you doing, Stell? How are you even able to talk or think straight with *him* next to you?'

'With great difficulty.' I blew out a breath. 'Earlier he was putting sun lotion on my back and... let's just say I found it *very* enjoyable.'

'Shit. I can imagine! So if you like him, why don't you just go for it? I know what happened was crappy, but that was years ago. I'm not trying to downplay what you went through. Remember, I was there. I saw how you suffered, but maybe you can push it to the back of your mind somehow? I'd hate to see your past ruin your future.'

'I wish it was that simple.' I drained my glass. This wine was so good.

'Why not just take advantage of the situation? Use it for your own good. It's been ages since you had a shag, so can't you just be fuck buddies? Have a bit of fun in the sun? It doesn't have to be anything deep – just a holiday fling. Give your poor vibrator a break and get the real thing!'

'You're forgetting one thing: sex involves two willing parties. It doesn't matter if I'm attracted to Max. He doesn't feel the same way.'

'How do you know?'

'He said, at the beginning, that if we stuck it out for the week it wouldn't be anything romantic.'

'You're forgetting that *you* also hated his guts at the beginning, but now you feel differently.'

'Even when I was standing in the pool topless, Max didn't show the slightest bit of interest.' I ignored her comment, which was annoyingly accurate, and drank more wine to console myself.

'He was being a gentleman!'

'And the only reason he put sun lotion on my back today was because Jasmine suggested it and he probably felt bad saying no.'

'I doubt that.'

'He was so repulsed by touching me that he only lasted two minutes before stopping and diving into the pool. Oh, and he's avoided me for most of the day. Those enough reasons for you?'

'Maybe he was hot. And you said he's the CEO, right? He probably had work stuff to do.'

'I don't know. He was acting weird. Anyway, I'm not going to make a fool of myself. If he's interested, which like I said, I doubt, *he'll* need to make the first move.'

'Come on,' Sammie sighed. 'This isn't the 1900s! Did Beyoncé teach you nothing? We're strong, independent women! We don't need to wait for a man to make the first move. If you want to have some fun with Max, tell him. The least he owes you is an apology fuck.'

'I don't want an apology fuck!'

'Yeah, you do! Think about it. If he's really sorry, he'll do whatever he can to make it up to you. He owes you twelve years of orgasms! It's time to collect!'

As I pictured Max with his head between my thighs sucking on my clit, tingles shot up my spine.

Sammie was right about one thing. It *would* be nice to experience an orgasm that wasn't given to me by my vibrator.

But for all of the reasons I'd already mentioned, I wasn't sure that declaring my attraction to Max was a good idea.

'I'll think about it.'

'Good!'

'I'd better get ready. We've got a beach barbecue and party tonight. I hope they have more of this wine or those delicious cocktails.'

'What wine? Are you drinking right now?'

'Maybe. I had a few cocktails by the pool and now I'm on the wine from the other day.'

'Whoa... easy, tiger! You should pace yourself. You know what a lightweight you are.'

'I'll be fine.'

'If you say so. You're so lucky to be going to a barbecue *and* a party on the beach! Speaking of that, don't forget to wear one of those thongs your mum gave you, in case you do get *lucky* tonight!'

'Bye, Sammie,' I said.

'Laters, sweetie!'

As I put the phone down, a naughty giggle slipped from my lips. Must be the alcohol making me feel lightheaded.

I went to the wardrobe and opened the drawers. Coincidentally the 'Touch Me' thong was right at the top.

Just the thought of Max touching me made me quiver with excitement.

My inhibitions were evaporating faster than the wine in my glass.

Which was probably why I plucked the red lacy thong out of the drawers and slid it on.

Just in case...

23

MAX

Tonight was the night.

It was time to do the thing I'd avoided for years: explain my bad behaviour to Stella.

Even though I knew it'd kill all the progress we'd made, I just had to suck it up. That was the least she deserved.

I buttoned up my white linen shirt, zipped up my khaki shorts, slid my feet into my flip-flops, then headed to the beach.

When I arrived, Stella was already there.

I swallowed hard.

She looked like a wet dream.

I thought that having a wank in the shower earlier would've helped, but nope. My dick was still ready for action and from the way it was twitching right now, there was only one woman that would make it satisfied.

'You're *here*!' Stella ran over, grinning and clutching a colourful drink.

That was strange. She seemed happy to see me.

'Yeah,' I frowned. 'Didn't you think I'd turn up?'

'*You've* been avoiding me!' She poked my chest.

Ohhh. She was tipsy. That was why she was being so friendly.

'How many of those have you had?'

'*These*?' Her voice went up an octave. 'Not sure! But they're *delicious*! It's called a *Tinto* de something. *Tinto de Veranda*! Here!' She thrust the glass in my face. 'Try it!'

I didn't have the heart to tell her it was Tinto de *Verano* – a summer drink with wine and some lemonade-type stuff. A bit like a sangria. It wasn't normally strong so she'd either had a lot of them, or had mixed her drinks.

'Nah, I'm good. I was hoping we could talk.'

'*Talk*?' Her brows knitted together. 'This is a *party*! Dance with me!'

The bass from a reggaeton song vibrated around the beach.

Stella grabbed my hand and dragged me to an area where some other guests were dancing.

Just as I was thinking of how to convince Stella to go somewhere quieter so we could talk, she started grinding against me.

Fuckkk.

My dick was already excited, but the sensation of having Stella's tits pressed against me made it shoot up faster than a rocket. I attempted to pull away before Stella felt my boner, but she wrapped her hand around my waist and pulled me into her.

Jesus fucking Christ.

She felt so damn good.

If I had my way, I'd push Stella on the sand right now and bury myself inside her.

'Mmmm,' she purred. 'Feels like I'm not the only one who's excited! Is that a gun in your trousers or are you just happy to see me?' Stella giggled as she continued pushing her body onto mine.

'Stell,' I said, using one of her old nicknames. 'You're drunk. This isn't a good idea.'

'Your dick doesn't think so!' she shouted over the music. 'I can feel that you're hard, Max. Shall we go somewhere and fuck?'

My brows shot up. Stella was never afraid to say what she wanted in the bedroom, so that wasn't what shocked me. What did, though, was the shift in her feelings towards me. I knew she'd thawed and we were getting on better. But there was still an ocean between that and having sex. As much as I wanted to, she was drunk. And we really needed to talk.

'Maybe I should take you back to your room...'

'Oooh, yes, please!'

'To *sleep. Alone.* You're not thinking straight.'

'I'm thinking perfectly fine! I'm on holiday and I want to have fun. I'm horny and I want to have sex! And you owe me, Mister!' She poked my chest again. 'Mmmm... so firm. So sexy. I can't wait to run my hands all over it.' Stella bit her lip and started trailing her palms over my pecs, past my stomach then down to my...

'Stop!' I moved her hand away, then scooped her up and threw her over my shoulder. 'Come on. I'm taking you to sober up. No arguments.'

'My hero!' She laughed again.

'Everything okay?' Jasmine came over. I supposed, given the tension between me and Stella, it didn't look good that I was carrying her off.

'Yeah!' Stella piped up. 'Me and Max are going back to my room to fuck! *Finally!*'

'Oh!' Jasmine's jaw dropped.

'We're not.' I shook my head. 'She's had too much to drink. I'm taking her back to her room to sleep it off.'

'Okay. Good idea... Have a good sleep, Stella.'

'We're not *sleeping!*' she protested. 'Max is going to give me his big cock and lots of orgasms! I won't be able to walk tomorrow!'

Jasmine winced. If Stella realised what she was saying right now, she'd be mortified.

'I'd better go.' I lifted Stella higher up on my shoulder.

'Probably best...' Jasmine stepped aside and I strode off to Stella's room.

When we got to the door, I found her key in her handbag and once we were inside, I lowered her onto the bed.

'I have condoms,' Stella said. 'Lots and lots of condoms! Ribbed ones, extra-large ones, thin ones! Take your pick!'

'We won't need them.'

'Why not?'

'I told you, because we need to talk.'

'Why don't you want me?'

'I'm getting you some water.' I walked over to the fridge, took out a bottle then brought it over. 'Drink this.'

She guzzled it down then fell back on the bed.

Minutes later, she was sleeping.

After taking off her shoes, I pulled the sheet over her.

The Stella I knew was really careful with alcohol. If she was still like that, she might throw up. It didn't feel right to leave her alone.

And I really needed to have that talk with her. If I left, I'd chicken out.

Right then I decided I'd stay here until Stella woke up.

I was determined to clear the air.

Once and for all.

24

STELLA

As daylight streamed through the curtains, I blinked, taking in my surroundings.

My head was pounding. It was like there was a bongos festival happening in my brain and my throat was drier than the Sahara.

I attempted to lift my head off the pillow. When I eventually dragged my neck upwards, I gasped. Max was on the floor.

What the hell? Why was he in my room? Did we have sex? If so, why was he on the floor and not on the bed?

No. That couldn't be right. He still had his clothes on.

I peeped under the sheets and saw that I was fully dressed too.

Just as I reached for the glass of water on the bedside table, a flashback popped into my head.

No, no, no!

I only remembered bits and pieces. I'd drunk multiple glasses of wine when I was getting ready. Then when I got to the beach I'd had a couple of those delicious rum cocktails. Max still wasn't there, so I'd had those drinks that tasted like sangria. I didn't remember having much to eat, though.

Then I think Max turned up. And then... wait. I think I danced with him and, oh yeah, he was hard, so I'd suggested...

Shit.

I think I'd suggested we go back to my room.

What happened after that, I had no idea.

A loud groan shot from my lips. This was why I never drank a lot. I couldn't hold my alcohol. But it was an all-inclusive hotel so they were handing out drinks and cocktails *for free*. And they all tasted sooo good!

After my conversation with Sammie, I supposed I just wanted to loosen up and have fun.

'Morning,' Max croaked, slowly sitting upright and rubbing his eyes. 'Shit.' He stretched his hand over his shoulder and winced. 'My back.'

'I'm not surprised. Why did you sleep on the floor?'

'It wasn't right to be on the bed. I only planned to crash for a few hours to check you were okay, but I must've been more tired than I thought.'

'Did we...?'

'No way,' he said quickly.

'No need to sound so relieved!' I snapped.

'It's not because I'm relieved. It's because you were really drunk.'

'I didn't do anything embarrassing, did I?' I held my breath, waiting for his response.

'You were...' he paused. '*Happy*. Friendly. Don't worry about it.'

'Oh, God.' I squeezed my eyes shut. I was going to ask for more details, but now I wasn't sure that I wanted to know.

'Listen, Stella. Another reason I stayed was because I need to talk to you about what happened between us. It's been the elephant in the room and if it's okay with you, I'd like to try and explain.'

I didn't have the energy to protest. And he was right. I'd avoided it. Tried to pretend it didn't matter, but it did. It was time to rip the plaster off.

'Okay.' I sat up reluctantly. Max's eyes widened. I think he was surprised that I hadn't brushed him off.

'So.' He stood up, put the kettle on and pulled out two mugs. 'As you know, when I got the call to join Manchester Athletic, I was so happy. It'd always been my dream.'

'Yeah.' I nodded. At that point, we'd been dating for two years and I thought we were madly in love. I knew I was.

Every weekend, whatever the time and come rain or shine, I'd stand on the pitch sidelines cheering him on.

Max was amazingly talented and I knew it was only a matter of time before he got signed and went pro.

When the call came, everything happened so quickly. He had to move to Manchester. He told me nothing would change, so there was never any question in my mind that we'd stay together.

I'd go to see him every other weekend and he came down when he could. It was difficult, but that was what you did for love, right?

'And it wasn't just me, my family and friends who were excited. The whole town went crazy. There was a big buzz around a local guy going to play for a Premier League team.'

That was an understatement. Max was splashed all over the local papers. They even featured him on the London evening TV news. Suddenly my boyfriend was famous. But to me, he was still my Max.

'But with the buzz came pressure,' he continued. 'From my dad not to mess up and my coach who obviously expected me to perform. I was barely twenty, living away from home for the first time, I'd just been given a dream opportunity and I really wanted to prove my worth, you know?'

'Yeah,' I nodded.

'And of course, I wanted to continue our relationship, that's why we did the long-distance thing for the first couple of months. But it was hard.'

'That's why I offered to move there. To support you.'

'But that meant you'd drop out of uni.'

'I wanted to be close to you.'

'But you'd always wanted to go to that uni. I didn't want you to sacrifice your dream for me. We were so young. And I needed to focus. I couldn't blow my big chance.'

'So you dumped me,' I scowled. 'On national TV.'

'It wasn't like that!'

I was getting ready to visit Max and tell him the good news that I'd deferred uni for a year so that I could be with him in Manchester whilst he settled in, when Mum called me to the living room because Max and his dad were being interviewed on TV.

The presenter asked Max how he was enjoying living in a new city.

'You're a handsome young man,' she'd said. 'You must have lots of women throwing themselves at you.'

'He's got no time for women,' his dad had jumped in.

'Rumour has it that you have a girlfriend back in London?'

At that point, my heart had bloomed. I was that girlfriend and Max was about to tell the world about us.

'That's all over now,' his dad had said.

'Good news, ladies!' the presenter had grinned. 'Max Moore is single!'

I'd slumped on the sofa, but then I'd told myself it was fine.

Any minute now Max would tell his dad and the presenter that wasn't true because he was in a happy relationship.

Except he didn't.

'I'm committed to football,' Max had said instead. 'That's my focus. I'm determined to be an important member of the Manchester Athletic team.'

And just like that, my whole world crumbled.

I'd cried for hours. When I tried to call Max, he didn't answer. So I got the train to Manchester. I had to see him. I needed an explanation.

Max's dad had opened the door and told me Max didn't want to see me. But I'd insisted. I wasn't leaving until I'd spoken to him.

When Max finally appeared, he couldn't look me in the eye.

'I'm sorry,' he'd said. 'I'm finding it difficult to manage everything. I think it's better if we... break up.'

Even though I'd already seen him dump me on TV, I still refused to believe it.

'Where's this coming from?' I'd pleaded. 'Is it your dad?' He'd never liked me, even before Max got signed.

'It's for the best,' he'd said. His gaze was still fixed to the floor. 'Please. Don't make this more difficult than it already is. There's too much riding on this, Stella. I have to make this work. I have to focus. I'm sorry.'

I ran out of there, crying. Hoping Max would follow. But he didn't.

When his dad saw me, he grinned. The arsehole got a kick from knowing my heart had just been shattered into a million pieces.

'Come on then,' I said, bringing my thoughts back to the present and propping a pillow behind my head. 'If it wasn't like that, how was it?'

'The truth was,' Max took a deep breath, 'Coach didn't like us having girlfriends. Said they were a distraction. That they affected how we played. And my dad, well, you know his thoughts. He wanted me to live, breathe, eat and sleep football twenty-four-seven. So when that presenter asked that question, he saw his chance to ruin things between us. For good.'

'But you could have denied it. You could've said he was wrong. Instead you confirmed it by saying football was your focus.'

'No! They edited it. I told her she was right, that I had a girl-friend in London and that the long-distance thing was hard, but they cut that out.'

'Why would they do that?'

'For better headlines.'

'Even if that's true, that still doesn't make sense. When I came to see you, you still ended it.'

'Like I said, I was under pressure. The coach was worried about my performance. And then Dad dropped two bombshells.'

'What?'

'He told me he'd been laid off from his job and that Mum was sick so it was up to me to take care of the family. He warned me that if I messed up and didn't give the game a 100 per cent focus, the family would be homeless and we wouldn't be able to get the treatment Mum needed.'

'I didn't know your mum was ill. Why didn't you tell me?'

'She didn't want anyone to know. She was too proud. Same with Dad. So I had to do what he said. Although you won't believe me, I was just as cut up about our break-up as you. But I felt like I didn't have a choice. The irony is, after we broke up, I started playing worse. And the worse I played, the more desperate I became. Which was why that shitty tackle happened. And just like that, my career was over. I went from hero to failure in less than a year. I lost everything. My career, my dreams and you.'

Shit.

I sat there, speechless.

I had no idea. I thought he just abandoned me. Like my dad did, all those years ago.

'I didn't realise.'

'I know.' Max scrubbed a hand over his chin. 'How could you?'

'But when you came back to London, I tried to see you.'

'I know. But I was in a dark place. I didn't speak to anyone. Not even Colton. I blocked everyone out. I realise now that I was in a deep state of depression. I was grieving. And I couldn't see you. You were a reminder of how I'd messed everything up. So I locked myself away.'

'And you moved away.'

'We had no choice. My parents weren't working. We had no money so the bank repossessed the house. We had to move into my grandma's, which was a nightmare. It took a while before we were back on our feet. Mum was making homemade soaps and skincare products which started to do well. Then she got sick again. And this time, she didn't recover.'

'I'm so sorry.'

His mum was never my biggest fan, but she usually tried to make an effort to smile or say hello. Which was more than Max's dad ever did.

'Thanks.' He swallowed hard. 'Anyway, people kept asking to buy her products, even when she passed. I saw how she made them and knew the ingredients she used, so I decided to try and do something with them. I never made my dream happen properly, but I thought if I could make Mum's products take off, all the shit I'd been through wouldn't be for nothing.

That's why I started the business. And I've been focused on that ever since.'

Wow and double wow.

I felt like all of the air had been knocked from my lungs.

'I... shit.' I sat up straighter. 'Sorry. Just trying to take this all in.'

'I know it's a lot. Especially so early in the morning. But at least now you know.'

'Yeah.'

'I thought about calling you to explain so many times, but the more time passed, the more difficult it got. I should've fought harder for us. But at the time it felt like there was no way out. I'm really sorry. I didn't mean to hurt you. I understand if you don't want anything to do with me, but I needed you to know the truth. I'm gonna go now. Give you time to digest everything.'

Max got up. His eyes were red, but I couldn't be sure if it was because he was tired or upset.

As the room door closed, I sat there frozen.

For years I'd wanted an explanation.

But now I'd got one, I had no idea what to do with it.

25

MAX

I slept through breakfast and the morning briefing. I was exhausted. Not just from my terrible sleep on Stella's bedroom floor, but mentally.

The relief that flooded my body when I left Stella's room was intense. I'd carried that burden and guilt for years. So to finally give her the full story felt like a thousand bricks had been lifted from my shoulders.

Now Stella knew the truth, the ball was in her court. It was up to her to decide what she wanted to do with it.

But dredging up my past was difficult. That was the darkest period of my life for so many reasons. Everything I knew and loved was ripped away from me. My dreams, the love of my life, my home, my sanity, then my mum.

Football had been a huge part of my life since I was a toddler. From the minute I got my first football, Dad was relentless in training me.

Every spare minute was spent practising in the garden. I got a place on the school football team. Then went from getting scouted to going semi-pro and finally getting the call to go professional for a team I'd always loved.

I thought I had my whole career ahead of me. But thanks to my injury, I barely lasted a year.

Losing Stella was also a massive blow. Dad had been against our relationship from the beginning. He thought she was a distraction. And if I was being honest, although he never admitted it out loud, I think the fact that she wasn't white was an issue for him too.

But I didn't care about what he thought. I loved Stella and wanted to be with her. So when I moved to Manchester, I was determined to make it work.

Sometimes, though, things just aren't that simple. Like I'd said to Stella, the pressure from Dad and my coach got too much. And I thought it'd be selfish to stay with her just because she made me happy.

With Mum and Dad out of work, it was my responsibility to take care of the family and give my all to the opportunity I'd been given. So I did what they wanted: I broke up with her. And I've regretted that every day since.

When my career ended and Stella came to visit, all I wanted was for her to hold me and tell me everything would be okay. But I pushed her away. Mum didn't want anyone to know she was sick, so didn't want any visitors. Dad was embarrassed that I'd failed so he felt the same. And I didn't leave the house because I couldn't face anyone either.

The only bright spell during those times was the interest Mum started to get in her beauty products.

Thinking about this stuff again was fucking difficult. That was one of the reasons I left Stella's room. I was starting to tear up and I didn't wanna cry in front of her.

Anyway, the past was the past. Feeling sorry for myself wasn't gonna help.

I checked my phone.

There was a message from Jasmine to say today's activity was a boat trip and we'd be leaving at six. *Good.* The only thing I felt like doing right now was staying in bed, but hopefully I'd feel better later.

Just as I was about to put my phone down, a message from Stella popped up.

Hi. Are you okay?

A warm feeling flooded my chest. She was checking on me. Which meant she cared.

Maybe she didn't hate me after all.

26

STELLA

As Jasmine continued chatting to the other guests around the pool, I slid my phone in my pocket.

I'd just sent Max a text because he hadn't come for breakfast or the briefing. I hoped he was okay.

I got up from the sun lounger and was about to return to my room when I spotted Jasmine walking towards me.

'Hey,' she smiled. 'How's your head?'

'I've got the headache from hell, but I'll survive.'

'It was so sweet of Max to carry you to your room like that.'

'He *carried* me?' My brows knitted together. 'How drunk was I?'

'Um... you were very happy and, er, *talkative*...'

'Oh, God! I didn't say anything embarrassing, did I?' I winced.

'Everyone says silly things when they're drunk, so you're *fine!*'

Jasmine waved her hand in the air as if it was no big deal. But the look on her face and the way her voice went all high-pitched when she said *fine* told me otherwise.

'What *silly things* did I say?' My heart raced. 'Please. Tell me.'

'You sure you really want to know?' She avoided my gaze.

'Yes!'

'Okay, well...' She took a deep breath. 'You kind of said that you and Max were going back to your room to... *finally fuck*.'

'*No!*' I gasped. '*Seriously*?'

'Yes.' Jasmine nodded.

'Please tell me that's all I said?'

That was bad enough, but I had to be sure.

'Well, after that, you said... listen, it doesn't matter.'

'Jasmine, *please*!'

'You said that Max was going to give you his big cock and lots of orgasms and you wouldn't be able to walk tomorrow.'

My stomach plummeted about a zillion miles below the earth and my jaw crashed to the floor so hard, I was surprised it didn't shatter the concrete path.

'Oh, God!' I covered my face with my hands. 'I'm so embarrassed!'

'Please, don't be. I'm sure I've said much worse after I've had a few.'

Jasmine was trying to make me feel better, but that was impossible.

'What did Max say?'

'He just said you'd had a lot to drink and he was taking you to your room to sleep it off.'

'Shit.'

Poor guy must've been horrified. Having a drunk woman falling all over him wasn't exactly attractive. He didn't fancy me before, so he definitely wouldn't like me now.

'I can't go on the boat trip.' I shook my head. I had no idea how I was going to look Max in the eye now knowing what I'd said.

'Why not?'

'Too embarrassing.'

'The thing is,' Jasmine gestured to a table and chairs for us to sit at, 'when we're drunk, we lose our inhibitions and that's often when the truth comes out. I know you and Max have had your differences, but although the delivery and wording wasn't exactly what you might've chosen if you were sober, do you think there might be some truth to what you said?'

I didn't even need to think about it. The answer was *yes*. But I couldn't let Jasmine or Max know that.

'It's complicated.'

'I hear you. Have you and Max spoken about what happened in the past yet?'

'We spoke this morning.' I winced again, as I wondered what he must have been thinking about my behaviour last night.

'And?'

'Now I understand why he acted the way he did.'

'Do you think you can get past it?'

'The logical part of me says yes. But my heart's a different story.'

'I understand,' Jasmine nodded. 'It's up to you, but as an outsider with a lot of experience with observing couples who come here, you two are a great match. You might not see it yet, but trust me. Max is one of the good ones. If there's a chance, even if it's 1 per cent, that you two could make it work, it's worth a try.' She stood up.

'Maybe,' I mumbled.

'And life's for living, right? So at the very least maybe you could you know... enjoy each other's *company*...' She grinned suggestively. 'Good orgasms are hard to come by, so if Max is willing to give you some, it might be worth considering... See you at six for the boat trip.'

As Jasmine walked away, her words replayed in my mind.

She was right. Sammie had said the same thing.

I shouldn't be overthinking this or worrying about what would happen afterwards. I should just relax and live for the moment.

I'd come here to enjoy myself.

I'd come here to find a man that I liked. And despite our challenges and complicated, messy past, however much I'd tried to fight it, I liked Max.

A lot.

And I wanted him.

The question now, though, was whether he felt the same.

27

MAX

'Hey,' I said softly as I slid onto the fancy coach seat next to Stella.

'Hi,' she replied. 'How are you?'

'Okay, thanks. You?'

'Truthfully?' Her voice lowered. 'Really embarrassed.'

'Why?'

'Can we... maybe talk later?' Stella gestured to the couple in front who seemed to have stopped their conversation to listen to ours.

'Good idea.'

For the rest of the journey, we went through photos from the previous day that Jasmine had taken and thanked each other for the playlists we'd sent over earlier. I was relieved that the songs Stella had chosen were all positive and upbeat like mine.

After that, we took in the views from the window.

When we pulled up at the port, Stella's eyes bulged. I didn't blame her.

Jasmine said we were going on a boat. But this wasn't a boat.

It was a super *yacht*. The body was sleek, white and so shiny someone had probably spent the whole day waxing it.

'Welcome!' Jasmine said as we stood in the main area, which was like a living room with a bar area and plush leather sofas. A waitress started handing out glasses of champagne but I took some water instead. 'In a few minutes we'll set sail so you can admire the beauty of Malaga from the sea. A candlelit dinner for two will be served in individual cabins to give you and your match some privacy. I'll let you know when everything's ready. In the meantime, keep an eye out for sunset. It'll be great for creating some more beautiful new additions to your memory book. Enjoy!'

The sound of flamenco music played in the background and I found myself tapping my feet as I breathed in the sea air.

It was another warm evening, so it was nice that there was a bit of breeze out on deck.

We found an empty seated area towards the back of the yacht and looked out at the views of the coastline.

'Beautiful, isn't it?' Stella said.

'Yeah. And this yacht really is something else. I thought we'd be travelling on a little tourist boat.'

'Me too! When we boarded I had to try and stop my jaw from trailing on the floor and act like I hung out on super yachts all the time.'

'You mean you don't?' The corner of my mouth twitched.

'Surprisingly not!' she laughed. 'I should've remembered that The Love Hotel always pulls out all the stops.'

'Definitely.'

'Listen, Max, I just want to say a couple of things. Firstly, thanks for telling me the truth about what happened. I know it can't have been easy for you to talk about everything you went through. I appreciate it.'

'Thanks. That means a lot.'

'And I hope you don't mind me asking and if it's too difficult to talk about, you don't have to, I just wondered...'

'Go on. Ask me anything.'

'What happened to your mum?'

I sucked in a breath. Damn. She was right. It was difficult. I didn't like talking about it, but I didn't want to hide anything from Stella any more.

'For her whole life, Mum always thought she was invincible. She ate whatever she wanted, even if that meant having fry-ups and cream cakes, every day. And she smoked. A lot. Then there was the drinking. Like Dad, she drank more than she should.'

At that point, my mind drifted to my dad. I wondered if he was still alive. I'd cut all contact from him years ago. For all I knew, he was drunk in a ditch somewhere. I shouldn't care after what he put me through, but a tiny part of me still did.

'I'm sorry.' Stella touched my hand. 'It's okay if you want to stop.'

'I'm okay.' I took a sip of water. 'Hearing that Mum had high blood pressure and cholesterol shouldn't have been a surprise and even when she got diabetes she didn't take it seriously. She still kept eating and drinking the same shit. It was only when the doctor said she was morbidly obese and was at risk of a heart attack that she finally took action.'

'Shit. What did she do?'

'She started to eat better and got interested in organic food. She even became obsessed with checking the ingredients in all the products she used. That's what led her to try making her own natural soaps and stuff using olive oil. She wasn't working so had loads of time on her hands. That's how her Olibella products were created.'

'But didn't her lifestyle changes help?'

'She tried but by the time she tried to reverse the damage, it was too late. In the end, she died of a heart attack.'

'Oh, Max.' Stella shuffled up closer and rubbed my back. 'I'm so, so sorry.'

'Yeah.' I swallowed the lump in my throat. 'Thanks. I'm happy I was able to carry on with her products so at least that's her legacy.'

'I think it's great that you were able to do that. I'd love to try some of your products. You'll have to send me a link of where to buy them.'

'You don't need to *buy* them,' I smiled. 'I'll give you some!'

'Oh, no, that wouldn't be fair. They cost money to make, so I wouldn't expect them for free.'

My chest inflated. Most people were happy to take freebies and didn't give a shit about the costs, but not Stella. She'd always been a good person.

'Consider it a gift. For putting up with me.'

'Well, in that case, you better send a whole truckload of products!' she laughed and my chest swelled even more. I was glad we'd lightened the mood. Shit was getting way too heavy.

'Deal.' I looked into her eyes. God, she had beautiful eyes. And a beautiful mouth. A mouth I wanted to kiss right now. To thank her for being so kind, understanding and thoughtful. Stella was fucking amazing.

She held my gaze and we sat in silence. Her leg was pressed against mine and her face was close. Almost close enough for our lips to touch.

Almost.

'Um.' Stella broke my gaze and I wondered if she felt the current of electricity pulsing between us. 'There was something else... I, I'm, er, really, really sorry about what I said on the beach. I was really drunk and I...'

'Did you mean it?' I edged closer.

I knew she was embarrassed and probably didn't want to talk about it, but I needed to know. A match had been lit inside me. I wanted Stella and I needed to know if there was any chance she felt the same.

'Mean what?' She pushed her sunglasses down from where they were resting on the top of her head to cover her eyes.

After dragging off my sunglasses, I whipped hers off her face.

'Look at me,' I commanded. 'You know what I'm asking. But seeing as you're asking me to spell it out, I want to know whether you meant what you said last night. Did you want something to happen between us?'

She swallowed hard and dropped her head to the floor. I lifted her chin and our eyes connected.

'I...'

'Tell me,' I growled. 'Last night you said we were gonna go to your room and *finally fuck*. Is that what you want? Do you want me to fuck you?'

Stella's eyes widened.

I inched closer, my heart thundering in my chest and my hard-on straining against my shorts.

She looked up at me, her lips parting before leaning forward.

Fuck. She felt it too.

After years of pining for her, yearning to see her again, we were about to kiss.

As I ran my thumb over her cheek, Stella squeezed her eyes shut and a moan slipped from her mouth.

Jesus.

Just hearing that sound drove me wild. I didn't care that we were on the boat with a group of other people. If Stella said the word, I'd do her right here. *That* was how badly I wanted her.

Our heads moved inwards, our lips now millimetres apart. I was just about to close the gap when the music stopped and Jasmine's voiced boomed from the speaker.

'Ladies and gents, dinner is served! Please come back inside so I can show you to your cabins.'

Stella and I sprang apart from each other like we were two teenagers who'd been caught screwing by their parents.

Talk about bad timing.

'I...' Stella stuttered. 'We should... I need to go to the toilet. I'll see you in there.'

Stella literally sprinted away.

What the hell just happened?

We were just about to kiss. I hadn't imagined the connection. One minute there were more sparks flying between us than at a fireworks display. Then, the next, Stella couldn't get away from me fast enough.

My mind raced.

I wanted Stella. So much.

Then again, maybe she was right to run.

All I could offer her now was sex and she probably wanted a relationship, which wasn't something I could give her.

I had too much going on at work and I hadn't had a proper relationship. Not since we dated.

Stella had only just forgiven me for my past fuck-ups. Hurting her once was bad, but twice? No way. I couldn't do that again.

Yeah. I nodded to myself. Now that I thought about it, the timing of Jasmine's interruption was perfect. She'd saved Stella from heartbreak and me from going through more years of guilt and regret.

I was glad that we'd cleared the air and were getting on better. But like I'd said from the start, this could never become anything romantic.

And I was relieved that Stella felt the same.

28

STELLA

As I walked back from the toilet and towards the cabin we'd been given, I replayed what just happened.

I couldn't believe I was about to kiss Max.

Yes, I liked him.

Yes, I wanted him to kiss me.

Ever since Jasmine had suggested earlier that we should enjoy each other's *company*, I'd barely thought of anything else.

And when he'd asked whether I really wanted him to fuck me, I'll admit, I also wanted to shout *yes please*!

The tingles between my legs were out of control by that point. I wanted Max so badly that if he'd suggested we do it in front of everyone, I would've agreed.

But now that I was thinking more clearly, I realised it would've been a *huge* mistake.

If Max fucked me once, would I really be able to walk away? I'd want more and something told me he wasn't able to give me that. I wasn't even sure if he'd fully come to terms with everything that had happened to him in the past. He still seemed so broken.

I had no doubt that Max would give me the ride of my life. But a few minutes of pleasure weren't worth the carnage that would come afterwards.

Things would get awkward. Especially when Max inevitably said he didn't see things going any further. It'd ruin the rest of our holiday.

Although it was tempting, it was better if we just stayed friends. That alone was more than I expected considering how I felt at the start of this trip, so I should just be happy with that.

As I remembered the way he stroked my cheek, goosebumps erupted over my skin.

No, no, no. Nothing can happen with Max.

Ever.

And the sooner my body got the message, the better.

When I stepped into the cabin, Max was already sitting at the table in the centre of the room.

I noticed that there was also a very comfortable-looking double bed and groaned internally. It would be so easy to fall onto that with Max, but I warned my brain again to shut down that train of thought.

'Hey,' Max said softly.

'Hi.' I sat down and Max jumped up to push my chair in then returned to his seat.

'So… about earlier…'

'Forget it,' I said quickly, dreading how awkward it was going to be sitting here alone with Max after our almost kiss. 'It's for the best.'

'Yeah,' he nodded before dropping his gaze to his empty plate.

I fiddled with the thick white serviette resting on the table as the silence stretched between us.

The waiter knocked at the door then came in to deliver the first course.

'Yay! Dinner!' I squeaked, grateful for the interruption. 'I'm starving!'

* * *

Breakfast with Max wasn't as awkward as I feared. Having photos to go through was a good distraction.

Originally when Jasmine mentioned the whole memory book thing, I thought it'd be a nightmare. But now, I was starting to enjoy the ritual of looking over photos from the day before over breakfast with Max. The pictures always came out much better than I thought. Jasmine was great at snapping candid photos and we never seemed to notice her taking them.

In the most recent selection, there was a cute pic of us on the boat staring out to sea that I'd picked as my favourite. And Max had selected a shot of us laughing at something together. Neither of us could remember what that could've been because after he'd told me the heartbreaking story about his mum, we'd lightened the mood and laughed multiple times.

Well, up until our almost kiss and the dinner in the cabin. For the rest of the night, we kept the conversation firmly on the food and how amazing the yacht and the views were, which helped relieve the tension a little.

We hadn't spoken about what happened, just like we'd agreed. I reckon Max was also relieved we'd avoided making a big mistake.

On the coach back, I fell asleep. Max had woken me up when we pulled up outside the hotel and he offered to walk me to my room, but I said I'd be fine. Partly because I wanted to avoid another awkward moment where we'd wonder whether or not we should do the goodnight kiss thing.

And also because although I knew that I shouldn't be having illicit thoughts about Max, I couldn't get him out of my head and I didn't trust myself not to do something stupid like invite him into my room.

So we'd kind of waved at each other awkwardly and said that we'd catch up at breakfast. And now here we were.

'Shit!' I looked at my watch. 'The briefing starts in five minutes.'

I downed the rest of my coffee and Max shoved the last piece of egg-white omelette in his mouth before we both got up.

As we walked to the pool area, we chatted easily, both agreeing to finish our playlist selections and upload them once we got back to our rooms. I already had a shortlist in my head.

See. This was good.

We did the right thing not kissing last night.

It was much better this way. As long as I didn't look into Max's eyes and avoided any accidental brushing of hands, legs or skin in general, I could get through this.

This was our seventh day here and although initially we'd said that a week was all we'd commit to, now it was clear that we were going to stay for the full fortnight.

From tomorrow we'd get to choose our own activities, so I'd make sure that I selected daytime trips that weren't too romantic. Then once we'd finished whatever excursion we'd been on, we could just do our own thing by the pool or chill separately in our rooms. That way, all potential temptation would be avoided.

Simple.

'Hi, everyone!' Jasmine shouted, causing the chatter around the pool to die down. 'Happy Friday and congratulations! You've completed your first seven days at The Love Hotel. Everyone still enjoying themselves?'

'Yes!' all the guests cheered.

'Great! So as we're entering our second week, we're going to switch things up. As you already know, now you'll be choosing the activities, with some support from us. But that won't be the only change.'

'Oooh!' Heidi, our new friend from last night, called out enthusiastically. 'Do tell!'

My pulse quickened. Jasmine really loved springing surprises on us. I started to think about whether or not I'd like it. Then I reminded myself that now Max and I were friends, there was no need to worry.

'At the moment you've been staying in separate rooms and mainly just meeting your partner for the daily activities. But part of a successful, long-lasting relationship is getting to know each other: *properly*. Usually people wait months, sometimes years to move in together, but we like to do things differently. So for the rest of your holiday, we're accelerating the process. We want to help you get to know each other better. Warts and all.'

Why did something tell me I wouldn't like the sound of where this conversation was going?

'How?' someone shouted from the front.

'You and your partner are going to move into a villa. *Together*. Isn't that wonderful?'

Oh.

Dear.

God.

I thought it was going to be a big enough challenge avoiding Max when we were staying in separate rooms.

But keeping my mind, lips and body from straying when we were living under the same roof?

How the hell was I going to be able to resist?

29

MAX

You've got to be joking.

As Jasmine fielded questions about the latest bombshell she'd just dropped about each couple moving in together, my brain scrambled.

This wasn't good.

My willpower was already hanging by a thread.

Ever since that almost kiss last night, I'd tried to keep my thoughts about Stella platonic, but I was fighting a losing battle.

The plan was to try and spend the minimum amount of time together. But if we were staying under the same roof, there'd be nowhere to hide.

'You'll each be staying in a two-bedroom villa, so there's no pressure whatsoever to share a bed,' Jasmine added. *That's something, I suppose.* 'And if anyone has any safety concerns, please don't hesitate to come and speak to me in confidence. I can't wait to introduce you to your new homes!'

I glanced at Stella. Her jaw was almost on the floor. At least I wasn't the only one who was surprised.

'Looks like we're going to be roomies!' I said, trying to lighten the mood.

'Yeah. I'm happy in my room, though, so I don't mind just staying there. You?'

'Same.' That'd definitely make things a lot easier.

'Let's go and talk to her.'

We both approached Jasmine, who was just finishing a conversation with another couple.

'Hi,' I said once she was free. 'Can we talk?'

'Stella, Max, hi! I was just coming to find you to brief you on today's activity. How can I help?'

'We just wondered if we could keep our rooms?' Stella asked. 'I'm sure the villa's nice but Max and I, we're happy where we are and considering our past, we already know each other quite well, so the whole getting to know you thing is better suited to new couples.'

'Ah,' Jasmine winced. 'I'm so sorry, but that's not going to be possible. The new arrivals are coming tomorrow so your rooms have already been allocated. All couples move into the villas on the property in the second week.'

'Is there really no way we can stay somewhere else, like separately?' I added.

'No.' She shook her head. 'Not really. I mean there are a couple of rooms, but they haven't been renovated yet, so they're...'

'We'll take them!' Stella and I shouted our agreement.

'I'll tell you what. Why don't I show you the rooms we have available and then I'll take you to the villa, which as I said has two completely separate bedrooms, and then you can decide. What do you think?'

'Cool,' I said. Stella nodded.

'Follow me.'

Jasmine led us away from the main part of the resort. It wasn't as well maintained, with overgrown bushes and trees.

When we arrived at the front door, the paint was peeling. There wasn't a key card to open it. Instead she pulled a rusty key out of her pocket and pushed it into the lock. After a few shoves, the door eventually opened.

A strong musty smell hit me as we stepped inside. The floral bed sheets looked like they were from the seventies. And the bright yellow walls and orange floors instantly gave me a headache.

'I see what you mean about it needing to be renovated,' Stella said.

'Yes,' Jasmine nodded. 'This was what all the rooms were like before. Strictly speaking, we don't allow guests to stay here because it's not up to the standard we like.'

'Can we see the villa now?' I asked. Stella's eyes bulged but I was pretty sure she didn't want to stay here any more than I did.

'Of course!'

Jasmine led us back to the main resort and along a path I hadn't noticed before. A row of luxury detached villas appeared in view. Each one had a garden with lush palm trees and colourful flowers.

When we stepped inside, I gasped. It was immaculate, like it'd just been built. The living room was open plan with a big comfy sofa and a widescreen TV.

The modern white and charcoal kitchen was straight out of an interiors brochure.

'Oh my God!' Stella rushed towards the huge glass patio doors, slid them open and stepped outside. 'It's a private pool!'

'Wow.' I took everything in. As well as the pool there was a table and chairs, sun loungers and a daybed just like the one by the hotel's main pool. And we had panoramic sea views.

'Let me show you the bedroom.'

We followed Jasmine back inside then down the hallway and after we passed the main bathroom, she led us into the grand master bedroom, which had a huge four-poster bed.

If that wasn't impressive enough, Jasmine slid open the huge glass double doors to reveal a hot tub.

'This is amazing!' Stella gasped.

It really was. I hadn't noticed before because I was so blown away, but the patio outside the master bedroom stretched all the way to the living room's patio, so we could access the private pool easily from here too.

Luckily the walls at the side of the villa were fairly high so we had privacy and our neighbours wouldn't be able to see what we got up to. Not that me and Stella were gonna get up to anything.

'Just imagine,' Jasmine said, 'chilling in the hot tub at the end of the day with a glass of bubbly. Or waking up and walking a few steps to take a dip in your own private pool. Or cooking dinner and then curling up on the sofa and watching a romantic film on that amazing cinema-style TV screen.'

'I love a good hot tub,' I said. 'And that TV looks impressive.'

'*Everything* about this place is impressive,' Stella said. 'Let me guess. You can't wait to watch the football on that massive screen!'

'No.' My chest tightened. 'Don't watch it any more.'

'What?' Stella frowned.

'This villa's amazing.' I quickly changed the subject.

'I agree.' Jasmine nodded. 'But if you'd really prefer to stay in the old-fashioned rooms, rather than staying in separate rooms in this idyllic five-star luxury villa, of course I'll honour your wishes.'

'No!' Stella shouted and I breathed a sigh of relief. 'I'm sure we can make it work so we can stay here, right, Max?'

'Totally.' As long as I didn't look at Stella for too long and avoided all forms of physical contact, hopefully I'd be able to keep my cool. 'You can have the master bedroom if you like and I'll take the other room.'

'Oh, no, I couldn't let you sleep in there. That bed looks much smaller. Your feet will hang off the edge.'

'I'm sure you'll find a solution!' Jasmine said. 'So are we good? You're both happy to stay here?'

'Yeah,' we replied.

'Excellent! If you let me know when you've packed up your things, I'll send Simón, the Suitcase Superintendent, to move everything here.'

'Thanks,' I said.

'Right, I'll leave you to it!' Jasmine walked towards the door then paused. 'Oh!' She slapped her forehead. 'I totally forgot to tell you about your activity for today!'

My heart jolted, then I realised it'd be fine. All the activities so far had been fun. Whatever Jasmine had up her sleeve would be no different.

'What is it?' Stella asked.

'Your couple's massage lesson!' she beamed. Stella and I stared at each other, bug-eyed. 'It's all booked on the beach for two hours from five until seven o'clock to give you time for your lunch to settle. You're going to love it!'

Two hours.

With Stella running her hands over my body.

Me running my hands all over hers.

Whether our lunch had settled or not was the least of our problems.

If I got a boner after a few minutes of her putting sun lotion on my back, how the hell would I survive Stella massaging me properly?

30

STELLA

I liked Jasmine. I really did. She was sweet, kind and caring. But sometimes I wondered if she got a kick out of seeing us suffer.

First she sprang the *moving into the villa together* thing on us. Then she casually dropped the bombshell about the couple's massage lesson.

I'd forgotten all about that and I wished she had too. I should've known she wouldn't have missed an opportunity to force us together.

'So, I suppose we should pack our things...' I tried to avoid looking at Max. I wondered how he felt about this.

Maybe I should worry less about him and should focus more on how *I* was going to keep my cool. He'd made me wet just applying sun lotion on me for two minutes, so God knows what state I'd be in if he started kneading his palms into my back or skimming the top of my arse with his big manly hands.

Shit.

'Yeah. If I don't see you at lunch, I'll see you at the beach for the... *massage*.'

Max said the word 'massage' like it was a double root canal

without anaesthetic. Yep. Just like I thought. He was dreading it too. Probably for different reasons, though.

'Bye,' I said, practically racing out the door and back to my room.

I was stood in front of the outdoor massage area, waiting for Max. The teacher was already here and she seemed like a no-nonsense type. That was a good thing because she'd keep the atmosphere frosty. And frosty was exactly what I needed to calm down my libido, which was out of control.

After I'd packed and organised my room, I'd planned to take my new vibrator in the shower. Determined that I wasn't going to be caught out without batteries again, I'd upgraded to the rechargeable version.

But I'd forgotten to charge it.

So here I was, hornier than a dog in heat, about to get a massage from the hottest man alive.

Help.

As Max strolled towards me, I swallowed hard. The man looked like a god with clothes on, so touching him with just a flimsy towel covering his butt would be a new kind of torture.

'Hi,' he smiled, then looked at his watch. 'I'm not late, am I?'

'No, no,' I said, wishing that for once he had been, or better still missed the whole thing altogether. 'You're right on time.'

We both stepped inside the outdoor massage suite. It had a square white wooden structure, but instead of windows, it had roll-down blinds and floaty white curtains.

Inside there were two single beds, covered with crisp white sheets and fluffy towels on top.

'*Hola*,' the woman said with little emotion. 'I am Olga – your Relaxation Facilitator.'

Max snorted just as a giggle flew from my lips.

'Sorry,' I said immediately. I'd been here a week but still hadn't got used to their crazy names.

'Something is funny?' she said in her strong Spanish accent.

'No, sorry,' Max added, his mouth still quivering.

After we'd filled out forms and Olga asked us some questions about our skin and general health, she said it was time to start.

'You.' She pointed at Max. 'Take off your clothes and get on the bed.'

'Okay,' Max said as she drew the curtains and rolled down the blinds.

'Should we wait outside?' I said.

'You are together, *sí*? This is nothing you have not seen before.'

Technically I *had* seen it all before, but I'd seen younger naked Max, not *all man* naked Max. Something told me the two were very different.

His physique was bigger and I couldn't help wondering whether his dick was too. Presumably it'd stopped growing after puberty, but I'd be happy to check. Purely for market research purposes, of course.

I reminded myself yet again that I was supposed to be keeping my cool, not turning up my horn-o-meter.

'We should give Max his privacy.' I turned my back.

'It's okay,' Max replied. 'I'll wrap the towel around me to take off my shorts.'

Of course, my dirty mind then decided it would be a good idea to picture Max sliding his shorts down his solid thighs.

'Ready,' he called out.

Olga walked to the bed. Max already had his face in the hole at the top and his back facing us.

'The towel should be lower,' Olga said. 'Your girlfriend will move it down, okay?'

'Um, yeah,' Max stuttered as my eyes bulged.

'How low are we talking?' It was sitting above Max's waist.

'Lower, so you can touch all of his back,' Olga said.

'Like this?' I shifted it down a few centimetres, trying to control my shaky hands.

'Lower,' she commanded. I moved it down, resisting the urge to lick my lips. 'Better. *Señor*, you do not wear the paper pants?'

'Paper pants?' Max asked, his voice muffled. 'I didn't see them.'

'My mistake.' Olga shook her head. 'I did not put them on the bed. I am sorry. You want to wear them now?'

'I'm okay,' he replied.

OMG. Max was completely naked under this towel. My nipples hardened. I hadn't even touched him yet and I was already turned on.

'Let us begin,' Olga said, snapping me out of my illicit thoughts.

After switching on some relaxing spa music, she took a bottle of oil from the warmer and instructed me to pour it onto my palms then rub them together. 'Start at the neck and shoulders,' she advised.

As my hands connected with Max's skin, desire surged through me. His shoulders were huge and although they were solid, the skin was beautifully soft.

'Perhaps you should be firmer,' Olga suggested. 'Ask what he likes.'

'How do you like it?' I asked before realising that sounded sexual. 'I mean, how's the pressure?'

'It's...' Max paused, 'fine.'

I was hoping for more than just *fine*, but I'd only just started.

At various intervals, Olga gave me instructions, for example to count to thirty slowly in my head for every section that I massaged, so everywhere received a balanced amount of attention.

The more I relaxed and stopped worrying about whether I was doing it right, the more natural it felt. Running my palms over Max was heavenly.

Once I'd massaged his shoulders, neck and the centre of his back, my hands glided lower. When I got to the area above Max's arse, he flinched.

'Sorry,' I said, worried I'd scratched him.

I continued kneading my thumbs into his hot, soft flesh like Olga had showed me, every touch sending a new wave of need ricocheting through me.

Trying to push the erotic thoughts out of my head at this point was pointless. My knickers were sodden, my nipples were harder than steel and I'd bitten my lip so much I was surprised it wasn't bleeding.

My head was high with desire. I couldn't even remember why I wasn't supposed to like Max any more. And I didn't care. I just wanted him.

'That is the end of his massage now,' Olga announced.

Already?

I glanced at my watch and, sure enough, an hour had passed. We'd probably spent at least ten minutes filling out the forms, talking to Olga and taking photos for our memory book at the beginning so it made sense.

'*Señor*, please get up.'

'Um.' Max lifted his head from the face hole. 'Maybe it'd be better if I stay here with my face down in this whilst Stella gets ready on the other bed. Just to, er, give her some privacy whilst she changes?'

'*Señora*?' Olga asked.

'Makes sense. Do you have the paper knickers?' I asked her. The ones I was wearing were ruined.

I turned away, removed my vest, wrapped a towel around me and took off my bra and skirt before sliding off my damp knickers and rolling them up into a flannel. I then put on the paper ones Olga had given me.

Next I lay face down on the bed, pushing the towel as low as it could go around my waist. Definitely better that I did it. The less Max touched me, the better.

'You are ready?' Olga asked.

'Yes,' I confirmed.

'I... okay,' Max said. He didn't sound sure. 'Should I... get dressed?'

'You are fine,' Olga replied.

I heard her give him the same instructions that she gave me and seconds later, I felt his hands on me.

Holy. Shit.

As Max ran his delicious palms over my shoulders, I squeezed my eyes shut and clenched my thighs.

There was no way I could make it through an hour of this without coming on this massage table.

How could he make me feel so good just by touching my bloody shoulders? What the hell would happen if he flicked his thumb on my clit?

God, I really, really wanted to find out.

I wanted him to do so much to me.

I wanted him to touch me everywhere.

Max's hands glided down to the centre of my back and every nerve ending in my body came alive.

A deep moan flew from my mouth. I couldn't stop it.

'You okay?' Max asked.

'*More* than okay,' I said, my breath ragged.

I was too relaxed, too turned on to hide how I was feeling. My brain was mush, my body was on fire. I was this close to telling Olga that three was a crowd and booting her out of here so I could pull Max on top of me.

As Max's palms skimmed the top of my arse, I ground my hips into the bed.

I swear to God, if he kept going, I was going to explode.

Just as Max ran his fingertips lower, I heard a voice call Olga's name from behind the curtain.

'So sorry to interrupt Max and Stella,' it was Jasmine, 'but I have an urgent message for Olga. Olga, there's an important call for you in the office. I need you to come with me. Will you two be okay to carry on by yourselves for fifteen minutes or so?'

'Yeah,' Max replied.

'Yes,' I panted.

'I am very sorry about this.' Olga sounded flustered. 'I will be back as soon as possible.'

'I hope she's okay,' Max said, continuing to run his hands all over me.

'Are we alone?' I asked.

'We are,' Max said. 'And looks like we'll be that way for fifteen minutes...'

'Mmm,' I groaned. 'As long as you keep touching me like that, I don't care if she leaves us alone for hours.' I wasn't bothered if he knew I liked him or not. I'd wished for Olga to leave and now that the sex gods had granted my first wish, I wished that Max would want to take advantage of the situation.

'On the boat, I asked you a question,' Max said, 'but you didn't answer.'

'What question?'

'I asked,' his fingers skimmed my lower back, sending shockwaves through me again, 'if you meant what you said when you were drunk. If you really wanted us to go back to your room and fuck.'

Hearing him say that word sent my pulse racing.

'Yes,' I panted. 'I meant it.'

'And do you still want me to do that?'

'Yes.' My heart thundered through my chest.

'Good,' Max growled. 'And would you like me to fuck you right here, right now on this massage table?'

'Yes.' I bolted upright, causing Max's hands to drop. My breasts were exposed but I didn't care. 'I want you.'

'I don't just want you, Stella. Right now, I fucking *need* you. Feeling your hands all over me drove me crazy. I nearly came on that damn bed. And touching your body, feeling your skin, hearing you moan...' His eyes were the colour of charcoal. 'I... my cock wants you so bad that if I don't bury myself inside you right now, I feel like I'm gonna die.'

'I need you too.'

Max stepped forward, leant down, then crushed his mouth onto mine. As our lips moulded together, fireworks erupted within me.

Our mouths moved hungrily against each other's, like we'd been apart for twenty years rather than twelve.

I'd forgotten how amazing this was. Max was always a great kisser, but now? He was so skilled at snogging he hadn't just graduated with honours. The man had got his kissing Master's *and* a PhD.

'Oh, God,' I cried out, running my hands through his scalp, then dragging my nails along his back.

I parted my lips and Max slid his tongue inside. As our

tongues flicked against each other it was like no time had passed. There was no awkwardness. It was like kissing Max was the reason my lips were created. I could literally do this all day, all night, all week.

And then I remembered. We only had fifteen minutes. Probably less than ten minutes now.

'Max,' I moaned into his mouth. 'I need you. But we don't have long.'

'Shit.' He dragged himself away. 'You're right. You sure you still want this, though? Like you said, I'm gonna need to be quick.'

'Yes,' I said breathlessly. 'I'm so close right now I'm not even sure I'll last more than a few minutes.'

'Lucky you. I'm worried about blowing my load in seconds. As much as I want to do this, if you want, we can wait. So I can fuck you properly.'

'No! You can't go back on your word. You said you wanted to screw me right here, right now, so that's what you need to do.'

'If that's what you want.'

He rushed over to his shorts, pulled out his wallet then a condom.

Max returned to the bed and stood in front of me.

'Last chance to back out. Remember, this is risky. Jasmine and Olga could come back at any minute and we're on the beach in broad daylight. Even though no one can see us because the blinds are down, the way I want to fuck you right now, they're gonna hear us.'

'Don't care.'

Without saying a word, Max dropped his towel.

Oh. My. God.

As I took in the sight of his huge erection, I gasped.

I remembered Max being big, but not *that* big.

'You okay?'

'I will be when you put that inside me.'

Max ripped the packet, then rolled the condom down his long, hard length.

'Ready?' He pulled the towel off from around my waist, causing it to drop on the floor, then trailed his fingers along the edge of the paper knickers, before dipping them underneath. 'Fuck, Stella. You're so wet.'

'I told you, I want you.'

'You asked for it.' He ripped the knickers off in one swift tug.

Max pulled me to the edge of the bed, lined his cock up at my entrance then plunged inside me.

We both groaned loudly as Max pummelled into me. I held onto his waist, revelling in the sweet sensation of him filling me up. The more he thrusted, the more I wanted.

'Harder.' I dug my nails into Max's back as he gripped my hips tighter.

'Fuck, Stella,' he said, rubbing his thumb against my clit. 'You feel so good.'

'I-I,' I stuttered. 'If you keep touching my clit, I won't be able to hold on,' I said, feeling the wave already building inside me.

'Good,' Max whispered into my ear. 'Come for me.'

He circled my clit, still pounding into me and I knew it was game over. I squeezed my toes as the sensations raced through me at lightning speed.

Max dropped his head, taking my nipple into his mouth. As he sucked on it, I felt like a volcano was erupting inside me.

He continued thrusting faster, fucking me so hard the bed began to move. It crashed into a little table which had products on top, sending them plummeting to the ground.

'Don't you dare stop!' I warned. 'Oh, God.' I grabbed his arse, pushing him deeper. 'Oh, God!'

'That's it, Stell. Let go.'

'Ohhhhh, fuck!' I screamed, my orgasm ripping through me like a tsunami.

As my body slumped, Max continued thrusting, a feral growl shooting from his mouth.

'Fuucckkk!' he groaned as he finished inside me, before falling forward, his chest pressed against mine and his heartbeat racing. 'Jesus,' he panted. 'That was...'

'I know,' I said. I didn't want to say it out loud but that was the best sex I'd ever had.

Our chests heaved against each other, our bodies slick with sweat.

If I had to give Max one of the silly titles this hotel loved so much, it'd have to be something like *Sex Supremo*, *Orgasm Oracle* or *Pussy Professional*.

The man had *skills*.

Just as I started to relive all the delicious sensations I'd experienced, I heard voices coming towards us.

'You are hurt?' Olga's voice sounded from outside. 'I heard somebody scream.'

'We're back!' Jasmine called out loudly.

'Shit!' We both jumped up. 'Can you give us a minute?' I called out.

Just as Max and I reached for our towels, Olga pulled back the curtains then gasped.

'What is happening?' she shouted as Jasmine followed behind her.

Max was able to cover himself in time, but my towel was stuck under the table leg, so Olga got an eyeful. Of *everything*.

When Max saw I was standing there in the buff, he whipped his towel off and held it in front of me, which meant that although I was covered, now his massive dick was on show.

It didn't take a genius to guess what we'd been up to. But if Olga had any doubts, the fact that Max was wearing a used condom made everything crystal clear.

'Oh, *my*!' Jasmine bit her lip and Olga's eyes flew from their sockets. 'Why don't we, er, give them some time to sort themselves out...' Jasmine quickly ushered Olga outside.

Fuck.

I slumped on the bed with my head in my hands and groaned.

First I showed my boobs to the entire hotel. Now I almost got caught screwing on a massage table and managed to flash my tits and fanny to my bloody Love Alchemist and Relaxation Facilitator.

Ground. Swallow. Me. Up.

31

MAX

'You okay?' I stepped in front of Stella. I didn't care that they'd seen my cock. *Shit happens.*

I knew Stella would care about them seeing her, though. That was why when I realised she was naked, I didn't have to think twice about using my towel to cover her up.

Stella's eyes were wide. She was still in shock.

'I'm so embarrassed,' she winced. 'Can we just get out of here?'

'Course.'

After I'd rolled off the condom, wrapped it a tissue, thrown it away and cleaned myself up as best I could, I got dressed.

When I looked round, Stella already had her clothes on and was clutching a flannel which was rolled into a ball.

'What's in there?' I asked, stripping the bed we'd just shagged on and putting the towels in the laundry basket in the corner. Didn't feel right to leave it for Olga.

'My knickers,' she answered sheepishly.

'Why don't you put them on?'

'They're too wet.'

Hearing that made my dick jerk. I knew we'd only just had sex, but if we hadn't been interrupted and Stella was up for it, I would've had her all over again.

Getting caught wasn't ideal, but for me, it was worth the risk.

Sex with Stella was incredible.

Everything was so much better than I'd imagined.

The way we kissed.

The way we fucked.

We were like a couple of wild animals on heat and I enjoyed every damn second.

When I entered Stella, I felt like I'd come home. Being inside her seemed like where I belonged.

Like I'd said from the start, I would've preferred it if we could've taken our time. But after being apart for so long, the idea of waiting another second felt like a lifetime. And even if we were given ten hours together instead of ten minutes, something told me that wouldn't be enough.

'Give them to me,' I growled.

'What?' Her brows furrowed. 'Why?'

'I can put them in my pocket.'

'O-okay.' She handed them over and I stuffed them in my shorts pocket.

'Ready?'

'As I'll ever be.'

When we stepped outside of the massage room, Jasmine and Olga were standing several feet away.

'Wait here,' I said. 'I'm just gonna apologise.'

'I should come too.'

'You can if you want, but I've got this.'

'You sure?'

'Yeah. See you back at the villa.'

'I'll apologise later too. I just need to get cleaned up.' Stella hurried off.

'Olga, Jasmine.' I walked towards them. 'My sincere apologies for what you just saw. I didn't mean for you to be exposed to... well, I hope I didn't offend you.'

I didn't regret what I did with Stella, but of course I didn't want to make them feel uncomfortable.

'You could not wait to do *that* in your room?' Olga sneered.

'It's complicated. I know it sounds lame, but it was a kind of heat of the moment thing. It wasn't planned. It just... happened. Me and Stella, we were together before and...'

'Max, with your permission, I can explain to Olga. I appreciate your apology, though. Go back to the villa. I'll come and see you both later.' Jasmine was so professional that I couldn't tell whether she was pissed off.

'Okay,' I nodded, wondering what the consequences of getting caught would be.

When I arrived at the villa, the bathroom door was closed and I heard a tap running. Any minute now, Stella would be going in the shower. I wished I could join her, but I had to respect her boundaries.

Instead I went to my room and took out some fresh clothes. There was only one bathroom so I had to wait until Stella finished to clean myself up properly.

As I reached in my pocket, I remembered I had her underwear. I pulled out the flannel, ready to put it in the laundry basket, but as I tried to unravel it, Stella's knickers fell on the floor.

I bent down to pick them up. Fuck. Stella wasn't joking. These were soaked. And knowing that she was so turned on and wanted me that much instantly made my dick hard.

Before I knew it, Stella's lacy panties were under my nose and I squeezed my eyes shut as I inhaled her delicious scent. *Jesus.* What I wouldn't give to taste her right now. I'd love to run my tongue over her clit. If we'd had more time, I would've devoured her with my mouth and made her come all over again.

Reluctantly, I put her knickers on the bed and headed to the kitchen. I needed a glass of water to help cool me down.

Just as I was going back to my room, Stella came out of the bathroom.

'You're... back.' She paused in the hallway. As I took in the sight of the towel wrapped tightly around her, I tried to ignore how sexy her shoulders looked. 'I was just about to get in the shower, but I forgot my face wash. What did Jasmine and Olga say? Are they kicking us out?'

'Not sure,' I shrugged. 'Jasmine said she'd speak to us later.'

'Shit.' She shook her head. 'We shouldn't have been so reckless.'

'Do you regret it?' I asked. 'Because I don't.' I walked towards her and she stepped back, her body pressing against the wall.

'You don't?'

'Not. One. Bit.' I fixed my gaze on Stella and she swallowed hard. 'There is one thing I regret, though.'

'What?' she said, her chest rising and falling rapidly like she was struggling for breath.

'That I didn't get to fuck you again.'

'What's stopping you now?' she said.

'Give me the green light and I will.'

'Consider *this* my green light.' She tugged the front of her towel and it dropped to the floor, revealing her magnificent body.

'Jesus, Stella. Do you have any idea how beautiful you are?' I ran my hands across her shoulders, down the centre of her chest, then gently circled from the outside of her tits, inwards until I reached her nipples. A soft moan flew from her lips.

Next my hands travelled down her belly, then between her legs. As I grazed my fingers over her clit, Stella groaned and pushed out her hips.

'Fuck, Max,' she pleaded. 'Please. I want you.'

'I want you too. But this time, I'm gonna do things properly. Open your legs.'

She spread herself open for me like I'd asked and I dropped to my knees.

'I've missed kissing you, I've missed being inside you and I've missed tasting you.'

'I haven't showered yet!' she gasped.

'Don't care. It's your scent that I want on my tongue. Nothing else.'

I leant forward, parted her lips and licked her slowly from her clit to her opening.

This time, Stella moaned loudly with pleasure and the sound sent a jolt of electricity straight to my dick.

As I flicked her clit gently with my tongue, then grazed it with my teeth, Stella's legs shuddered. She grabbed my hair, pushing my face deeper into her.

Knowing she was enjoying it and wanted more was all the encouragement I needed to continue.

As I sucked on her sensitive bud, she cried out.

'Oh my God,' Stella gasped. 'How are you... so... *ohhhh*!'

I could tell she was already close, but I wasn't done with feasting on her yet. I slid two fingers inside Stella and she cried out again, louder this time. As I fucked her with my fingers, I continued lapping at her clit, her delicious juices dripping onto my tongue.

'Max!' she screamed. Hearing her call out my name almost made me come in my shorts. 'I can't!'

I flexed my fingers inside her and picked up the pace, licking and sucking her like I hadn't eaten in days and she was my first meal.

Her body began to shake and she gripped my hair tighter. As her orgasm exploded, her legs gave way and she slid down the wall.

I lifted my head away and drank her in.

Her gorgeous chest heaved and there was a satisfied smile across her face.

'Good?' I said.

'Y-you really... have to ask?' She struggled to speak.

'Yeah. I need to know that you're satisfied.'

'*More* than satisfied.'

'Good.'

'I'll return the favour... in a minute.' She paused. 'Just need to catch my breath.'

'Thanks for the offer. Trust me, I'd love that, but like I said before, I'd like to fuck you properly. That was just a bit of foreplay. The starters. Now that you've come, let's move onto the main course.'

'Yeah?' She tugged at my shorts. 'What's on the menu?'

'Today's special is a large serving of cock with all the trimmings.'

'Sounds delicious,' she said. As my shorts dropped to the floor, my dick sprang free. Stella started stroking it and I nearly lost my damn mind. 'And where will this main course be served? In the bedroom?'

'If you've got no objections, I'd like to *serve* you against this wall.'

'No objections from me.'

That was all I needed to hear. After I reached in my shorts pocket to pull out my wallet, I rolled on a condom and wasted no time in burying myself inside her.

And I knew once we'd finished, I'd want to do it all over again...

32

STELLA

The sound of a phone notification jolted me out of my sleep. I slowly opened my eyes and squinted as I took in my surroundings.

For a second I was confused about where I was, then I remembered I was in the villa now. This was my new bedroom.

As I sat up in the bed, I winced. My whole body ached like I'd just done a marathon gym workout.

Then I remembered.

Max.

It wasn't a dream.

We'd hooked up. Multiple times.

After he'd gone down on me, he'd fucked me against the wall. Then we'd showered together and were supposed to get ready for dinner, but we'd fallen asleep. When we woke up, it was after midnight and we were horny so we did it again on the bed. Twice.

I'd had more sex in the last twenty-four hours than I had in probably the last two years. And I felt bloody amazing.

Although I tried to deny it, I knew from the moment I saw

him again that me and Max would have insane chemistry in the bedroom. We had an incredible connection when we dated and time and experience had only intensified that.

Getting caught on the massage bed was embarrassing but I wasn't going to lie: I'd never been so turned on in my life. Knowing that it was forbidden in so many ways heightened the pleasure. When Max had his hands all over me, I didn't care about the fact that someone might hear or walk in on us. I had only one objective: to feel Max inside me. And once I'd experienced that feeling, I couldn't get enough of him.

And oh, my, *God*. When he went down on me in the hallway: Jesus. I'd never experienced pleasure like it. Max and I dabbled in oral sex when we dated, but we were only in our late teens. At the time, of course, we thought we knew what we were doing, but I could confirm with 100 per cent certainty that Max had mastered his technique now. He'd picked up an arsenal of new skills and I was happy that I got to benefit from them.

After experiencing how talented he was with his tongue, the *Pussy Professional* title didn't do him justice on its own. The man was an *Oral Aficionado*.

Speaking of Max, I wondered where he was? I threw off the sheet, swung my legs out of the bed, then hobbled to the window to draw the curtains.

My poor vagina felt like it had been rubbed with sandpaper, but I wasn't complaining. The soreness was worth it.

Once I'd brushed my teeth and washed my face, I went to look for him.

Max's bedroom door was open and the bed was made. I didn't even know if he'd slept there or with me. The villa seemed empty.

When I went into the kitchen, there was a note pinned to the fridge.

Morning!
   Hope you slept well. Gone to get some stuff for
breakfast.
   Back soon,
   M x

My heart fluttered. That was so sweet of him.

As well as some bread and fresh fruit, luckily the hotel had stocked the fridge with ham, milk, butter and cheese, so last night we didn't go hungry. But we'd eaten most of the food, so I was glad Max had gone to get more.

Now we had a kitchen of our own, it made sense to eat here sometimes instead of always going to the restaurant. It was more intimate. The Love Hotel organisers knew what they were doing by moving the couples in together.

I laughed to myself as I thought about the fuss we'd made when we were told we'd be sharing this villa. And look what happened. Hours later we were here fucking like rabbits.

If I was being honest, we both knew that this would happen. We'd tried to fight it, but in the end the pull between us was too strong. Even if they'd put us in rooms at separate ends of the hotel, sooner or later we would've ended up screwing. Sometimes, chemistry couldn't be denied.

There was a reason I was trying to deny the attraction though: I didn't want to get hurt. But I wasn't going to worry about that for now. I just wanted to enjoy myself.

I heard the villa door close and Max came in the kitchen.

'Hey!' he smiled. 'You're awake!'

'Only just,' I grinned as my eyes scanned him from head to toe.

Max was so gorgeous. His hair was wavy, his tanned skin glowed and those muscular arms were incredible. I was so glad that I didn't have to admire them from afar any more. Now, I could run my hands all over them.

'Good morning.' Max put the shopping bags on the floor, strode over to me and crushed his lips on mine, giving me a long, slow kiss. My body fizzed with excitement.

'Mmm,' I said when we eventually came up for air. 'That's definitely a good way to start the morning.'

'Yeah. I could think of an even better way,' he licked his lips, 'but after our workout last night and earlier, we need to eat. I'm gonna make breakfast so go and relax on the patio and I'll let you know when it's ready.'

Now we were in charge of our own activities, we didn't have morning briefings.

'Ooh! Thanks!' I said, thinking that no one had offered to make me breakfast before. 'If you're sure you don't need a hand, I'll go and have a shower first.'

'I'm good. Go for it. And help yourself to the products.'

When I went in the bathroom there was a whole selection of shower gels, soaps and creams from Max's company. Everything looked so amazing I couldn't wait to try them.

I took much longer in the shower than I should've, but those Olibella products were divine. I didn't think my skin had ever felt or smelt so soft. Having access to all of these products was a dream.

Once I'd got dressed, I checked in on Max, who said he needed another half an hour, so rather than lounging around on the patio whilst he was hard at work in the kitchen, I offered to collect yesterday's photos.

It'd also give me time to call Sammie. She'd texted last night to see how the villa move and massage had gone, but I was *otherwise engaged.*

Seeing as I had time to kill, I took the long route to reception via the beach.

There wasn't a single cloud in the bright blue sky and as the gentle waves rolled towards me, I closed my eyes and inhaled the salty sea air.

I took off my flip-flops and exhaled, my feet sinking into the soft, warm sand. This was miles away from trudging along the cold, wet pavements to the post office like I did every day in London. This place was paradise.

When I first arrived and saw Max, all I wanted to do was rush home, but I was so glad I'd stayed. Everything right now was like a dream. No. It was better. It was like I was living in a romance novel. I was so happy I never wanted to leave.

I pulled out my phone and dialled Sammie's number. After a few rings, she picked up.

'So, have you and Max shagged yet?' she asked.

'Wow. Not even a hello, how are you?'

'Sorry, hon. I don't have time to beat around the bush right now. I'm getting ready to see my gran for lunch and I'm running late. So come on then! Spill! Did you jump him on the massage table thingy?'

I paused, thinking how scarily accurate she was.

'Kind of...'

'*No way!*' she gasped. 'I was only joking! What happened? Did you ask him to roll on his back so you could straddle him? I need details!'

As I explained how we'd gone at it like animals after Jasmine called Olga away, Sammie screamed so loudly, my eardrums almost burst.

'That's fan-fucking-tastic!' she cheered as if I'd just won a lifetime achievement award rather than just screwing my ex.

'Yeah, it really was. Until Jasmine and the massage therapist, sorry, the "Relaxation Facilitator" walked in on us.'

'*Nooooo!*' Sammie screamed again. 'They caught Max giving you a beef injection? That's hilarious!'

'A *beef injection*?' I shook my head even though I knew she couldn't see me.

'Yeah! I heard someone call it that the other day and thought it was funny! They also called it *hiding the salami*, which is also accurate! Anyway, you're distracting me. So they walked in as Max was giving you a good pounding? How long were they there before you realised? Did they take any photos for your memory book? Can I see them?'

'No!' I laughed. 'Of course not! Luckily we'd finished... *just*. But they saw us naked. Max covered himself, but I didn't get to my towel in time.'

'You're becoming a right flasher!'

'Not intentionally, believe me. Anyway, when Max saw I was naked, he put his towel in front of me, which meant they got an eyeful of his dick and the full condom.'

'Oh my God!' she shrieked. 'That's hilarious!'

'It wasn't hilarious! It was mortifying!'

'For you, maybe! But that was nice of Max to try and shield you. What a gent! Is he still as well hung as before?'

'Bigger! I'm not even sure how that's possible, but it's true.'

'You lucky cow! So what did your Love Alchemist woman say? You're not gonna get arrested for public indecency, are you?'

'We're still waiting to hear what our punishment will be. But so far, no police have come knocking.'

'Good. So have you hooked up since then?'

When I told Sammie how Max went down on me and that we'd been at it like dogs on heat ever since, she screamed with so much excitement, I was surprised she hadn't lost her voice.

'So yeah, he's making me breakfast and I'm on my way to get the photos.'

'You are living the dream, my friend! I'm so happy for you! Maybe I need to apply to this Love Hotel place. Sounds a million times better than scrolling through the apps.'

'Definitely.'

'You owe your mum the biggest bouquet of flowers for setting you up with this holiday. Does she know what's happened with you guys yet?'

'No. You're the first person I've told and I don't want her to get too excited.'

'Why not?'

'Because this can never be anything serious. It's just sex. Knowing Mum, she'll start planning our happy ever after and for once, I'm just trying to have fun, y'know?'

Hearing myself say out loud that I was about to dive headfirst into a holiday fling was weird.

I'd always been a relationship kind of girl, and once I'd got my head around the fact that I was coming to this hotel, I secretly hoped I'd find my perfect match, but I had to be realistic. Whilst now I realised Max still fancied me, I was pretty sure that he didn't have any interest in settling down. So instead of overthinking things like I normally did, I was going to just try enjoying the moment and go with the flow for a change.

If I had zero expectations, I wouldn't be disappointed.

'I hear you. I think you're doing the right thing. Just enjoy yourself. Try not to get too in your head about what it means and what'll happen next, okay.'

'I'll do my best. Oh, shit.' My eyes widened as I saw Jasmine walking towards me. 'I've just seen my Love Alchemist. Better go. Say hi to your gran from me.'

'Will do! Happy shagging!'

I laughed and hung up.

'Jasmine!' I said in my brightest voice. 'I was hoping to bump into you. I wanted to apologise. I'm so embarrassed and I'm so sorry if our actions offended or upset you and Olga in any way. I know this is a professional establishment and public indecency is wrong and we could've been arrested, but *please*. Don't report us to the police or throw us out. I'm really starting to like it here.'

'Don't worry! I won't be reporting you to the police!' Jasmine smiled and my shoulders loosened. 'This is private land anyway, so although I'm not a lawyer, I'd imagine nudity isn't a criminal offence.'

'Oh, thank God!' I blew out a breath.

'Shit happens, right?' For a second I was surprised to hear Jasmine swear, because she always seemed so professional. But I guessed she was a hot-blooded woman with needs, just like me. 'The way I see it, you can't expect to put perfect matches together and not expect fireworks.'

'True,' I nodded. 'But I'm sure other people are able to make it back to their room before they go at it. Honestly, I don't know what came over us.'

Well, that wasn't strictly true. I challenged anyone not to run their palms over Max's body, then feel him running his hands all over them and not instantly want to jump his bones.

'At least you were shielded by the blinds. Let's just say I've caught some guests in more compromising situations than what you and Max got up to. Honestly, don't worry. I'll take care of Olga.'

'Thank you.'

'I came by the villa last night to talk to you both and reassure you, but you sounded erm, *busy*, so I don't think you heard the doorbell.'

She must've heard us screwing.

'Sorry,' I winced.

'No worries! So, this is good news, though, right? If you two are, y'know, *getting intimate*, that's a great sign!'

'Yeah...' I replied, reminding myself that I wasn't going to overthink it.

'Anyway, I'm so glad you've got a second chance at love!' Jasmine beamed.

'Oh... no. This isn't a *love* thing!' I laughed. 'It's just... *sex*. It's like you said. I'd be silly not to grab the chance to enjoy some orgasms.'

Like I'd said to Sammie earlier, I had no expectations of anything more than that. After what happened before, it'd be too messy and complicated. A holiday fling was a much better idea.

'Right. Yes, yes, *of course*,' she smiled. 'My mistake.'

'Anyway, thanks again, for y'know, understanding. I better get the photos and go back to the villa. Max is making breakfast.'

'How romantic!'

'We'll do our playlist updates later too. We didn't get round to it because...'

'No need to explain,' she grinned. 'I look forward to seeing what songs you two select for each other. Enjoy your breakfast.'

'Thanks, we will.'

Once I'd collected the photos, I headed back and when I saw what Max had done, bubbles of excitement flooded my stomach.

He'd laid a table outside, but it wasn't just the normal cutlery he'd set out. There was a little vase with a single red rose and what looked like a bottle of champagne was chilling in a silver bucket.

'*Señorita*.' He stepped into the living room to greet me. 'If you'd like to come with me, I will show you to your table.'

I followed him, a wide grin covering my face. Max pulled out a chair and I sat down.

'Wow,' I said, taking in the views of the sea in the distance. 'This looks like the best seat in the house.'

'Only the best for you! Wait here.' He left then returned with a plate which he laid in front of me. 'You still like French toast, right?'

'I *love* French toast!' As I glanced at the plate, my mouth watered.

'Thank God! It's been a while since I've made it. I try not to eat too much fried food, but a little holiday treat shouldn't hurt.'

Max brought out his own plate, a bowl of fruit salad and freshly squeezed orange juice so we could make a Buck's Fizz with the champagne.

'Thanks for all this,' I said.

'My pleasure. Whatever happens, I want us to remember our time here. I want it to be special.'

'When you say *whatever happens*, is that a polite way of saying if this only ends up being a holiday fling?' I teased.

I should play the lottery. I knew that was what Max had wanted.

Max's eyes widened then dropped to the table. I took his silence to mean *yes*.

'I'd kind of hoped we could stay in our bubble a little longer, but I guess we're only delaying the inevitable.'

'The inevitable?' I asked.

'Yeah. *The talk*. We should have a chat about what happened last night and what it means, for us.'

He was right. It had to be done.

It was better that we both knew where we stood from the beginning.

I'd be lying if I said I wouldn't be chuffed if he confessed his undying love for me, but deep down I knew that wasn't what Max was about to say...

33

MAX

I poured the champagne into my glass and topped up Stella's Buck's Fizz, then took a large glug.

'So.' I paused, thinking how best to word this. 'About last night and this morning. I think it's obvious that I thought it was fucking incredible. Everything was even better than I could've imagined. And hopefully the feeling's mutual.'

'You know I enjoyed it too.' Stella licked her lips.

'Good. And I really like you. A *lot*.'

'*But...*' she jumped in.

'But, as bad as it sounds, I was thinking with my dick, not with my head. I mean, the head on my shoulders, not the other head...'

'I know which head you meant,' she laughed. 'And?'

'And I think the reason I was against the whole moving into the villa thing was because I knew it wasn't a good idea. Right now, I don't know what I want. I don't know if I'm cut out for something serious. There's still so much I need to do with the business and every relationship I've attempted since you has been a shit show. But the thing I worry about the most is hurting you. I fucked up once and I don't wanna risk doing it again. So maybe it's best if we draw a line under what happened and go back to trying to be friends, like we were before the massage. What d'you think?'

I exhaled and my shoulders loosened. I felt better now I'd got that off my chest.

'Why do you assume that I want something serious with you?' Stella raised her eyebrow.

'Oh.' I swallowed hard. 'I just thought that... well, we're at *The Love Hotel*, a place where people come to find *love* so I just assumed that you were looking for something long term.'

'But you're here too and you've just said you're not looking for love either.'

Touché.

'True. There's nothing wrong with people wanting that. Colton is crazy in love and blissfully happy with his wife and kid. All I'm saying is, I don't know if that's for me. And I wanted to be upfront about it. Like I said, the last thing I want to do is lead you on or hurt you. I'm just trying to be honest.'

'I appreciate that. But for me, last night and this morning was just sex. Not all women want marriage and babies, you know! I was horny, my vibrator wasn't charged and I thought you'd be good in bed, so I thought, why not?' She shrugged like it was no big deal.

'Oh.' My jaw dropped. 'Right. Okay.'

Of all the things I expected Stella to say, it definitely wasn't *that*.

Of course, I knew plenty of women enjoyed having no-strings sex just like men did. I just didn't know Stella was one of them. I guessed people changed. I hadn't seen her for twelve years and we hadn't really spoken about her relationship history.

Now I felt like a fucking idiot. Here I was worrying about

how to let her down gently, when she had no interest in getting into a committed relationship with me in the first place.

'So to answer your original question,' Stella said, 'yes, we can go back to being friends if that's what you really want?'

'Y-yeah,' I stuttered. 'Friends is good.'

Trying to keep things platonic with Stella was gonna be torture. There was nothing friendly about the fantasies that'd been racing through my mind about all the different ways I'd like to fuck her. But I had to push those desires out of my head. It'd only end in tears.

'Great! Is there any more French toast?' she said casually like we'd just been discussing the weather.

'Um, yeah. I'll get some.'

As I walked to the kitchen, a strange feeling of emptiness washed over me and I didn't know why.

Stella had agreed we could go back to being friends. I'd been honest with her and said I couldn't commit and she'd told me it didn't matter because what we had was just sex anyway.

We'd cleared the air. Clarified things. We'd reached an agreement without any arguments.

I'd had sex with no strings.

I'd got what I'd wanted.

So why did I feel so disappointed?

34

STELLA

I climbed out of our private pool, reached for the towel, sat on the sun lounger and started drying my skin.

There was no sign of Max in the living room. Once he'd wolfed down his breakfast, he'd said he had to do something and left.

I knew Max wasn't expecting me to say I wasn't bothered about him not being able to commit to something long term. I'd caught him completely off guard. And I wasn't surprised.

A week ago, if someone told me I would've been so casual about sleeping with a guy (especially Max), I wouldn't have believed them. But now that I had, I felt kind of strong. Powerful. Like a woman who knew what she wanted and went for it.

More often than not, it was men who called the shots. And yeah, I kind of waited for Max to make the first move, but I was also clear about the fact that I wanted him.

What I'd said to Max was true. I was horny. My vibrator wasn't charged and I knew he'd be good in bed. I had an opportunity to solve my sexual frustration so I grabbed it with both hands.

The thing I said about not every woman wanting to settle down and make babies was also true.

Full disclosure: yes, I did want that at some point, but when we were on that massage bed, I wasn't thinking about living happily ever after. I was caught up in the heat of the moment and wasn't thinking any further ahead than getting some good old satisfaction.

Right now, playing happy families with Max wasn't what I wanted. We both had bigger priorities. Max said he needed to focus on his company and I had aspirations too. I wanted a career I loved and I needed to find my own place. Once I had that, *then* I could consider finding someone.

I knew Mum was hoping I'd come here and find the love of my life. And I admit, once I'd got my head around coming here, part of me also wished for that too, but seeing as it wasn't on the cards, there was no point dwelling on it. Mum also wanted me to enjoy myself and live my life, which was exactly what I was doing. And it felt good.

The last thing I needed was to repeat my past mistakes by making Max the centre of my universe, wasting my days dreaming of us falling in love and having a relationship, only to end up devastated all over again.

When I got back to London, I didn't want to be sitting by the phone wondering if he'd call or trying to decode what his text messages meant. That was why I'd agreed to us being friends.

It was better that way. Safer.

Was it going to be difficult to keep my hands off Max? Definitely. If I had my way, I'd ask him if he wanted to pick up where we left off in the early hours of this morning. But that wasn't a good idea.

I was glad we'd had that talk this morning, before either of us started catching feelings. At this stage, it was easier to nip any emotions in the bud.

We'd be fine.

I walked to the other end of the patio and slid open the bedroom doors. I spotted Max in the hallway.

'Hi,' I said.

'Hey.'

'What you up to?'

'Just finished some work stuff. Was thinking about going for a walk on the beach. Wanna come with me?'

I would very much like to come with you.

'Okay,' I said, warning my mind to get out of the gutter. 'Can you give me ten minutes?'

'Course.'

Once I was dressed, we dropped off our memory book photo selection choices to reception then headed down to the sea.

'Beautiful, isn't it?' I slipped off my flip-flops so I could feel the sand beneath my feet. It was quickly becoming one of my favourite things to do.

'It really is. Gonna be so hard to go back to reality after this.'

'What sort of stuff do you do at your company?'

'The short answer is *a lot*. I kind of oversee everything, product development, marketing, looking at different markets to expand into, meetings. It's endless.'

'Don't you have staff to help?'

'Yeah, but I like to be hands-on, y'know?'

'Well, not really. I've never run a business before so...' I shrugged.

'I know you mentioned before that you do design but what kind of clients do you work for?'

'At the moment, I work for my mum.'

'Oh yeah? So we're both involved in family businesses, that's cool! What's her company?'

'You promise not to laugh?'

'Laugh? Why?'

'She makes sexy underwear.'

'Really?' Max's eyes widened. 'I remember she used to work at a factory before making underwear, but that was vanilla stuff, right?'

'Yeah. Don't get me wrong, we do still sell normal knickers, but our bestsellers are the personalised ones.'

'Tell me more about these personalised knickers,' Max smirked.

I explained and Max asked lots of questions. Not just about the kinky requests, but the business too. He seemed genuinely interested.

'So yeah, I handle all the orders and admin. When I first started, I redesigned the website and marketing materials but now that's done, there's not much need for design work, apart from the odd promotion or creating visuals for social media stuff.'

'Do you think you'll ever branch out and do stuff for other clients?'

'I'd love to. I miss the creativity. As much as I enjoy working for Mum, I don't want to do it forever. I'd like to run my own free-lance graphic design business, take on my own clients, challenge myself.'

'You should do it!' Max said. 'Good graphic designers are hard to find. We're having a nightmare with the company we use at the moment.'

'Why?'

'I think they've got complacent. We've used them for a couple of years now and the stuff they sent over for a new olive oil body care range was pretty terrible. The branding looked so dated.'

'I could do some designs for you if you want?' The words shot out of my mouth before I had a chance to think. I shouldn't have said anything. Now Max would feel awkward. 'No obligation. You don't have to pay me or anything. I genuinely love your products and they deserve to do well so maybe if I did some sketches or something it could give them some direction.'

'I'd love that,' Max replied.

'Really?' I couldn't hide the surprise in my voice. I thought he'd just fob me off. Then again, I basically said I'd do it for free so he had nothing to lose.

'*Yes, really*. But of course I'll pay you. Your work has value and I respect that.'

'Oh. Thanks. Send me the brief and I'll do some brainstorming later or tomorrow.'

'You're on holiday. I can't ask you to do that!'

'I don't mind. I can do it by the pool or something. As long as you keep me topped up with cocktails!'

'You sure?'

'Yeah. I wouldn't say so otherwise. I enjoy it. I wish I could do it full time.'

'Then you should. It's important to follow your dreams.'

'Yeah, but Mum needs me.'

'Who's taking care of things whilst you're here?'

'Believe it or not, Mum's roped in the vicar's wife!' I chuckled.

'No!' Max laughed and the sound made butterflies dance in my stomach. 'That's hilarious! Do you think she'll take some of those thongs home and wear them for her husband?'

'Who knows? Maybe Mum made her one that says "Sinner"!'

'Yeah!' He laughed again. 'So do you have any of these sexy thongs?' His eyes darkened.

'Max!' I gently slapped his bicep playfully. God, it felt so good. 'That's not a question that *friends* ask each other.'

'Why not? It's a totally innocent question!'

'That's for me to know and for you to find out,' I flirted.

'Is that an invitation?' The corner of his mouth turned up into a smile.

'No comment,' I said.

I was actually wearing one of the thongs Mum had given me right now, but I wasn't about to tell Max that.

'Anyway, if you really want to go out on your own, you should go for it. I'm sure your mum will support you.'

Hearing Max's encouragement warmed my heart. Maybe one day I'd think about branching out, but not yet.

'What do you want to do for lunch?' I said.

'I don't mind cooking in the villa. It's nice to have a kitchen.'

'Do you like cooking?'

'Yeah. I like being able to control what ingredients are used. Making things exactly how I like them.'

'You're a real health enthusiast, aren't you? The working out, the salads... You were always careful, but it seems like you're into it a lot more now.'

'I am.' His voice went low. 'Because of what happened to Mum. That motivated me to take better care of myself.'

'Makes sense. I'm no chef, but I'm okay in the kitchen. I make a mean macaroni cheese. Not exactly healthy, but it's one of my signature dishes.'

'Maybe you can make it for me sometime.' Max faced me.

Our eyes locked and my stomach fluttered. All I wanted right now was for him to lean down and kiss me.

'I'd love to. I can do something healthier like ginger and chilli salmon.'

'You'd make that for me?' Max said, brushing away the strand of hair that had blown onto my cheek.

'Yeah,' I murmured. Max's thumb was still brushing my cheek and even though it was another hot sunny day, the heat from his palms sent goosebumps scattering across my skin.

'You're really easy to talk to,' Max said. 'I like spending time with you.'

'I like spending time with you too.'

As his head moved closer to mine, my heart started to race.

'I like doing so much with you.'

'What else do you like doing with me?'

'I can't tell you.'

'I thought you just said I was easy to talk to?'

'You are.'

'So tell me then,' I insisted.

'It's not just *talking* that I like doing with you.' Max's eyes darkened. 'And that's the problem.'

'If you could do anything with me right now, what would it be?'

'You don't want to know.'

'I wouldn't have asked if I didn't. Tell me.'

'First, I'd kiss you.'

'Hmm-hmm.' Shockwaves raced up my spine.

'Then I'd lay you on the sand, pull up your top, unhook your bra and suck on your beautiful nipples.' His eyes were now the colour of charcoal.

'And after that?' I asked, wetness pooling between my legs.

'I'd lift up that skirt to see if you're wearing one of those thongs, then I'd drag it to one side, make you come again with my mouth, then fuck you until you begged me to stop.'

'I wouldn't ask you to stop.' I ran my hands over his chest.

Max stepped forward and his erection pressed into my belly. God. I wanted him so badly.

He took my face in his hands, dipped his head then kissed me. Hard. Fast. Passionately.

I groaned into his mouth, grabbed his bum and pulled him into me.

Just as his hand slid up my skirt, the sound of someone clearing their throat loudly vibrated in my ears.

We both pulled apart then spun around to see Olga scowling at us.

'You have a room at the hotel, *sí*?'

'Hi, Olga!' Max smiled. 'So nice to see you again! Erm, yeah, funnily enough we do.'

'Well, I think that you should use it!' She stormed off.

'Oh my God,' I laughed. 'She must think we're a couple of exhibitionist-nymphos.'

'I suppose we can't blame her. Every time she sees us, we're in a compromising position out in the open.'

'So much for just being friends,' I grinned.

'I know. I shouldn't have kissed you. I'm trying to stick to the platonic thing, but you're so fucking addictive, Stella, I can't help myself.'

I felt the same way. When Max was around, all logic fell away.

'Maybe we need to be realistic,' I said. 'We're going to be living in the same house for another six days, we're clearly attracted to each other so we can either spend the rest of our time here sexually frustrated and miserable or we can just enjoy ourselves. *Together*.'

'So just whilst we're at the hotel, then we walk away?'

'Yeah,' I nodded.

'And you're okay with that?'

'Yep.'

'In that case, we better take Olga's advice and go to our villa so we can continue what we started.'

'Our conversation?' I teased.

'My mouth will be moving, but what I plan to do to you won't involve any talking. And if I'm doing it right, you'll be so turned on you'll feel like you can't even breathe, let alone speak.'

Hearing that made the elastic in my thong snap.

'Well, what are you waiting for?' I took his hand. 'Hurry up and take me back to bed.'

35

MAX

'Just checking you're still alive,' Colton's voice boomed down the phone. I was on my way to reception and thought it'd be a good time to return all the missed calls he'd left over the past few days.

'Sorry, man. I've been kind of busy.'

'Busy, or *getting busy*?'

'How did you know?' I laughed.

'C'mon. It was only a matter of time before shit happened between you two. How long did you last before jumping each other's bones?'

'Friday.'

'Damn. That was quick. So have you been holed up in your hotel room since then?'

I told Colton all about the move to the villa and what happened during our massage.

'You dirty dog!' he laughed.

'We've left the villa a couple of times since then for walks and stuff, but the rest of the time, well, like I said, we've been *busy*.'

Ever since we'd agreed on Saturday to continue what we'd

started, I'd been in a hedonistic haze. I'd lost count of the amount of times Stella and I had sex.

We'd screw then rest. Once we got the energy, we'd drag ourselves away from the bed, the sofa, floor or one of the other surfaces we'd defiled and get something to eat. Then we'd end up kissing and the same pattern would be begin again: fuck, sleep, eat, repeat.

We were both insatiable. But now it was Tuesday and we only had four full days left here, we both agreed we needed to actually leave the villa and reconnect with civilisation.

Surprisingly we'd kept up with our daily Love Tasks. We'd taken selfies in bed. I'd sneaked a few photos of Stella in the pool in one of her many sexy bikinis and we'd both creepily taken pics of each other sleeping.

Keeping up with the playlist thing was easier than I thought. We'd gotten used to putting on music to drown out the noises we made during sex, so we picked a handful of songs from that selection.

I'd chosen tracks like 'I Want to Sex You Up' by Color Me Badd, 'Too Close' by Next and 'Coming Home' by Usher, 'Pony' by Ginuwine and 'Sexual Healing' by Marvin Gaye and Silk's 'Freak Me'.

Stella's selection included Madonna's 'Sex', 'Freak Like Me' by Adina Howard, 'Physical' by Olivia Newton-John, Ariana Grande's '34+35', 'Kiss It Better' by Rihanna and 'Hotter than Hell' by Dua Lipa.

I smiled as I thought about how things had changed since the angry playlist Stella first sent me. In the beginning it was hard for us to be within three feet of each other without all hell breaking loose. Now, if she didn't have her arms or legs wrapped around some part of my body, I didn't feel right.

But it was fine. I wasn't getting attached. I just liked being around her, that was all.

'I'm happy for you, bro!' Colton said. Even though I couldn't see him, I could tell he was grinning.

'Thanks.'

'So are you two officially together now?'

'No, we're just... it's a casual thing.'

'Does *she* know that?'

'It was Stella's idea. The morning after stuff happened, there I was worrying about hurting her when I explained I wasn't ready for a relationship and she basically laughed in my face and asked why I assumed she'd want anything serious with me! She said she was horny and my dick was available, so she thought, why not?'

'Sounds like you've met your match!' he chuckled.

Under different circumstances, I would've agreed. If ever I was interested in a relationship, I'd want someone strong and confident like Stella. But anyway, that wasn't gonna happen. Work had to come first.

'Col. I better go. Gotta arrange the car for our trip today.'

'Where you going?'

'I'm taking Stella to Córdoba.'

'Isn't that one of your favourite cities in Spain?'

'Yep.'

'So let me get this straight: you flashed two hotel staff so you could give Stella your towel and protect her modesty, you've spent days holed up in the villa together because you can't tear yourself away from her arms, you've cooked for Stella and now you're taking her to your favourite place, but it's just casual, right?'

When he put it like that, it did sound sus. But what he

thought wasn't important. Me and Stella knew it was just a friends-with-benefits situation and that was all that mattered.

'That's right, it's not serious. Córdoba's a nice place. If you came to Spain, I'd take you there too.'

'Yeah, but you'd take me to see the factory that's nearby, not to wander the streets holding hands like you're about to do with Stella.'

'Gotta go,' I said, avoiding his comment. 'Say hi to Betty and Natalie.'

'Laters.' He hung up.

When I got back from organising the car, Stella was ready and so we set off straight away.

I could lie and say we spent the journey there talking and admiring the scenery, but the truth was, we spent most of it kissing.

When the driver sheepishly announced that we'd arrived, we dragged ourselves apart and out of the car.

'I didn't even get to ask you where we were going!' Stella straightened her skirt and attempted to fix her hair.

'This is Córdoba: one of my favourite cities in Spain.'

'I haven't heard of it before. What's here?'

'I'm about to show you.' Before I even realised I'd done it, I took Stella's hand and led her through a large ancient gate which was surrounded by high stone walls and battlements. 'This is the old Jewish Córdoba, which is called *La Judería*.'

I showed Stella some of the famous Cordovan courtyards or *patios* as they were known as in Spanish.

'It's really pretty,' Stella said, taking in the beauty of the courtyards which were decorated with colourful flowers planted in pots, hanging from the walls or on the stone paving. Some courtyards even had wells, fountains and antique furniture.

Hearing her say that she thought the city was pretty caused a warm fluttery sensation in my chest. I loved this place and really wanted her to like it too. So seeing the awe written across her face made me so happy.

'Every May they have a competition here to find the best *patio*.'

'That sounds amazing!'

My heart swelled again as we continued walking.

'This is *Calleja de las Flores*,' I pointed. 'It's one of the most popular streets here.' The whitewashed walls were lined with blue flowerpots filled with bright pink flowers.

After we'd taken some photos, I led Stella to the famous Great Mosque of Córdoba which had a cathedral inside.

Annoyingly, Colton was right: Stella and I strolled around admiring the stunning architecture hand in hand like our palms were moulded together. The only time we separated them was when we went to the toilet.

And I was kind of embarrassed to admit that when Stella released her palm from mine, I missed the warmth and softness instantly.

Shit. I sounded like some loved-up teenager.

'That was incredible!' Stella said as we stepped out of the mosque. 'I've never heard of a cathedral being built inside a mosque before. And how did they build everything so beautifully all those years ago?'

'No idea, but it's impressive. You hungry?'

'Yeah.'

'Let's go eat.'

I took Stella to one of my favourite restaurants and she tried the *Salmorejo*, which was a cold soup that was a traditional dish from Córdoba, made from tomato, olive oil, breadcrumbs, garlic and vinegar topped with Serrano ham and pieces of boiled eggs.

'This is actually really nice.' She scraped the last spoonful from the bowl.

'Glad you liked it.'

'Thanks for bringing me here. It means a lot that you took me to one of your favourite places. It's like you're letting me in.'

'Letting you in?'

'Yeah. Like you trust me.'

'But I *do* trust you.'

'Yeah? Will you answer a question for me then?' She leant forward and looked deep into my eyes.

'Anything,' I said quickly. Damn those eyes. I shouldn't have left myself too open. But I couldn't help it. I felt so comfortable around Stella and whenever her gaze was locked on me, I was putty in her hands. Right now, if she asked me to rob the Bank of Spain, I'd agree.

As Stella opened her mouth, I braced myself.

'Why have you cut yourself off completely from football?'

Damn.

Stella's question hit me like a punch in the gut. I sucked in a breath and my brain scrambled. I didn't know what I thought she'd ask, but I wasn't expecting *that*.

My immediate thought was to shut down. To tell her I didn't want to talk about it, like I always did whenever anyone tried to raise it. But Stella had some kind of magical power that made me feel like it was okay to open up and be honest.

After inhaling again, I tried to speak.

'I...' My voice shook. 'I don't... Watching people do what I used to. What I wanted to keep doing but couldn't, it's painful. I had it all. My whole career in front of me and then... It's hard to watch someone living your dream knowing you'll never make it happen.'

'I get that,' Stella rested her hand on mine, 'but it seems like you've blocked out *all* mentions of football for years and I'm just wondering how well that's worked for you?' She paused. 'Do you feel better, denying yourself?'

Good question.

'Honestly? Not really. Still hurts.'

'That's what I thought.' Stella paused again. 'When we first went to the villa and we were talking about the TV, you said you don't watch games any more. Have you really not seen or been to one since your injury?'

'Nope.' I shook my head.

'Football is everywhere, so that must be exhausting. How do you avoid it on TV or online and in the newspapers?'

'I don't watch TV and I'm always working so I don't have time to read newspapers.'

'Colton used to love football too, didn't he? Didn't you ever want to go to a match with him?'

'He asks me all the time,' I sighed, 'but I always say no.'

'Have you ever tried?'

'Once. Years ago. About a year after my injury. But when I arrived at the stadium, I started shaking. I couldn't move. Colton had to take me back to his place. I was too embarrassed to go home.'

His mum said it was probably some kind of panic attack, but I wasn't sure. All I knew was that it was better if I stayed away from football. Too many bad memories of that fateful day an ill-timed tackle resulted in my right leg being shattered in two places.

I hoped once it healed and if I kept up with the physio that I'd be able to play again, but nope. Even after seeing countless doctors and specialists, it was clear. My career was over.

'That sounds awful. Did you ever see anyone? Obviously I know you had physiotherapy and stuff, but I mean like a therapist. To help mentally?'

'Nah. I was still living with my parents at my gran's and you know what my mum and dad were like. If I mentioned wanting to see a shrink, they would've laughed me out of the house.'

'And now?'

'Don't know,' I shrugged.

'Might be worth thinking about seeing a therapist and trying to get your love for football back again. Of course it won't be easy and it won't be the same, but eventually I reckon you could find some joy from it again – in a different way. I mean, we're in Spain and weren't Real Madrid one of your favourite football teams?'

'Yeah,' I smiled. 'I'd always hoped I'd play for them one day.'

'Well, just because your old dreams didn't happen, doesn't mean you can't make new ones.'

Of course Stella was right, but I'd never really thought about doing anything else.

My life had always been mapped out for me.

It was only ever gonna be about football. Nothing else mattered.

But then that was ripped away.

And when I finally dragged myself out of the black hole I'd spiralled into, I threw all of my energy into getting Mum's business off the ground instead.

As far as I was concerned, my dream had expired, so that was it. I'd missed my one chance. Although it sounded strange now, I'd never really considered the fact that I could have another roll of the dice.

Stella's question swam around in my mind.

If I could create a new dream, what would it be?

I didn't know the answer right now, but for the first time in what seemed like forever, I felt like maybe the world was open to me again.

And that maybe I deserved another shot at happiness.

36

STELLA

As I chopped vegetables in the kitchen, I thought about how great it was to spend time with Max today in Córdoba. It was a beautiful city and I was so grateful that he'd taken me there.

It felt like we'd really bonded. I loved the way he held my hand the whole time. The sensation of my palm snuggled in his was so comforting. Sounds corny, but he made me feel safe. Treasured.

And the thing was, I wasn't even sure if either of us realised we were holding hands until we'd been there for a while, because everything felt so natural. Like we'd been doing it for years.

Max finally talking about why he'd completely cut himself off from his passion also made me happy. I knew it was difficult for him, but choosing to open up showed he trusted me. Which meant a lot.

I didn't know much about football, but when players got injuries or had to retire, I knew some of them still stayed in the industry, becoming coaches or commentators. Maybe that didn't interest Max, but to go from football being your entire life to avoiding it completely seemed extreme. Especially seeing as it hadn't stopped his suffering.

Seeing how broken he was shattered my heart. I wanted to help him. And ever since we got in the car back home, I'd been mulling over an idea of how to do that. I'd messaged Jasmine to see if she could help, so hopefully she'd reply soon. In the meantime, I was going to try something else that I thought could be useful.

As Max came out of the shower, he strolled into the kitchen with a towel wrapped around his waist. The sight of his bare muscular chest sent my pulse racing.

'Mmm.' I licked my lips.

'You ogling me again?'

'It's hard not to when you insist on walking around half naked.'

'I can cover up if you want?'

'No, no!' I replied quickly. 'I like you just the way you are.'

'Awww, thanks.' Max wrapped his arms around my waist, then kissed my forehead. 'What are you making?'

'Chilli and ginger salmon with roast potatoes.'

We'd stopped off at a supermarket on the way back to the hotel and whilst Max took a work call, I went and got all the ingredients.

'Sounds great! What d'you wanna do after dinner? Go for a drink at the beach bar?'

'Actually, I was hoping we could have a night in and, y'know, just chill.'

'*Netflix and chill*, eh?' He raised an eyebrow. 'I'm surprised after all the walking we did that you have the energy for sex. Even *I'm* tired.'

'Not *that* kind of night in. This has nothing to do with sex. There's a series I've wanted to see for ages that I thought we could watch together.'

'Wow. Watching a TV series together. Isn't that straying into coupledom territory?' he smirked.

'Friends with benefits can watch TV series together too you know.' I rolled my eyes.

'I'm just teasing. I'm up for it. I'd ask you what the series is, but I've probably never heard of it anyway, so you can surprise me.'

'Great! Dinner will be ready in half an hour.'

Once we'd eaten, I got everything set up in the living room whilst Max loaded the dishwasher. When I thought about it, this whole situation was really weird. It only felt like yesterday that I hated Max. Now here we were living under the same roof, cooking meals for each other, him organising the dishes, and we were about to snuggle up on the sofa to watch TV together. Jasmine wasn't wrong when she said this whole villa thing was designed to fast-track relationships.

Not that this was a *relationship*. It was just a... friendship thing. Once we went back to London, who knew if we'd even see each other again?

Anyway, I wasn't going to overthink. I tipped the popcorn I'd also bought earlier into a bowl and put it out on the coffee table.

'All done.' Max strolled into the living room.

'Ready?'

'Yep.' He sat next to me on the sofa and wrapped his arm around my back. 'So, hit me with it. What are we watching? A romcom series?'

Under different circumstances, that would've been my first choice. But tonight I'd selected something because I hoped it'd help Max.

'It's a show called *Ted Lasso*. It's got that Jason Sudeikis guy in it.'

'Oh, cool! What's it about?'

'Now don't freak out, but it's a comedy…'

'Why would that freak me out?'

'About… football…' I waited for his reaction.

'Stella,' Max sighed. 'I know you're trying to help and I appreciate it, but I don't think…'

'Hear me out. It's about an American football coach who's hired to manage a British football team. But the thing is, he knows nothing about football. It's won loads of awards and is supposed to be hilarious. I thought it might be a fun way to ease you back into the football world.'

'I'm not sure.' Max shuffled uncomfortably in the sofa.

'It's only half an hour. Why don't we try one episode and if it's too difficult, we can stop.' I squeezed his hand.

'Okay,' he murmured.

Yes!

I picked up the remote control then pressed play. Max's body tensed and I started to question my suggestion, wondering if it was a bad idea and whether I was pushing him too much too soon. But within minutes of starting the show, from the corner of my eye I saw his shoulders relax and it wasn't long before he started chuckling.

After that, the laughs kept coming. Especially when it got to the part where Ted Lasso was thrown straight into a press conference and bombarded with questions about 'soccer', all of which he got wrong.

When the credits for the first episode rolled, I pressed pause.

'So? What do you think?'

'It's really funny,' Max smiled and relief flooded my veins.

'Want to watch another one?'

'Go on then.'

I hit the button for the next episode and Max pulled me closer into him. I rested my head on his shoulder and every time Max laughed, the joyful vibrations erupting from his chest filled my heart like a helium balloon.

He was enjoying it. He was happy. And knowing that made me so glad I wanted to get up and do a celebratory dance around the living room.

Episode two quickly turned into episode three, then four and before we knew it, we'd binged the entire first season. We'd only moved to go to the loo or to get more drinks and snacks. Other than that, anyone would think we were glued to the sofa. And to each other.

'Season two?' Max asked, glanced at his watch then gasped. 'Shit! It's three in the morning! I didn't even realise.'

'It's crazy. The time just flew by.'

'You know what they say. Time flies when you're having fun. Thank you.' He leant forward and kissed me softly on the lips. 'I'm really enjoying it.'

'Glad to hear it! I'm not exactly a football fan, but I'm loving it too.'

'So maybe we can pick up on season two tomorrow night?'

'Maybe. I might have something planned for your activity, so I'll let you know.'

I'd been so engrossed in watching the show that I hadn't checked my phone, which was charging in the bedroom.

'Mmm... I'm intrigued. Okay then, bed?'

'Definitely.'

Max went to the bathroom to brush his teeth and I headed to the bedroom to look at my phone. Jasmine had replied.

That's a great idea! I made some calls and it's all sorted! Come to reception at five tomorrow to allow enough time to get there.

Yes! Butterflies erupted in my stomach. That was brilliant news.

Now I just had to hope that when Max found out what I'd planned he didn't freak out...

37

MAX

I signed out of my emails and took a sip of the bright orange cocktail Stella had got me earlier, then put it on the table next to the daybed.

We'd spent most of the afternoon chilling by the hotel pool. Even though we had a private one in the villa, because we only had a couple of days left, we thought we'd come here and soak up the atmosphere.

Plus, as nice as it was to have our own kitchen, sometimes it was good to enjoy food and drink we hadn't had to make ourselves.

Whilst Stella had been reading beside me, I'd spent a couple of hours replying to work emails. Looked like some distributors in Australia were interested in taking on our products.

And I'd finally heard from a factory in the US who could manufacture a new range for us. I was in talks with a huge distributor too. If I secured those deals, it'd transform the business's fortunes and catapult us into the big league.

Now that I'd replied to their messages, I needed to wait to

hear what the next steps would be, so I couldn't get too excited yet, but I was happy with how things were progressing.

Speaking of happiness, even though I was still tired, yesterday was pretty much a perfect day. Walking around one of my favourite cities with Stella, enjoying a nice meal then cuddling on the sofa.

There were moments when it felt kind of like we were a proper couple, which of course we weren't. But even though a relationship wasn't something I wanted, it didn't feel as scary as I thought it would.

So many things about the last twenty-four hours surprised me. The way I'd opened up to Stella and not only binge-watching a TV series, which was something I didn't do, but one that was football related.

And surprisingly it really was great. I didn't remember laughing so much at a programme. The combination of the feel-good vibes the show gave off and having Stella curled up in my arms was... nice.

Not boring nice. *Good nice.*

It was cool that we were creating these memories. Once we were back in London living our normal lives, I'd look back on these times and smile.

'We should get going.' Stella put her Kindle down.

'Okay.' I locked my phone and picked up the towel. 'Still not gonna tell me where we're going?'

'Nope! It's a surprise.'

'How will I know what to wear?'

'*Please.*' She rolled her eyes. 'It's not as if you need to know whether to wear heels or flats.'

'Heels are *always* my first choice of footwear,' I joked.

'They wouldn't be if you had to spend hours walking in them!'

'So we're *walking* somewhere for hours?'

'Stop trying to get it out of me! Come on.' She grabbed my hand and led me up the pathway to our villa. 'We need to shower and get dressed.'

'Yes, boss!' I did a mock salute.

An hour later, we were in the chauffeur-driven car. Stella filled me in on the conversation with her mum earlier who was excited to tell her that Marjorie, the vicar's wife, had requested a thong to take home. She hadn't mentioned what message was on the back, because of 'client confidentiality', but Stella was sure her mum would let it slip sooner or later.

We also dissected all the episodes of *Ted Lasso* we'd watched and struggled to decide on which of the characters were our favourites. It was currently a toss-up between Roy Kent and Ted Lasso himself. But we were fans of most of the other teammates too.

It was funny, watching the show reminded me of some of the players I'd worked with during my time. Luckily, before I had a chance to get fully lost in my thoughts, the driver announced that we'd arrived.

As I looked out of the window, I swallowed hard.

Shit.

My body temperature spiked.

'So...' Stella reached for my hand. 'As you can see, we're at a football stadium. I know you're worried, but I thought we could try and watch a game. *Together*.'

'Stella, I don't know. I appreciate what you're trying to do, but...'

'This is the stadium for Cádiz. They're in the Premier League or *La Liga* I think it's called in Spain, right? But their stadium isn't as big as some of the others, so I thought it might be less daunting. Oh, and they're playing Real Madrid tonight...'

'Seriously?' I bolted up and my eyes widened.

'Yep,' she nodded, a smile touching her lips.

As I watched the crowds filing into the stadium, I swiped the back of my hand over my forehead.

My mind raced. I wanted to watch the game. I really did. I mean, *come on*. It was Real Madrid: one of the greatest teams in the world. But I didn't know if I could.

What if I freaked out again?

I didn't want to embarrass myself in front of Stella.

'I-I...' I opened my mouth to speak but my throat dried up.

'Yesterday you were worried about watching a football-related TV show but you tried and enjoyed it. I know this is harder, but I wouldn't suggest it if I didn't think you were up to it. And remember, if it's too much, we can just leave. We don't have to watch the whole match. You can just dip your toe in the water. What do you think? Want to try?'

I paused and the silence stretched for what felt like minutes but could've only have been seconds as I weighed it up in my mind.

Anyone else would think my fear was ridiculous. That it was no big deal to watch a game, because they didn't understand. But luckily Stella did. I believed her when she said she thought I could handle it. And somehow, knowing she believed in me made all the difference.

'Okay.' My heart thudded against my chest. 'I'll try.'

Stella threw her arms around me and squeezed me so tight I almost couldn't breathe.

'Come on.' She flung the car door open and jumped out excitedly. 'We've got a football match to go to!'

* * *

As the referee blew the half-time whistle, I blew out a shaky breath.

I did it.

For the first time in well over a decade, I'd watched a match and survived.

At first it was difficult. Joining the thick crowd as we made our way to our seats, seeing the players coming out on the pitch for the first time, hearing the cheers from the fans and of course watching the players, particularly the strikers, do what I used to love so much made my chest tighten. It brought back so many memories. Some good, many bad. My mind was quickly flooded with regret and thoughts of what could've been.

But Stella had taken my hand and every time she squeezed it, a shot of adrenaline rocketed through my veins, giving me the courage to stay and see the game through. And after the first twenty minutes or so, I started to relax.

Now I was even looking forward to the second half.

'You okay?' Stella said, checking on me, just like she'd done repeatedly since we first stepped into the stadium.

'Yeah,' I smiled. 'I'm good. Really good, actually.'

'You okay to stay?'

'Definitely,' I nodded.

The second half was even better than the first. Obviously the team were completely different from the days that I played, so I didn't know any of the players, but they were super-talented. Watching them was so inspiring. Even though I wasn't out on the pitch, I felt so pumped. So... *alive.*

I even felt comfortable enough to take some photos. Stella took some of me by myself and then some selfies together. This was a big turning point for me, so just in case I woke up tomorrow and thought it was a dream, these photos would prove that it actually happened.

In the end, Real Madrid won 3-1, which was brilliant. As we left the stadium hand in hand and walked towards the taxi, my heart felt full.

'That was incredible!' I scooped Stella up in my arms and spun her round. With so many fans coming out of the stadium, it probably wasn't the best thing to do, but I was happy and I needed Stella to know it. 'Thanks again!'

'You're welcome! I'm glad you enjoyed it!' she beamed. 'I did too, strangely.'

'I'm buzzing, though! I don't think I'm gonna be able to sleep tonight!' I put her back down on the ground.

'We don't have any activities tomorrow during the day – just the leaving date, so we can stay up late then have a lie in.'

The mention of the leaving date made my heart sink. I'd volunteered to organise our last activity and although I'd already briefed Jasmine on what was needed and it'd all been set up for tomorrow night, I wasn't ready to leave this place. I wasn't ready to leave Stella either.

'Good plan,' I said, pushing it out of my mind. I didn't want to think about the future. I just wanted to focus on what I'd achieved today.

On the car back to the hotel, I talked Stella's ear off, gushing non-stop about the game. She was probably bored stiff, but didn't show it. It was like all of the football talk and enthusiasm I'd bottled up for years came flooding out all at once.

I texted Colton some photos and he replied to congratulate me.

Once we'd reached the hotel, it was pretty late.

'What do you want to do now?' Stella slid off her sandals and closed the door. 'Watch *Ted Lasso*?'

'Later.' I stepped in front of her. 'Y'know what I've realised?'

'What?'

'Tomorrow's our last full day here and we haven't used the hot tub.'

'You're right!'

'You've spoilt me tonight, now it's my turn to spoil you. Why don't you get in the tub and let me bring you some treats. I'll be your personal hot tub butler.'

'Okay!'

I went to the kitchen to prepare everything. I already had some champagne chilling in the fridge and there were still some strawberries left.

Once I was ready, I rinsed off under the shower, put on my trunks, got the tray I'd prepared from the kitchen and brought it to Stella.

Even though most of her body was covered by the bubbles, I could still see the tops of her breasts in her bikini top and the delicious sight made my dick thicken instantly.

Fuck, she was gorgeous.

'Wow,' Stella smiled as I rested the tray on the ground and took off my flip-flops before sinking into the tub. 'Champagne, strawberries *and* a handsome butler! What more could a woman ask for?'

'Don't forget the stars.' I pointed to the dark sky and slid up beside her, the water instantly heating my skin. 'And I even brought you the moon.'

'So you did. And the sea air.' She inhaled deeply.

'Cheers to this amazing villa.' I handed her a glass of champagne, then picked up my own.

'Definitely. Cheers!' She clinked her glass against mine, holding my gaze, then took a sip.

'Hold up.' I reached for my phone which was on the tray. 'Let's take a pic for the memory book.'

After a few snaps, I put the phone down and leant back.

'So, how you feeling now?' Stella asked.

'Fucking great!' I took a glug of champagne. 'And it's all because of *you*.' I fixed my gaze on her.

'Y'know I didn't score those goals, right?' she smiled.

'You arranged for me to see the game. You wanted to help me. And you did. In a big way.' I inched up closer to her. 'You made me feel amazing. So now I want to do the same to you.'

I leant forward and pressed my lips against hers.

Stella looped her arms around my neck, then kissed me back.

Within seconds, the kiss became frenzied.

Our tongues flicked hungrily and Stella let out a moan which sent a jolt of electricity straight to my dick.

Still kissing her, I lifted her up and placed her on my lap. She didn't waste any time straddling me and pressing her pussy onto my rock-hard cock.

Reaching around to her back, I quickly undid her bikini top, exposing her beautiful tits. Tearing my lips away from her mouth, I trailed my tongue down her neck. Ignoring the taste of warm chlorinated water, my head dipped to her breasts and I slid her hard nipple in my mouth, whilst circling the other one with my thumb.

Stella threw her head back and cried out, grinding herself on me as she gripped onto my back.

'Fuck, Stella,' I groaned, slipping her nipple from my mouth. 'I want you so much.' My hips jerked forward.

'Here?' she panted.

'I would but, it's probably not a good idea. Hot tub sex looks cool on films and shit, but the chlorine isn't great for condoms.'

'Yeah, probably not good for my poor vagina either.'

'Right. And I really like your pussy, so I need to take care of it. Hold on tight.' I stood up and Stella wrapped her legs around my back. I climbed out of the tub, then carried her across the patio to our private pool area, then laid her down on the daybed. 'We can stay here or I can carry you back to the bedroom.'

'Here,' Stella said, a naughty smile touching her lips.

'Glad you said that. It's not every day we get the opportunity to make love under the light of a thousand stars. Wait here.'

I got up and quickly went to get a condom. Thank God Stella's mum had given her so many. I'd only bought a pack of three which we'd finished on our first night together. I wasn't expecting to get so lucky.

When I returned, Stella was under the outdoor shower.

Naked.

'Thought I'd wash the chlorine off,' she said as I drank in the delicious sight of her body. I really was one lucky man.

'Good idea,' I replied, watching her move to the daybed before removing my shorts. My cock sprang free and Stella's eyes widened.

When I finished rinsing off under the shower, I strode over to where Stella was laid out on a towel, her legs spread open, ready for me. I was desperate to be inside her, but my dick would have to wait.

I dropped to my knees and flattened my tongue between her legs, dragging it slowly down her clit and to her opening. Stella cried out.

As I flicked my tongue against her, I felt like I was in heaven. I could spend my whole life devouring her.

Stella fisted my hair, pushing my head deeper. I slid one finger inside of her and her hips jerked up off the bed. I slid in another finger and felt her tremble. I loved how Stella's body responded to my touch.

It wasn't long before her orgasm ripped through her. She

quickly pushed her hand to her mouth to stifle her screams and I had to really focus to stop myself from coming.

'Jesus, Max.' Her chest heaved. 'You are seriously talented.' I wiped my mouth and slid up beside her.

To my surprise, Stella got up and moved her head down in between my legs and wrapped her hands around my cock, which was already leaking pre-cum.

'Don't you want some time to recover?'

'No. You've made me happy, now I want to do the same for you.' She licked me from base to tip and I almost lost my damn mind.

'Fuck!' I grunted.

'I want to make you come.'

'God.' I struggled to speak as she slid my dick in and out of her mouth. 'Th-that feels amazing, but I really want to come inside you.'

Without saying a word, Stella reached for the condom then rolled it onto my dick.

Just as I was about to climb on top of her, Stella straddled me then lowered herself down onto my cock and we groaned as I filled her up.

Stella rode me and the sight of her on top of me, her tits bouncing, her pussy gripping my dick was almost too much for me to handle. My eyes rolled back in my head.

This was... *wow*.

This was what fantasies were made of. This wasn't like sex that I'd had before. This wasn't even like the sex Stella and I had been having all week. It felt different. I didn't know how it was possible, but it felt *better*.

Deeper.

As I looked at the pleasure written across Stella's face as she tipped her head back and dug her nails into my chest, adrenaline pulsed through me. I felt lightheaded. High.

Stella wasn't just sexy as hell. She was kind and caring. The more I thought about what she'd done for me, the more intense my desire became.

I was desperate to come, but I didn't want these sweet sensations to end. Ever.

This felt like how it used to be with Stella.

We weren't fucking any more.

It was like we were making love.

Then I remembered what I'd said to Stella earlier.

I hadn't said we'd be screwing. I'd said we'd be *making love* under the light of a thousand stars. It was like I already knew tonight was gonna be different.

And it really was.

But right now, I couldn't think about what it meant or what would happen after tonight.

All I knew was that I was enjoying pleasure like I'd never felt before and I wasn't gonna let anything stop it.

38

STELLA

As I continued riding Max, I struggled to catch my breath. I couldn't believe I was here, outside on the daybed in our villa's patio.

I didn't know if it was the thrill of having sex under the stars, with the sound of the waves crashing against the sand, the crisp sea air tickling my skin, the feel of Max's hard muscular body beneath me, or a combination of everything, but tonight, something was different.

Max and I always had a strong sexual attraction. But as I rocked on top of him, this didn't feel like it was just sex. The connection felt deeper.

When we got busy on the massage bed, that was just fucking. We were like a couple of horny wild animals. But tonight wasn't crazed and frenzied screwing. It was slow and sensual.

The way Max was looking at me with awe-struck eyes, the way he caressed my breasts as they bounced above his chest, the way he went down on me earlier, devouring me like his only purpose in life was to give me pleasure, didn't feel like I was just a holiday fling.

This felt like *something*.

Something *more*.

'Stell.' Max's eyes rolled back into his head as he moved his hands down to grip my arse. 'I don't know how much longer I can last. You're just too...' He squeezed his eyes shut.

'Same,' I panted. The wave had been building, but I was doing everything I could to hold it back. I didn't want these sensations to end.

When Max swiped his thumb against my clit, I knew I was fighting a losing battle. His touch was so powerful it made me powerless. There was nothing I could do but surrender.

I threw my head back, succumbing to the inevitable. As I rode Max faster, my orgasm ripped through me like wildfire.

Max thrust once, then twice before groaning loudly. His body stiffened beneath mine.

I collapsed onto him, our damp chests sticking together and our hearts racing.

Max wrapped his hands around me, stroking my hair then kissing the top of my head.

I didn't know how long we stayed like that, but it wasn't long enough.

'Stell,' Max whispered in my ear. 'Sweetheart, I need to take off the condom.' I reluctantly rolled myself off Max and onto the daybed. 'Back in a sec,' he said.

As I took in the sight of his gorgeous naked body as he strode through the patio doors, I pinched myself. Even in my wildest dreams, I couldn't have imagined this would be possible. I was so happy.

Max returned with the tray which had the bottle of champagne, strawberries and a flannel in a bowl of water. Underneath he had a blanket and fresh towels.

After putting the tray down, he climbed back on the daybed.

'Thanks for the flannel.' I'd wanted to clean myself up when we finished, but those two orgasms had used all my energy. The bathroom seemed like a million miles away. I reached for the bowl.

'Let me.' Max parted my legs and ran the damp flannel between them, slowly wiping me. God. This man. Normally the post-sex clean-up was the least enjoyable part, but somehow Max made it sexy. 'There.' He put the flannel in the bowl which was now on the ground. 'All done.'

'Thanks,' I said.

'My pleasure.'

After handing me a towel, he picked up the blanket and covered us.

Max stretched out his arm, inviting me to come closer. As I snuggled up into his chest, I exhaled. Here I was, outside, under a sky full of stars, wrapped up in the arms of the most amazing man.

This was perfection.

I couldn't think of a single thing that would make this moment more magical.

I wanted it to last forever.

I knew it couldn't, though. In less than forty-eight hours, I'd be back in London. Back to normal life and Max would just be a memory.

Which was why it was more important than ever to enjoy every precious second of this bliss whilst it lasted.

* * *

When I woke up, I was in bed, the sheets wrapped tightly around me. I turned over and saw Max, sitting up beside me.

'Morning!' he smiled and my stomach flipped.

'Morning,' I croaked. 'Did you carry me to bed? Last thing I remember was making love under the stars, but even that feels like it was too good to be true.'

'Yeah?'

'Yeah. It was... incredible. Out of this world.' I pictured Max's head between my legs, then relived the sensations that pulsed through me when I rode him.

I also remembered Max cleaning me up, which was sweet.

Although Max didn't comment on what I said, his wide smile told me he'd enjoyed it just as much as I had.

'It's late, so I thought we could have a brunch picnic on the beach, seeing as it's our last day here?'

My stomach sank. We were going home in the morning and this amazing experience would be over. I wished that every minute for the next twenty-four hours could last an hour. But even then, it wouldn't be long enough. I wasn't ready to say goodbye to Max.

'Sounds lovely,' I said.

'Oh, and Jasmine messaged to say we have to submit our final playlists and photos by two. So we can go through yesterday's photos and send them the ones we took in the hot tub.'

'Good plan. And we could do our playlists on the beach if we bring our headphones.'

'Okay. I'm gonna shower now. Feel free to join me.'

'I might take you up on that. Give me five and I'll be there.'

'Cool.' Max climbed out of bed and walked towards the door. 'And Stell?'

'Yeah?'

'I *did* carry you to bed after we made love under the stars. And you were right: it really was out of this world.'

As he left the bedroom, butterflies erupted in my stomach.

He'd felt it too.

He'd said we'd *made love*.

Before we'd agreed that this wouldn't be anything serious.

I'd promised myself I wouldn't catch feelings and swore I'd be happy with a holiday fling.

But now things were different.

Now I'd changed my mind.

Shit.

39

MAX

Whilst Stella went to reception, I headed to the beach with the picnic basket I'd got from the restaurant. I laid the blanket on the sand, sat down and exhaled.

It was another beautiful day. The sky was so blue it didn't look real, and even though it was only just before noon, the sun was already blazing. If it got any hotter, I'd have a dip in the sea to cool off.

I was glad to have a moment alone to try and get my head straight. Then again, even if I sat here for hours, I doubted my opinion would change.

It was obvious. I was in deep shit.

I had feelings for Stella. *Strong* feelings. And I didn't know what the fuck to do about them.

In twenty-four hours we'd be on our way to London and back to our normal lives. That was exactly what I'd wished for the first night I'd arrived here. But now, the thought of going back to the monotony I called a life made my chest tight.

These past two weeks with Stella had been fantastic. Yeah, we'd got off to a rough start and there were times I questioned whether we'd make it through the day, never mind the first week. But we did. And it'd been even better than I hoped.

When Stella told me she thought last night was out of this world and I'd agreed, I'd lied. Saying it was *out of this world* didn't come close to describing how I felt. Making love to Stella wasn't even in this stratosphere.

No wonder she questioned whether it was real. Everything about it was like a dream. The way Stella looked at me. Her touch. Our connection.

Then there was the way we held each other afterwards. How we talked and laughed together under the stars. If I'd seen that scene in a film, I'd think it was corny, but experiencing it was like magic.

After she'd fallen asleep and I'd carried her to bed, I'd watched her sleeping for a few minutes. Taking in the sight of her soft skin, the tiny scar on her left cheek that I used to love stroking and those full lips that I never wanted to stop kissing.

A flashback of her mouth wrapped around my dick popped into my head and made my pulse rocket. I was crazy to ask her to stop, but at that moment, I just needed to feel her. I wanted to be closer to her and have that connection. The stuff I'd never felt with anyone else. That feeling of intimacy.

I didn't want to fuck Stella. I wanted to make love to her.

See? Like I said, I was in deep shit.

I didn't want tomorrow to be the end, but after the emails I saw this morning, that was the only option.

My meetings in Australia and the US were confirmed and my secretary was planning the flights for a series of business trips that would start after I got back from Dubai.

I'd be in Australia and the US for two weeks each. Looked like I'd be visiting multiple places in Europe too, which would add another few weeks to my travels.

People always thought business trips were glamorous but most of the time they were just one long sales trip. Meeting after meeting, trying to convince strangers to take on our products or get them to agree to the best price to manufacture them.

It'd be lonely, exhausting and hard work, but hopefully worth it. Getting Mum's products into the hands of a worldwide audience had always been her dream and I was determined to make it happen.

All that meant that however much I wanted to, I wouldn't have time for a relationship with Stella, which was a damn shame.

Maybe I was getting carried away, though. She'd said from the beginning that she didn't want anything serious and that once we left the hotel we'd walk away from each other so I was probably worrying about nothing. I was sure it'd come up in conversation naturally, so until then, I was just gonna enjoy our last day together and not overthink it.

'Got them!' Stella appeared, snapping me out of my thoughts.

'Let's see.' I shuffled up on the beach mat then brushed off the sand that had blown onto it so Stella could sit down.

She snuggled up to me, looping her arm in mine and resting her head on my shoulder as I opened the envelope.

Warmth flooded my veins. I loved when Stella laid her head on me.

As I looked through the photos from the game, my heart swelled. I was so grateful she'd arranged it for me. I was already excited to watch another game when I got back from my trips.

'Definitely that one!' Stella pointed at a selfie. The players were on the field in the background, but that wasn't what caught my eye. It was the fact that Stella was kissing my cheek and I was grinning at the camera like a lovesick teenager who'd just been touched by a girl for the first time.

That was how I felt whenever I was around Stella. Like I was eighteen again.

'It's a great shot,' I agreed. All of them were. In the end, I settled for a photo Stella asked a woman behind us to take. We were smiling as we watched the game and I had my arm wrapped around Stella's back.

'Done! Oh, I bumped into Jasmine. She said we both have individual debrief sessions this afternoon. Think she wants to get our feedback on the experience. She said she'll text us the time and location.'

'We better finish all our Love Tasks so we don't get in trouble!' I laughed.

'As soon as we've eaten we can do our playlists. Then we'll have the rest of the afternoon to enjoy the beach.'

'Let's get stuck in then.' I opened up the picnic basket.

Stella and I finished all the food, then once we'd sent off our playlists, we laid on the blanket, arms and legs wrapped around each other.

'This place is so beautiful,' Stella said into my chest. 'I don't want to leave.'

'Me neither.' I paused. Maybe now was a good time to bring up the future. Well, the sad fact that we didn't have one together. 'So.' I paused, thinking about how best to phrase it. 'We should talk about...'

The sound of my mobile ringing made us both jump. I stretched out to where I'd left it after we'd taken our last set of selfies.

'It's Jasmine,' I mouthed as I accepted the call. 'Hi. Yeah, course. I'm on my way.' I ended the call. 'She wants to do my debrief now and yours afterwards.'

'Okay. What did you want to talk about?' she frowned. 'Before Jasmine called there was something you wanted to say.'

'Oh, er,' I stuttered. 'Nothing that can't wait.'

'Sure?'

'Yeah.'

Maybe Jasmine's interruption wasn't a bad thing.

Waiting a few more hours to talk wouldn't make a difference. Would it?

40

STELLA

I was on my way to the restaurant for my debrief with Jasmine. Max had messaged ten minutes ago to say she'd be ready to meet me in half an hour and he was heading to our villa to shower and start packing.

With the final surprise date that Max had arranged in just a few hours, we wouldn't have time later so that was a good idea.

Knowing that I also had a lot of packing to do, I decided to get to the restaurant earlier just in case Jasmine was free.

When I arrived, there was no one at the front desk and the restaurant was empty. Laughter sounded from the kitchen, then Jasmine appeared with a massive smile on her face and a chef followed behind her.

Interesting...

I caught them staring into each other's eyes, still smiling, and wondered if they were together.

The sound of a text notification boomed around the room and their heads snapped to the door where I was standing.

'Stella!' Jasmine's eyes bulged. 'I wasn't expecting you until four.'

'Sorry.' I backed away. 'I can come back if you like?'

'No, no.' She waved her hand. 'Let's get started.'

'I will see you later?' the chef said.

'Yes.' She switched back into professional mode. 'If you could have everything prepared for around seven, that'd be perfect.'

He nodded, then returned to the kitchen.

'Sorry about that.' Jasmine pulled out a chair at a table by the window, sat down and invited me to join her.

'No need to apologise. Er, I hope you don't mind me asking, but are you two *together*?'

I knew it was none of my business, but I was curious. And seeing as I knew Jasmine was about to grill me about my own love life and seemed friendly, I thought it was worth asking.

Okay, so I was nosy. It wasn't a crime.

'With Alejandro? Oh, no!' Jasmine shuffled uncomfortably in her seat. 'He's *much* younger than me.'

'So?' I replied. 'He's handsome and was definitely looking at you like he was interested.'

Alejandro had thick dark hair and olive skin. I wasn't sure if he was Spanish, but he had an accent. And as much as Jasmine tried to deny it, I could tell she was attracted to him.

'He doesn't see me like that.' She waved her hand dismissively. 'Alejandro's my *colleague*. Well, technically he reports to me for client events so there's that whole power dynamic thing too, which is why we *absolutely* could *never* get involved. He's strictly off limits.'

'Right,' I said, thinking there was no way they didn't want to get it on. There were so many sparks flying between them I was surprised the restaurant hadn't caught fire.

'Anyway.' Jasmine pulled a notepad out of her handbag. 'My love life isn't important right now. What I'd like to know is how everything is with *you*. Obviously today's your last full day here, so I wanted to have a catch up. How are you feeling: about going home tomorrow?'

'Sad. Wish I could stay. I know that sounds crazy, considering how much I wanted to leave that first night.'

'I get it. Seeing Max for the first time after all those years was a shock. But you stayed and worked through it. You should both be really proud of yourselves.'

'Thanks.'

'And how are things with Max, romantically speaking?'

'Great, actually. We've reconnected really well.'

'It certainly seemed that way! I was so glad when you two got together.'

'Yeah. Sorry again about the whole massage *incident*.'

'No need. I got the feeling you needed a little nudge, so I was happy to lend a hand...' she smirked.

'What do you mean?' I frowned and Jasmine raised an eyebrow. A light bulb went off in my head. 'Wait. *No way!* Did you *plan* that? Did Olga really have a call?'

'It's funny because I was sure she did. But when we got back to the office, the line had miraculously gone dead. It was the strangest thing...' Jasmine's cheeks quivered like she was trying to stifle a smile.

'You set us up!' I gasped before bursting out laughing.

'I cannot confirm or deny,' she smiled. 'But we're called Love *Alchemists* for a reason. We're experts at creating situations which allow magical things to happen.'

Mind blown.

I had to hand it to Jasmine. I had no idea.

I wondered if Jasmine had deliberately orchestrated other things like sending me on the Caminito del Rey walk knowing that I'd be scared and Max would step in and help me.

And now that I thought about it, I reckoned she deliberately showed us that shitty hotel room, knowing that we'd choose to stay in the luxury villa together instead.

Sneaky. But *genius*. I was glad she'd done her alchemy thing.

'Thank you. I've had the best time and Max is... *amazing*.'

I didn't even need to look in a mirror to know I had the biggest heart eyes. Every time I thought about him, I swooned.

'He's definitely a keeper. Speaking of which, what are your plans? Are you going to continue your relationship in London?'

Good question.

'What did Max say?'

'Sorry but I can't share what he told me. These one-to-ones are confidential.'

Dammit. I guessed if I really wanted to know, I had to ask him.

We'd need to have a proper chat. I knew that originally we'd agreed that we'd enjoy each other whilst we were here, then walk away. But that was before, right? Maybe he'd changed his mind.

I got the feeling Max wanted to raise it on the beach earlier, but then Jasmine called.

'I understand.'

'I really do hope you do stay together, though. You two have something special.'

I thought we did too. But it took two to tango.

'If you don't mind, I'd like to check in with you again in a few weeks, once you're back home. See how things are going. Would that be okay?'

'Course,' I said.

'Great! Well, that's all for now. I know you must have packing to do so I'll let you go. The hotel will send a feedback questionnaire in the next couple of days which we'd love you to complete

ASAP whilst everything's still fresh in your mind. Enjoy your date tonight!'

After I left the restaurant, I made my way to the villa.

Although I had to pack, there was something more important I needed to do first.

It was time to have a chat with Max. To find out if he wanted to change our agreement and give this relationship thing a try. I knew I did.

I just had to hope that he felt the same way...

41

MAX

When Stella came back from her chat with Jasmine, I was on a call to the office having a conversation that was best had away from the villa. So I told Stella I'd be back soon, then walked towards the beach.

'That's fine,' I confirmed with Rita, my secretary. 'Go ahead and book it.'

'Will do,' she said. 'And I've arranged for a car to collect you from the airport tomorrow.'

'Thanks.'

'Colton's in meetings this afternoon, but he asked me to tell you that you're expected at his house on Sunday for breakfast.'

'We'll see,' I groaned inside, knowing breakfast was just a ruse for what it was really going to be: an interrogation. 'Depends if I have time before my flight to Dubai.'

'He's already asked me to arrange a car to pick you up from his house to take you to the airport.'

'Right,' I said, knowing that sounded just like him. 'Thanks.'

'Have a safe flight and speak to you on Monday.'

'Yeah. I'll call you from the show when we break for lunch. Have a good weekend.'

I hung up then saw Jasmine had texted to confirm that everything had been prepared for tonight, so I headed back to the villa.

As soon as I stepped in the hallway, I heard the shower running, so went straight to my room to get dressed.

Half an hour later, my phone chimed with a message to let me know the car was waiting at reception.

It was only a short drive to the secluded spot that I'd chosen. We could probably walk there, but I wasn't sure if Stella would be wearing heels, so I wanted to make it more comfortable for her.

We should really have a proper talk about how we were feeling at dinner. Then again, if the conversation didn't go well, it'd ruin our last night. I'd just have to play it by ear.

As I stepped into the living room and saw Stella by the patio doors, with her back to me, my jaw dropped. She looked amazing. Stella was wearing an orange and yellow sleeveless mini dress which hugged her curves in all the right places.

The woman was a goddess. I wished we could stay here alone, but we had a dinner to get to. A *leaving* dinner. Thinking about the fact that this could be the last night we ever spent together made my gut twist.

'You look incredible!' I said.

When Stella spun around and I saw her smile, my pulse raced.

'You don't scrub up too badly yourself.' She bit her lip.

Knowing she found me attractive made me feel ten feet tall.

'Cheers. Shall we go?' I held out my hand.

Stella walked towards me and placed her palm on mine,

instantly sending my body temperature through the roof. Now everything felt better.

I led her through the villa door and down to the car.

The chauffeur opened the door to the sleek black Mercedes. We barely travelled for five minutes before he announced we'd arrived.

'That was quick!' Stella slid out of the car. 'Can't wait to see what you've organised for our last night.'

'Ladies first.' I gestured towards the path.

'Oh my God!' Stella gasped as she saw the set-up.

Pretty pink flower petals lined the path which led down to a private candlelit table for two on the beach.

A giant love heart had been drawn into the sand and the table was directly in the centre. The edge of the heart was surrounded by red candles in glass jars.

'Like it?' I asked.

'*Like*?' Stella's eyes widened. 'It's *amazing*! Look at the views!' She pointed at the stunning blue sea and the orange and yellow sky. The sun was starting to set and she was right – the views were just as incredible as I'd hoped. 'And the *table*!'

It was covered in a crisp white tablecloth, with a gold candelabra in the centre, matching gold crockery and cutlery and a stand holding a shiny gold bucket with a bottle of champagne chilling inside.

'Not bad, eh?' I smiled.

'An intimate candlelit dinner on a private beach is what dreams are made of! And wait...' Stella sniffed the air, taking in the scent of barbecued fish. 'Is that...?'

Stella's head swivelled as she noticed the chef further down the beach who was manning a barbecue and standing by a fire grilling skewers of small shiny silver fishes over an old fishing boat.

'Wait? We have our own chef too?' Her eyes were like saucers.

'Yep! Only the best for you.' I wrapped my arm around her waist. Seeing her so happy made my heart swell.

'Hello, you two!' I recognised Jasmine's voice.

'Oh, hi!' Stella said as Jasmine stepped in front of us.

'Welcome to your last supper! Let me take you to your table.'

We stepped inside the heart in the sand. I pulled out Stella's chair, then sat opposite her.

A waiter approached, took the champagne from the bucket then poured it out.

'Something smells good!' Stella said to Jasmine. 'What's your *friend* cooking?'

'Oh, er...' for some reason Jasmine blushed, 'he's doing *espetos*. They're sardines seasoned with some olive oil and sea salt.'

'Sounds delicious,' Stella said.

'So as you can see, Max arranged this private dinner for you. Alejandro will be cooking a three-course meal and your dedicated Cuisine Champion will be on hand to serve you throughout the night. I'll be in different locations this evening, checking on all the couples, but if you need anything, before I return, please call me. Right, I better check how the *espetos* are coming along.'

Stella grinned as Jasmine walked over to the chef.

'What's that grin for?' I cocked my head.

'I think something's going on with Jasmine and that Alejandro.'

'Really?'

'Yeah. I asked her earlier and she denied it. If she's telling the truth and there isn't, I reckon it's only a matter of time.'

I glanced over just as Jasmine threw her head back, laughing at something the chef said.

'Oh… yeah, you're right. He's giving her the *look*.'

'What *look*?'

'The kind of look a man has when he's eye-fucking a woman he likes.'

'How do you know?'

'Because that's the way I look at you.' I brushed my thumb over her cheek, then leant across the table, moved the candelabra to one side, then kissed her softly on the lips.

'Mmm,' Stella groaned and I wished I could record that sound and play it on repeat. 'If we weren't in such a gorgeous setting with this amazing dinner you'd arranged, I'd like you to do more than just eye-fuck me.'

'Trust me, once we're back at the villa, if you give me the green light, it won't be my eyes that'll be fucking you…' My dick jerked in my shorts.

The waiter appeared, jolting me out of my thoughts.

'May I present to you the first course for this evening's meal: fresh *espetos*.' He laid two plates in front of us. '*¡que aproveche!*'

'What does that mean?' Stella frowned as the waiter left.

'Enjoy your meal,' I replied.

'Oh! Got it.'

'Cheers!' I lifted my glass in the air. Stella clinked her glass against mine, then we both took a sip.

'So.' Stella stabbed the sardine with her fork before realising I was eating with my hands then doing the same. 'How'd it go with Jasmine earlier?'

'Okay. You?'

'Good, I suppose. Thankfully she didn't gloat or say I told you so when I said we were getting on well.'

'Yeah. She saw something that we didn't right from the start.'

'Oh and she admitted that she set us up!'

'What?' I almost choked on the sardines, which tasted so good. I quickly swallowed my mouthful. 'How?'

'Remember the *urgent* call Olga had to leave for?'

'What about it?'

'There was no call!'

'You're joking!' My eyebrows shot up.

'Nope! I don't think that was the only thing either...'

As Stella explained her theories on how she thought Jasmine had arranged certain things to bring us closer together, it started to make sense.

'Wow.' I took the last bite of fish. 'Jasmine's like a silent romance ninja. You don't even realise she's playing cupid and has cast a love spell on you until it's too late.'

Stella and I looked at each other and our eyes locked.

I'd said the 'L' word by mistake and she'd picked up on it.

'Yeah.' She held my gaze. 'Jasmine said that's why she's called a *Love* Alchemist,' Stella added, placing an extra emphasis on the word *love*.

I supposed now was a good time to have that conversation.

'So, maybe we should...'

'Good evening.' The chef approached the table and spoke in a thick Spanish accent. 'You like the *espetos*?'

'They were delicious!' Stella replied and I agreed.

'Very good. The next course is almost ready. Your match requested fresh fish, including salmon and also barbecue chicken, this is good for you?' He faced Stella.

'I love barbecue chicken! *And* salmon!' A grin broke out on Stella's face.

'Perfect.'

The chef left and soon afterwards, the waiter brought over the next course which smelt amazing.

Stella and I spoke about loads of different stuff like what

countries were on our travel bucket lists, what we thought was gonna happen next in *Ted Lasso*, how many of the funny Love Hotel staff job titles we could remember... Everything except what we really needed to discuss.

When the waiter placed dessert in front of us, Stella's eyes widened.

'Chocolate mousse with sprinkles? I can't believe you remembered!'

'How could I forget?' I smiled.

That was always Stella's favourite. Apparently she tried it for the first time at a birthday party when she was a kid and had been hooked ever since.

'People always think it's childish to have the sprinkles, but I love the extra sweetness and texture! I haven't had this for ages. Thank you!'

My heart inflated. I was glad Stella had enjoyed the meal. I wanted this to be a memorable night so when she looked back on our time together, this time, she'd have positive thoughts.

'You're welcome.'

'This is so beautiful.' Stella looked up at the stars as she licked the chocolate off the back of her spoon.

That was when that I noticed the classical music in the background. I wasn't sure how long it'd been playing because I was only focused on Stella.

The way she squeezed her eyes shut and groaned with pleasure every time she slid a spoonful of dessert into her mouth.

The way her whole face lit up when I said something funny. Everything about her made the rest of the world fade into the background. When Stella was there, it was like nothing else existed.

I really wished we didn't have to leave tomorrow. I hated that we only had a few hours left together.

'Hi.' Jasmine appeared. 'Did you enjoy your meal?'

'Everything was fantastic, thank you both so much!' Stella reached across the table and squeezed my hand. 'This was the perfect last night. I really wish we didn't have to leave tomorrow.'

'I know.' Jasmine nodded. 'It's hard to say goodbye to such a beautiful place. But this shouldn't be a night of sadness. I'd like you to celebrate your experience at The Love Hotel and hopefully the long-lasting, loving relationship you've started. I know things were challenging in the beginning, but the transformation from, let's call it *uncertainty* to love, is wonderful. It's been a joy to watch you fall in love again! I have something for you. I'll be right back.'

As Jasmine walked over to the waiter, I wanted to call her back and tell her that it was too soon for the whole 'love' thing. We'd only been here for two weeks and 'together' for just half of that. Yeah, I had strong feelings for Stella, but it couldn't be *love*.

'I never thought I'd say this,' Stella said, 'but I'm really glad I came here. And I'm glad you were my match.'

'Same.' I leant forward and kissed her again.

Once we pulled away, we stared at each other in silence. Like neither of us knew what to say.

Really we should talk, but it didn't seem like the right moment.

Nah. I wasn't gonna raise it tonight. If Stella asked me, I'd tell her where I stood. But until then, I wanted to enjoy our last night together.

'I have something for you!' Jasmine returned, breaking the silence. She handed Stella a large red gift box as the waiter cleared the table. 'Here's your memory book.'

Stella lifted the lid then pulled out the photo album which had a soft red velvet cover. As she opened it, I saw the first set of photos we'd chosen.

'Wow!' Stella's face broke into a smile. 'I love it!'

'Great. I'll leave you to look back on your wonderful memories. See you tomorrow.'

After waving her off, I moved my chair next to Stella's then we started going through the book.

'Oh my God,' Stella winced. 'I'm still mortified about the bikini top incident!' She covered her eyes with her hand as we looked through volleyball game photos.

'I love this one,' I said, pausing at the photo of us on the bridge at the Caminito del Rey.

Every page sent happy memory after happy memory flooding into my brain.

We'd been through a lot together these past two weeks.

A link to the final playlists had also been emailed to us. I couldn't wait to listen to that.

'Thank you.' Stella looked up at me.

'For what?'

'For two amazing weeks.'

'Right back atcha.' I kissed her again.

This time it was hungry and frenzied like we hadn't kissed for weeks. I dropped the memory book on the sand, freeing my hands to roam across Stella's back then brushed against the side of her breasts.

'Oh... Max...' she groaned into my mouth.

Fuck. Hearing her call my name was like a match had been lit inside of me. Reluctantly, I pulled away. The chef was clearing up and the waiter was still here too. As much as I wanted to have Stella right here on the beach, this was our last night and I wanted it to be special.

'Shall we...?'

'Yeah,' she panted, knowing exactly what I was going to

suggest without me even having to finish my sentence. 'Let's go back to the villa.'

42

STELLA

My alarm sounded and as I slipped my hand out from the crisp, warm bed sheets to turn it off, I groaned. It only felt like five minutes ago that I'd gone to sleep.

After coming back to the villa, Max and I had made love again and then curled up on the sofa together watching multiple episodes of *Ted Lasso* before dragging ourselves to bed in the early hours of the morning.

Last night was magical. The food was incredible and as we looked through our memory book, champagne bubbles erupted in my stomach.

Every photo was beautiful. When they'd first suggested the idea, I thought it was ridiculous. But now I saw that capturing all those special moments and putting them into a physical book was genius.

And when Max and I raced back to the villa, hands and lips roaming everywhere, that was the cherry on top. As soon as he entered me, it felt like all was right in the world. He fit me so perfectly. The way our bodies connected was like two pieces of a jigsaw puzzle sliding together.

But with all the beach celebrations and being together when we got back, it meant we hadn't spoken about what would happen next.

I didn't want to ruin our last night by mentioning it. There was no hiding from it now though. In less than an hour we'd be leaving the hotel and potentially each other.

For good.

When I turned over, Max wasn't in bed. I threw back the covers and went to the living room. His suitcase was already by the door. I heard noises in the kitchen so went in and saw him loading croissants onto two plates.

'Morning,' I said.

'Oh, hey! I was gonna bring this to you in bed.'

My stomach flipped. That was so sweet.

'Thanks. Do you want to eat outside?' I asked. 'Soak up the last few sun rays before we go back to dreary London?'

'Good idea.'

'Actually, there's something I keep forgetting to show you!' I went back to the room, got my phone, brought it out to the patio then sat opposite Max. 'Here's some quick designs I did. They're only rough because obviously I've been trying to do it on my phone, but hopefully you get the idea. I thought we should celebrate the beauty of the olives you use in your products, that's why there's a lot of green and an emphasis on nature and...'

'I love it!' Max beamed. 'This is *exactly* the kind of thing I was hoping for.'

'Oh!' My eyes widened and butterflies erupted in my stomach. 'That's great.'

'Can you send me what you've done? I'd love to get Colton's thoughts. He doesn't work in marketing, but I trust his opinion.'

'Course.' I tapped on the screen, hit reply to the email Max had sent with the brief then clicked send. 'Let him know it's only rough though.'

'I will. Thanks again. And don't forget to send an invoice for your time.'

I waved my hand dismissively and bit into my croissant. Didn't feel right to charge him. I genuinely wanted to help.

Whilst we ate breakfast, Max gushed about how much he loved my designs. Then we talked about the weather, what we'd miss about the villa, our date last night... Everything except the one thing we needed to discuss.

After checking we hadn't left anything, we locked up the villa for the last time and pulled our suitcases to the hotel reception where Jasmine was seeing off some of the other guests. Once she'd finished, she came over.

'Awww, you guys! I'm going to miss you!'

'We'll miss you too!' I said. 'Are we allowed to hug you?'

'Course!' She opened her arms.

Max and I walked into them and we gave her a tight squeeze.

'Cheers for everything,' Max said.

'You're welcome. I wish you two a long and happy future together.'

Max's eyes connected with mine and I swallowed hard.

'I take your cases?' Simón, the Suitcase Superintendent, broke the silence.

'Er, please. Thanks!' I stuttered as he loaded them into the boot of the car. 'Well, keep in touch and good luck.'

'Good luck?' Jasmine frowned.

'Yeah. With your... *friend*,' I smiled.

Jasmine's gaze dropped and she fiddled with her blouse. She was always composed so seeing her flustered was strange. Her reaction confirmed what I suspected though. She definitely liked the chef.

'Car's ready,' Jasmine changed the subject. 'Safe journey home and I'll be in touch soon to see how you're both getting on.'

We waved goodbye, slid onto the back seat then shut the door.

As the driver set off, Max faced me.

'So,' he said, his face solemn. 'We probably should have *the talk*. About what happens when we get home.'

My stomach twisted.

If the look on Max's face was anything to go by, this wasn't going to be good.

43

MAX

'Let me guess,' Stella said. 'You like me but you're not ready for a relationship, right?'

Shit. She was spot on.

'Yeah,' I winced. 'But it's not so cut and dried. I wanna be with you, but I just don't think it can work.'

'Why?' Her face crumpled and my heart squeezed.

'The next few months are gonna be tricky. I've got a lot of travelling to do for work, so I don't wanna promise anything then let you down.'

'Travelling? Where to?'

'Australia, America, around Europe... I've spent ages trying to grow our export business and I've finally had some break-throughs. It's too important not to pursue it.'

'More important than a relationship.'

'Yes. No. I...' I blew out a breath. 'It doesn't mean you're not important to me. You really are. It's just... I need to get this done.'

'Fair enough.' She shrugged her shoulders like it was no big deal. I should've been relieved, but stupidly part of me was disappointed that she wasn't bothered. Maybe she didn't like me as much as I liked her. 'Well, maybe drop me a line when you're back and depending on the circumstances, we could meet up.'

'Circumstances?' My brows knitted together.

'Y'know. Maybe you'll meet someone. Or maybe I will.'

The thought of Stella with another man was like a knife to my gut. I didn't want her to be with anyone else.

I didn't want another man to touch her soft skin, to kiss her lips, to be inside her. But I had to accept that it was gonna happen because I couldn't give her what she wanted.

Even if I was considering the whole relationship thing, I couldn't expect her to wait months for me to come back.

Imagine the conversation: 'Hey, Stell, I wanna be with you, but I'm gonna be busy for a couple of months, so you okay to put your life on hold for me and not date anyone until I come back?'

That wasn't fair. It was selfish. I'd already wasted enough of her time. When I was in Manchester she spent time and money coming to visit me. I found out after we broke up that she even put her studies on hold for me. And what did I do? I broke her heart. I wasn't gonna do that again.

Nah. The only option was to let her go.

What was that saying? *If you love something, set it free. If it comes back, it's yours. If it doesn't, it never was.*

If Stella and I were meant to be, we'd find each other again, right? Just like how we both ended up at The Love Hotel after all those years.

I wanted to believe that, but part of me thought that we were already lucky once. Leaving our future in the hands of fate for a second time was asking too much. But like I said, I had no choice. I had to let her go.

'So that's it then?' I fixed my eyes on Stella, trying to read her reaction.

'What else is there to say? We said from the start that we'd keep it casual, that'd it'd just be for the holiday, so that's what we're doing. Sticking to our agreement.'

'And you're happy with that?'

'What does it matter?' she huffed. 'You've said you're too busy for a relationship, so that's all there is to it. I'm not going to beg if that's what you want.'

'I'd never expect you to do that, I just...' I had the feeling that the more I spoke, the worse it'd sound, so I decided to shut the fuck up.

'We've agreed it's the end, so let's just forget it and enjoy the views,' Stella said.

For the rest of the journey we sat in silence.

Stella's eyes were glued to the window, facing away from me whilst I sat at the opposite end of the backseat.

Sitting so far apart felt weird. The last few car journeys our lips, bodies and hands were super-glued together. Now we were like strangers. It was like we'd reverted to that first night at the hotel when she couldn't stand the sight of me. I hated it, but I'd made my bed, so I had to suck it up.

When we arrived at the airport, we checked the departure boards. Stella's flight was going to Gatwick and I was on the later flight to Heathrow, so we'd be checking in separately.

'So...' I said. 'Have a safe flight and...' I racked my brain, thinking of what to say. *Keep in touch* sounded so lame. That was what you said when you knew you weren't gonna speak to that person again. I didn't want that to happen. I really *did* want to see her again. 'Speak soon?'

'Yeah,' Stella said.

I went to kiss her lips, but she turned her face, causing my mouth to skim her cheek.

Fair enough.

'Bye,' I said.

As I watched her walk away, her silhouette fading into the distance, my heart cracked.

So that was that.

No more Stella.

No more holding her. No more feeling her head resting on my chest.

No more inhaling her delicious scent.

No more kisses.

No more hugs.

No more listening to the sound of her infectious laugh or stroking her soft skin.

Watching her walk out of my life didn't just mark the end of the holiday. It marked the end of one of the happiest times I'd ever experienced.

And right at that moment I knew that without Stella, my life would never be the same again.

44

STELLA

Once I stepped off the plane, I headed straight for the toilets. When I took off my sunglasses and caught sight of my reflection, I gasped. My eyes were red rimmed and although my skin was darker thanks to the sun, somehow it looked grey instead of brown.

That's what heartbreak does to you.

I didn't know why I was so upset or why I'd spent most of the plane journey hiding behind my sunglasses as I sobbed into my shoulder.

Max had said from the start that he wasn't looking for anything serious. And I was the idiot that assumed that just because I'd felt an intense connection towards him that it was mutual.

How could I blame him for what he'd said in the car when all he'd done was stick to our agreement? He was very clear about what he was able to offer. And I was the one that laughed at his suggestion that I might want a relationship from him.

I'd got exactly what I'd asked for. Something casual. That was why crying like a baby was stupid.

Instead of shedding tears, I needed to woman up, be grateful for the time that we spent together and move on. Simple.

After going to the loo and washing my hands, I headed to passport control. Luckily there wasn't a queue so it wasn't long before I was out of the airport and back on the train home.

As I looked out of the window at the dull, cloudy sky, my mind drifted. This time yesterday, I was on the beach, soaking up the sunshine, and listening to the waves gently caressing the sand.

I was inhaling Max's beautiful woody scent and the fresh sea air.

I was snuggled up on a picnic blanket whilst we talked and laughed together, eating our delicious brunch, looking through photos and picking the final selection of songs for our playlists.

The playlist. I hadn't even listened to it. I reached for my phone, then paused. There was no way I could play that now.

Instead, I continued looking out the window and reminded myself that the holiday was over. Just like my time with Max.

It was done. Finished. A distant memory. Time to get back to reality.

When I stepped through the front door, Mum was waiting, her eyes wide with excitement.

'You're back!' She gave me a big squeeze. 'I'll put the kettle on so you can tell me all about it!'

'Mum, I need to shower. And I'm a bit tired. Can we talk later?'

'Oh.' Her face fell and my stomach twisted.

'I'm so sorry.'

I knew she'd been waiting for me to arrive and tell her everything and I felt terrible about letting her down, but I really wasn't up to talking right now. I was doing my best to try and be strong and just get on with things, but for some reason it wasn't working.

'Don't worry. Have you eaten? I've made your favourite barbecue chicken stir fry.'

'Thanks. That's really sweet. Would you mind keeping it in the fridge so I can have it later if I feel up to it?'

'Is everything okay?' She put her hand on mine.

'I'm fine.' I squeezed her hand. 'I'll speak to you later.'

* * *

'What the hell?' I rubbed my eyes, then lifted my head from the pillow and squinted at my watch.

That couldn't be right. My watch said it was nine o'clock. In the morning. Which meant I'd slept for fourteen hours. Shit.

I sat up in the bed and my stomach rumbled. No wonder. I hadn't eaten anything since yesterday afternoon.

After I dragged myself to the bathroom, I headed down to the kitchen and was surprised not just to see Mum sitting there, but Sammie too.

'She has arisen!' Sammie bellowed in a deep voice.

'Awww! We were going to give it another half an hour before we went and checked again for signs of life!' Mum chuckled.

'I must've been a lot more tired than I thought.' I opened the cupboard and took out a mug. I needed coffee. Preferably drip-fed to me for the next twenty-four hours.

'That's what all that shagging will do to you!' Sammie threw her head back, laughing.

'Sammie!' I gasped. 'Not in front of my mum!'

'Oh, *please*.' Mum rolled her eyes. 'I was just about to say the same thing! I may be your mother but I'm still a woman who appreciates a good roll in the hay! How do you think *you* got here?'

'What? You mean the stork didn't bring me to you?' I smiled.

'Surprisingly not! If you like, I can share the story of how you were conceived.'

'No! Please *don't*,' I cringed.

'Why don't you tell us what's happening with Max instead?'

'Oh, God,' I groaned, pouring the fresh coffee into my mug and sitting on the stool opposite Mum and Sammie. 'Do I really have to?'

'Yes!' they both replied.

I'd have to tell them sooner or later. And I was glad that Sammie was here too. Not just to give me moral support, but also so I'd only need to tell the story once.

'Okay,' I sighed, reaching for the buttered toast in the centre of the table.

Once I'd finished explaining what had happened over the past twenty-four hours I blew out a breath, relieved I'd got it out of the way.

'And that's it. Max and I were just a holiday fling. He's going travelling for business for a couple of months, so it's over.'

'Oh, hon. I'm sorry,' Sammie said. 'You never know though. Maybe you could get together again when he comes back?'

'That's what I suggested. I said he could call me when he's back but I doubt he will. He'll probably meet some goddess in Australia or America and forget all about me.'

'No way! The way he looked at you in those photos didn't seem like he wanted to forget you. He was smitten. You're the only woman for him.'

'Yeah, right!' I scoffed. 'That's why he's desperate to commit to me.'

'Sometimes it's just about timing. It could just be a case of right guy, wrong time. Be patient.'

'I can't put my life on hold in the hope that he'll change his mind. I just need to forget him. What about you?' I looked at Mum, who was unusually quiet. 'Aren't you going to add your two cents?'

'What?' She snapped out of her thoughts. 'Sorry. I was just thinking. You said Max is going travelling?'

'Yes.'

'So instead of waiting to see where things stand between you when he comes back, why don't you just go with him? You've always wanted to see more of the world. Now's your chance.'

'I told you, Mum. He's going for business.'

'And?'

'And he'll be working the whole time. Plus, if he wanted me to come with him, he would've asked.'

I'd be lying if I said the thought of going to Australia and America didn't sound appealing, but there was no way I was going to ask him if I could tag along. That'd sound too desperate.

'Maybe, maybe not.'

'Plus I've just got back from holiday. I can't go swanning off again – and for two months! That's more than double my annual holiday allowance. And you need me.'

'Oh...' Mum shuffled in her seat, her gaze dropping to the table. 'About that. I wanted to talk to you about your position. I'm really grateful for all of your help, you know I am. But whilst you were away, Marjorie proved to be quite an asset. She was great with organising the orders and dealing with customers and we got on really well. So I was thinking that maybe you could think of finding another job?'

'Wait, what?' My jaw dropped. 'You're *firing* me?'

'No, of course not! I love us working together. But this isn't what you're meant to do. You deserve to do something much more stimulating than taking lacy thongs to the post office every day.' She reached across the table and grabbed my hands. 'I want to see you fly, darling. Maybe it's time to start looking for more freelance design work. Starting your own business like you've always wanted to.'

'I agree with your mum,' Sammie chipped in.

I took a sip of my cold coffee as I tried to gather my thoughts.

Of course I'd love to do that, but I didn't even know where to start. It was so daunting. I'd need to find clients and that wasn't easy.

'How long do I have before I'm unemployed?' I asked.

'You can work here for as long as you need. Maybe you could reduce your days and use that time to start working on your own thing? Don't worry about the money. Business is really picking up so I'll pay you the same and Marjorie can come in a couple of days a week to shadow you. Then when you're ready to take the leap, we'll have everything in place.'

Wow. Mum had really thought this through.

It was really kind of her to offer to pay me the same salary.

I racked my brain, trying to think of more excuses not to try, but the more I thought of it, the more I realised Mum had given me an incredible opportunity. The freedom to follow my dream.

Although I was scared shitless, I'd be crazy not to at least try.

Look at Max. He wasn't able to follow his dream and it crushed him. I didn't want to look back at my life with regrets. I owed it to myself to give it a go.

That was why, right there at that moment, I decided to do it. I was going to try and branch out on my own. To follow my dreams.

I wasn't able to make a relationship with Max work out, but I was determined to do whatever I could to finally make my career take off.

45

MAX

'You look like shit.' Colton opened the door to his house.

'Nice to see you too!' I replied, wheeling my suitcase into the hallway, slipping off my shoes then walking through the kitchen where Natalie and Betty were sitting at the table.

Colton was right though. I did look like shit, because last night I didn't sleep well.

Normally when I'd been travelling, even if I'd stayed at a fancy hotel, I was always happy to get home and sleep in my own bed. But last night, everything felt different.

No matter how hard I tried, I couldn't find a comfortable position to sleep in.

And everything felt so empty: the house and especially the bed.

I didn't smell Stella's gorgeous scent on my pillow or feel her tangling her legs in mine under the covers.

I'd lived in my house for years and had never had a problem with staying there alone. But last night I felt... lonely.

It just wasn't the same without her.

My mind racing all night can't have helped my insomnia

either. I must've spent hours trying to think of how to make it work.

I thought about asking Stella if she wanted to visit me somewhere whilst I was travelling. If we met up halfway through my trip, maybe the long-distance thing wouldn't be so bad.

But then I'd dismissed it. She'd just got back from a two-week holiday. Even though she worked for her mum, I was sure she couldn't take more time off work.

And I'd still be asking her to put her life on hold for me. A woman like Stella could have any guy she wanted. It wasn't fair to ask her to stop looking for a proper relationship with someone else, just in case I changed my mind about wanting one.

So I'd just have to cross my fingers and hope that when I got back she was still interested. Given how we'd left things at the airport though, I didn't rate my chances.

'Uncle Maxey!' Betty jumped off her seat. She ran over and threw her arms around my legs. Betty had her hair in two cute pigtails and was wearing the pink T-shirt I bought her on my last trip.

'Hey, you!' I quickly scooped her up, spinning her around the way I knew she liked.

'Did you like your holiday?' she asked as I placed her back on the ground. 'And did you stay until the end like you promised?'

'I did!'

'Yay!' she said enthusiastically. 'Did you bring me something?'

'Yep!' I went to the hallway, picked up a gift bag then went back to hand it to her.

'Sweeties *and* colouring pencils!' Betty beamed. 'Thank you!' She hugged my legs again.

'You're welcome. I know you like colouring. There's a notepad too.'

Stella had helped me pick the gifts when we visited Córdoba.

Stella.

Would it ever be possible for me to go five minutes without thinking about her?

'Why don't you help me in the garden.' Natalie gave me a knowing smile. 'Daddy and Uncle Max have some business to discuss.'

'On a Sunday?' Betty frowned. 'I thought business was what Daddy did at work. He doesn't work at the weekend.'

'This is a *different* type of business.' Natalie ushered Betty outside.

Once they'd shut the patio door, Colton pulled out a chair and sat directly in front of me.

'Spill,' he said.

I didn't even waste time trying to protest. Resistance was pointless. So I did what he'd asked and told him everything.

'And that's it. The end.'

'What d'you mean *that's it*? So you're just gonna give up?' Colton shook his head. 'I expected better from you, man. Especially after how you fucked up last time.'

'That's why I thought it was better to stop things now before I hurt her. Last time I didn't explain myself properly. This time I did. I've learnt from my mistakes.'

'You haven't learnt shit. If you had, you wouldn't let her slip through your fingers a second time.'

'So what was I supposed to do? Ask her to put her life on hold for me just in case I'm ready when I get back?'

'Newsflash: you can't always wait until you feel *ready* to do things. Otherwise you'd never do anything. Sometimes you just have to take the leap and hope that the parachute opens. Remember when Natalie first told me she was pregnant?'

'Yeah. You were shitting yourself.'

'Exactly. I didn't know anything about being a father. I hadn't had the best role model. I didn't feel ready. But I had to *make* myself ready. Even now sometimes I feel like I don't have a damn clue what I'm doing. There are days that I feel like the worst father in the world, but I keep going. Putting one foot in front of the other. All I can do is my best and pray that's enough. The same goes for relationships. They're scary. You'll make mistakes. But as long as you try your best and communicate, with the right person, you'll make it through and the highs will outweigh the lows.'

'That's deep.'

'It's the truth. Don't give up. You already have enough regrets. Don't add something that's easy to solve to that list.'

Maybe there was something in what he said, but I didn't agree that it'd be easy to solve.

'Let's just say I wanted to try, I still don't see how to make it work right now. Not until I've got these meetings overseas out of the way. I'm gonna be away for two months. It wouldn't be fair to ask her to wait for me.'

'So ask her to come with you.'

'I thought about it,' I rubbed the back of my neck, 'but she has to work. I couldn't expect her to drop everything for me.'

'I'd put money on the fact that Stella is just as miserable as you. And as for her job, didn't you say she wanted to do freelance design work? Those sketches you sent over were good. Much better than the other design agency.'

'We should hire her.' I paused. I didn't want Stella to think I was only asking her because I felt bad though.

'I agree. And if we did, she could work on the designs from anywhere in the world, right?'

'Right.'

I nodded, the jumble of thoughts I'd had in my head finally starting to unravel and slide together like a completed jigsaw puzzle.

'I'm gonna ask her. To do our rebranding. And to come with me. I'll work out the details this week whilst I'm in Dubai, then speak to her when I get back.'

'You sure you wanna wait 'til then?'

'Have you seen the time?' I pointed at my watch. 'I have to be at the airport in an hour and a half.'

'True,' Colton nodded. 'She's in South London, right?'

'Yep. So getting there now from here would probably take that long.' Like me, Colton lived in North London. 'And after all my screw-ups, I need to do things properly. I have to make sure it's an offer she can't refuse.'

'Finally the man starts talking sense!' Colton grinned.

Asking Stella to come with me was a big deal and there was chance that she'd slam the door in my face.

But if I did it right, she might just hear me out.

I needed to pull out all the stops. Show Stella how much she meant to me. I needed a grand gesture. Something that'd get her attention.

A light bulb went off in my head. And just like that, I knew what I planned to do.

It wouldn't be easy though.

Here's hoping I could make it work...

46

STELLA

It'd been a productive week. Hard, but I'd got through it.

Just.

Once Sammie left last Sunday, I'd spent most of the day holed up in my room, looking through the memory book like a saddo.

At first I'd told myself I didn't know what was wrong with me. I knew staring at the photos of me and Max together made things a million times worse, but I couldn't tear myself away from poring over the pages.

Then I'd start thinking about our last night and the things he'd arranged to make it special, like asking the chef to make my favourite food. Even after all of these years apart, Max still knew me better than any man ever had.

But by the time it got to Tuesday and I was still pining for him, I finally had to admit the truth: at least to myself.

I loved Max.

I didn't know if I'd ever stopped loving him.

Love wasn't like a tap you could just turn on and off. Real, deep love was like an endless river that flowed through peaks and valleys with no end.

I realised that my love for him had been dormant, but it'd never gone away completely. It was like my heart was always waiting for that moment that we'd see each other again.

And that was when I also realised that no matter what, as soon as Max was back from his travels, I'd go and see him. It was time to break down my walls. Let him in. I didn't want to be tough Stella. I wanted to be vulnerable, honest Stella. The woman he helped in the pool when her top flew off. The version of me that accepted his help when I was terrified of walking on that scary pathway.

At least if I told him how I felt instead of trying to pretend I didn't care, then I'd know that I did everything I could. I wouldn't have any regrets. Hopefully his feelings would've changed and he'd be willing to give us a go, but if not, I'd have proper closure and wouldn't have to wonder *what if*. I could move on properly with my life.

Once I'd come to terms with the fact that there was nothing I could do for the next two months, I threw myself into my work.

Marjorie said she was happy to work every afternoon which meant that once I'd gone through the emails in the morning and passed the orders to Mum, I could spend all afternoon and evening on my own venture.

There was so much to do, but I'd made a start on a business plan, drawn up a list of potential clients to contact and messaged some old colleagues to see if they'd heard about any design opportunities.

I'd also created a logo for my company: *Stellar Designs*. Next week I'd work on the website.

And I planned to look into taking a trip abroad.

Going to Spain had reminded me that there was a whole world out there to explore.

As much as I wanted to be with Max, I couldn't just wait around for two months. I'd wasted too much of my time sitting at home doing nothing. I didn't want to just exist any more. Now I wanted to keep living and enjoying life. Just like I'd done at The Love Hotel.

I didn't know yet whether or not I'd go on a solo trip or I'd invite Sammie, but I'd start by organising a weekend break.

I pulled out my desk drawer to get my passport. If I kept it out in full view, it'd motivate me every time I saw it.

That was odd. I continued rooting around the drawer but couldn't see it.

After jumping up from my desk, I went to the kitchen where Mum was working.

'Have you seen my passport?'

'Your passport?' she frowned. 'Why?'

'I thought it was in my desk drawer but I can't find it.'

'Maybe you left it in your suitcase. Do you have any plans for tomorrow?'

'Don't think so. I'll probably just keep working on my company stuff. You?'

'I was thinking of going for a walk near Kew Gardens. Want to join me?'

'Okay.' At least it'd get me out of the house.

Until then, I'd keep busy with my work.

Before I knew it, it was almost midnight. After I'd been to the bathroom, I climbed into bed.

I started tossing and turning. It'd been like this ever since I'd returned from Spain. I think the first night was an anomaly. I must've been so mentally exhausted I knocked out. But since then, I found it so hard to sleep.

I missed Max beside me.

I missed snuggling up in his arms.

I missed laying my head on his chest.

I missed the way he'd kiss the top of my head and hold me until I fell asleep.

Before I could stop myself, I reached for my phone and clicked the playlist link.

Even though I'd been desperate to hear what songs he'd added for our last day together, I'd managed to resist listening to it.

I knew that if I liked it, it'd ruin me. But I couldn't hold back any longer.

I started at the beginning where the songs were apologetic. With every song they became more emotional and heartfelt.

And when I reached the last set of songs, my heart melted.

He'd included 'Say You Won't Let Go' by James Arthur, John Legend's 'All of Me', 'Teenage Dream' from Katy Perry, 'Nothing Compares 2 U' by Sinéad O'Connor, 'The One That Got Away' by Katy Perry and 'I Will Always Love You' by Whitney Houston.

Max liked me.

He *really* liked me.

At that moment I wanted to call him. Speak to him. See his face, tell him how I felt, but it was two in the morning. Waking him up wouldn't be fair.

So instead I sent him a message.

> Hey. How are you? Can we talk?

There. Done.

Now I just had to hope that he replied.

* * *

When I woke up on Saturday morning, I reached straight for my phone, hoping there'd be a reply.

There wasn't.

I clicked on WhatsApp.

Max had read the message. Instantly, I panicked, thinking that he'd seen it but didn't want to reply. But then I tried to tell myself that maybe he was just busy. For all I knew, it could be the middle of the night wherever he was. I just had to be patient.

But when he hadn't replied hours later, I started to worry more. Maybe he wasn't interested like I'd hoped. After all, it'd been a whole week since we'd left The Love Hotel and he hadn't contacted me.

The slam of the front door snapped me out of my thoughts. Mum must've popped out.

I supposed I should get ready as we'd have to leave to catch the train then the Tube to Kew Gardens soon.

After showering and getting dressed, I went to the bathroom to do my make-up. Where the hell was my mascara? And my favourite lipstick? I went to Mum's bedroom to see if she'd borrowed it. We never usually shared make-up, but I was sure I'd left it in here the other day.

'You ready?' Mum called out. I didn't even hear her come back.

'Yeah. Have you seen my mascara?'

'Why?'

'Can't find it. Or my lipstick.'

'Can't you use another one?'

'They're my favourites!'

'Come on. We're going to miss the train!'

I quickly grabbed a lip gloss and my handbag then went downstairs.

Once we got to Victoria train station, we got the Tube which would take us directly to Kew Gardens. But when we pulled into the station, Mum didn't move.

'We're here.' I got up.

'Sit down a moment,' she said. 'We're taking a little detour. We're getting off at the next stop instead.'

'What? Why are we going to Richmond? I thought you wanted to visit Kew Gardens?'

Whilst my face was more creased than a pug's forehead, Mum was as cool as a cucumber and didn't say a word until the Tube pulled into Richmond station.

'Follow me,' she said.

I trailed behind her, wondering where we could be going. A few minutes later, I stopped in my tracks.

'Oh my God!' I gasped. 'This is so cool! This is where they film *Ted Lasso*. It's a TV show. I was watching it with Max...' My voice trailed off.

Shamefully I'd checked my phone throughout our journey here and there was still no reply from him.

My stomach twisted. I hated that I missed him so much.

'Really?' Mum said. 'Where did they film?'

'Look – over there!' I jumped up and down on the spot like I'd just been offered a giant slice of chocolate fudge cake. 'It's the pub! That's where Ted, the main character, and all the football fans go in the show. I didn't realise it was real!'

The name was different. This was called The Prince's Head whereas in the programme it was called The Crown & Anchor.

'That *is* very cool. Want me to take a photo of you in front of it?'

'Yes!' I replied.

As I stood in front of it and Mum snapped away, excitement flooded my veins. I couldn't wait to tell Max that I'd been here.

Then I remembered. I might not ever speak to him again. My stomach sank.

'We can go inside if you want?'

'I don't know.' My shoulders slumped.

'Come on.' Mum ushered me in. 'I need to use the loo.'

'Okay.' I followed Mum inside, dragging my feet, wondering if I should just send Max the photo anyway.

Mum stepped aside and when I looked straight ahead, I gasped.

No way.

It couldn't be.

If Jason Sudeikis aka Ted Lasso himself was here, I would've been less shocked.

But it wasn't an actor that had caused my jaw to crash to the floor.

It was the man I knew and loved.

Sitting at the bar was Max.

Flashing me that gorgeous smile that made my heart race and my knees weak.

I wouldn't have to send photos or message him because he was right here.

And I didn't think I'd ever been so happy to see anyone in my life.

47

MAX

For the past half an hour, my heart had raced so much that I thought it was gonna fly out of my chest.

And I'd used so many serviettes from the bar to wipe the sweat off my forehead I was sure the barman was gonna add it to my tab.

But when Stella spotted me and her face broke into a huge smile, all of the nerves vanished and every atom in my body came alive.

She looked happy to see me.

Thank fuck for that.

First hurdle down, several more to go.

God, she looked beautiful.

Stella was dressed in a long yellow floral dress and she looked like sunshine. All I wanted to do was jump up, pull her into me and kiss her. But I had to wait. Go at her pace.

I'd said to Colton that I wanted to do things properly and I meant it.

'Max!' she shouted. 'What are you... how come you're here?'

'Stell.' I took her hands in mine. 'I asked your mum to bring you here because there's something I need to tell you.'

'Mum?' Her head spun around to face her mum. 'You knew Max would be here?' She nodded. 'I... I have so many questions!'

'Maybe save them until later, love. He's trying to tell you something!'

'Yeah, course. Sorry!' Stella turned back to me.

'So, I'm not good at expressing myself but I... Even though it's only been a week since we came back from The Love Hotel, I missed you. *So much*. Those two weeks together were some of the best in my life. And I want more of it. I want more fun times together. I missed waking up with you. I missed you lying on my chest. I missed snuggling up on the sofa and watching *Ted Lasso* with you. I missed hearing you laugh, seeing your smile, touching you...'

'Ooh, hello!' Heather – Stella's mum – gasped. 'Oops. Sorry. Didn't mean to interrupt. Do continue!'

'I miss everything. I don't want to be without you, Stella. I love you and I want to be with you. If you're interested, I'd like us to be together.'

Stella stood there staring at me, her mouth open.

It was obvious she was in shock, but I couldn't work out whether it was good shock or *no fucking way* shock.

Seconds passed in silence, but it felt like hours. I knew she'd be surprised to see me, but I was hoping she was still interested.

When I played the songs she'd added on the playlist, which included Mariah Carey's 'We Belong Together' it seemed like it, but as the silence stretched, my nerves came back.

'Well, say something, Stella! Put the poor guy out of his misery!'

'Yes!' she shouted, snapping out her trance. 'Sorry, I was just, I wasn't expecting you to be here or to say all those things so I just needed a moment to take it all in. To check I wasn't dreaming. It seems a bit surreal. Being in the *Ted Lasso* pub with the man I've always loved telling me he loves me too and wants to be with me. This is real, right?'

'Yep.' I brushed my thumb over her cheek, then paused as I replayed what she'd just said. 'Wait. Did you just say you've always loved me?'

'I did,' she said quickly.

'Well, shit.' I grinned, my heart inflating like a hot air balloon. 'I thought I was the only one. The truth is, I never stopped loving you. I don't know if there was ever a day that I didn't think of you. Whenever I saw something funny or interesting, I always wanted to tell you about it. Or I'd wonder what you were doing and how you were.'

'Really?'

'Really. But I was never brave enough to get in touch. Not after how badly I'd messed things up. I didn't think I deserved to speak to you again. I thought you deserved someone better.'

'I wish you'd tried, but it doesn't matter now. That's in the past. Let's just focus on the future.'

'*Our* future. *Together.*'

'I like the sound of that,' she smiled and my heart swelled.

'Good. Can I kiss you now?' I grinned.

'I thought you'd never ask.'

I leant forward and pressed my lips onto hers. My body lit up like a fireworks display.

God, I'd missed the softness of her lips. As our mouths moved against each other, I wrapped my arms around her waist, then trailed my hands down her back.

After sliding my tongue in her mouth, the kiss deepened. Our lips grew hungrier, like it had been years since we'd kissed instead of just days. Stella's hand grabbed my arse and she pressed her body against me, my rock-hard cock prodding her stomach.

The loud sound of someone clearing their throat snapped us out of our kiss and we pulled away.

I'd completely forgotten we were in a busy pub. When I was kissing Stella, it was like nothing else existed.

'Sorry,' Stella apologised to the woman glaring at us.

'Don't apologise!' Heather chirped. 'This is wonderful! I'm so happy for you both! Are you going to tell her about the other thing?'

'What other thing?' Stella frowned.

'Oh. Oh, yeah!' I chuckled. 'I got a bit distracted. So.' I took Stella's hands and fixed my gaze on her. 'Remember how I was just saying that I didn't want to be without you?'

'Yeah,' she nodded.

'Well, remember I've gotta go away on business for a couple of months?' Stella nodded again and my heart thudded. 'I was kinda wondering if you'd like to come with me? The thought of being away from you for that long kills me. I'll pay for your flight and take care of all the expen...'

'I'd love to!' She threw her arms around me. From how tightly she was squeezing me, I could tell she was happy, which was a relief. My shoulders loosened. 'But when? I thought you had to leave soon?'

'Yeah. Flight leaves in four hours.'

'I didn't realise you were leaving today! I want to come, but I'd need to arrange cover for work. And find my passport which has disappeared so I couldn't do all that before check-in. And don't I need a visa or some official paperwork to travel too?'

'It's all taken care of,' I said calmly. 'Your mum's been really helpful. Between her and my secretary, Rita, they got everything prepared.'

Stella's mouth opened to speak, then closed again. I could hear the cogs in her brain turning at a million miles an hour.

'And I haven't packed. I don't have any clothes or toiletries!'

'Your mum packed a suitcase with the essentials. But if you need anything else, we can buy it there.'

'Oh my God,' Stella laughed. 'I don't know what to say. Thanks! Wait. Is that why I couldn't find my passport the other day, or my mascara and lipstick?'

'That's right,' Heather nodded. 'I packed all your favourites. Not your Waterfall Turbo 3,000 though. Didn't think you'd need it with Max around!'

'Mum!' Stella burst out laughing. I did too. She was lucky to have a mum who was so cool.

'There's some new thongs in there too. Max said you'd *lost* the others,' she winked.

I may have lied about them getting *lost*. I couldn't exactly tell Heather that I'd ripped them off her daughter because I couldn't wait to bury myself inside her.

'Thanks, Mum,' Stella smiled. 'How did you even get the suitcase to Max?'

'He collected it this morning.'

'That's why I heard the door?' Stella asked and her mum nodded. 'Wow! You two are good. Devious, but dangerously good!'

'I thought seeing as it's for a great cause, you wouldn't mind. I couldn't bear to see you moping around the house any more.'

At least I wasn't the only one who'd been moping. I expected Stella to brush it off, but she didn't.

'It's true.' She wrapped her arm around my waist and rested her head on my shoulder. 'I was really sad without you.'

'Me too. I'm sorry it took so long to get in touch. I wanted to call you sooner, but I needed to organise everything first. And I felt really bad about not replying to your text yesterday, but I knew if I did, I'd say something to spoil the surprise.'

'All is forgiven!' Stella kissed me softly on the lips.

'Thank God,' I said. 'There's just one more thing I need to ask you.'

'What's that?' Stella said.

'Your mum mentioned you've been busy setting up your own design business. And I wondered if you'd consider taking on a new client? As you know, we've got a new range coming out and we're looking for someone amazing to create our branding and marketing materials. I sent your sketches to my team and they loved them. Obviously you'll need to send us a quote and everything, but we'd like you to start as soon as possible. Maybe you could work on it whilst we're away. What do you think?'

'I'd love to!' Stella jumped up and down on the spot before throwing her arms around my neck. 'Thank you. I won't let you down!'

'You're welcome. And I know. You're so talented and now more people will get the chance to see that.'

Stella flashed the smile that I loved so much.

'Awww, you two.' Heather hugged us, tears rolling down her cheeks. 'I'm so glad you're together. I always thought you were made for each other. Right.' She broke away. 'I've done enough third-wheeling for today. I'll leave you lovebirds to it. Hope you have the best time together. Message me when you land and send pictures!'

'Will do,' Stella said. 'And Mum...' Stella moved her arms from my neck, grabbed her mum and gave her another big hug. 'Thanks so much for everything. Without you, I'd never have gone to The Love Hotel, I wouldn't have been reunited with Max again and I wouldn't be going to America and Australia! Still can't believe it!'

'You're welcome, darling. Take care of yourself and your lovely man.' Heather kissed Stella on the cheek. 'Love you.' She waved then left the pub.

'So.' I took Stella's hand and led her to two seats that had just become vacant. 'Fancy grabbing a quick bite and a drink here, then having a little wander around Ted Lasso's town before we head to the airport?'

'Sounds perfect!'

'Oh, and I've downloaded the final season on my iPad so we can watch it together on the plane too.'

'Amazing!'

'I'm so damn happy. Y'know, I always thought you were the one that got away. But now I know you'll always be *the one*. I love you, Stella Matthews.'

'I love you too, Max Moore.'

As our lips touched and we kissed again, I was so glad we'd been given a second chance to be together.

And I knew that the second time around was going to be even better than the first.

EPILOGUE
STELLA

Four months later

As the referee blew the final whistle, me, Max, Colton and Natalie all jumped up from our seats and cheered.

'What a brilliant game!' Max shouted. 'That goal Bellingham scored was perfection.'

'It really was!' I gushed.

The four of us had flown to Madrid for the weekend for some sightseeing and to watch Real Madrid play.

Ever since we'd got back from our travels, Max had watched a game every Saturday with Colton, which made me so happy. Max's passion for football was back on track.

We'd had a fantastic time in the US, Australia and Europe. As Max had said from the start, most of his days were spent meeting potential suppliers, manufacturers and distributors, but I didn't mind. I wanted to see his company do well. I wanted him to bring his mum's dream to life, so I supported him 100 per cent.

Plus, I was busy working on my own career. As well as finishing off my business plan and setting up my own website, I was flat out creating the branding for Max's new body care range, so it all worked out well.

In the evenings we'd met for dinner and at the weekends or whenever Max had time off, we'd gone sightseeing.

We'd visited the famous Sydney Opera House and went scuba diving at the Great Barrier Reef. An experience I'll never forget for as long as I live.

In the US we spent a day in New York and visited the Empire State Building and other epic attractions.

Although we didn't spend a lot of time visiting places in Europe because the schedule was tight, neither of us minded. It just meant we had an excuse to come back in our own time and visit each country properly.

Hence why I'd suggested we have a weekend away in Madrid. I remembered how much Max had enjoyed seeing Real Madrid play in Cádiz during our stay at The Love Hotel and thought it'd be nice for him to see them at Santiago Bernabéu – their home stadium.

Inviting Colton and Natalie to join us made perfect sense. Just like I was grateful to Mum for applying for me to go to The Love Hotel, I was glad Colton and Natalie had arranged for Max to go too. Without them, we wouldn't be together and so blissfully happy.

Colton had always been a rock for Max and Natalie was adorable. We both got on like a house on fire and I loved visiting them on Sunday mornings for breakfast and playing with Betty.

Speaking of houses, I wasn't living with Mum any more. Within two weeks of our travels, Max asked if I wanted to move in together when we got back. And of course, I said yes. I loved being with him and knew we'd get on well.

Now, instead of saving for a mortgage of my own, we'd talked about whether I wanted Max to put my name on his mortgage or buy somewhere new, together.

To anyone who didn't know us, it'd seem like things were moving fast. But when you'd already wasted years being apart from the person you loved, you didn't want to waste another second. Everything felt so right. Like we were both where we wanted to be.

My career was starting to take off (I also had two exciting new business meetings booked in for the next two weeks) and Max had learnt to have more of a work/life balance too. He delegated more, rarely worked late and he'd even started seeing a therapist to help him work through the trauma from his past. It was early days, but so far, he said it was helping.

The sharp ring of my mobile snapped me out of my thoughts.

'It's Jasmine.' I showed Max the screen.

'She's called a few times so you'd better get it.'

'Hey!' I answered. 'How are you?' Since leaving The Love Hotel, Jasmine and I had kept in regular contact. At first she just called to check how Max and I were, but now we spoke at least once a week. Max and I had even agreed that the next time we went to Spain we'd go and see her.

'Not good...' Her voice shook.

'Why?' I frowned. 'What's up?'

'It's Alejandro. Something's happened between us. We...'

Jasmine had tried to deny her attraction to the chef for ages, but I always knew she liked him. There was a loud commotion in the background.

'Hello? Jasmine? Are you still there?'

The phone line cut out.

'What's up?' Max said.

'Not sure,' I said, trying to redial Jasmine's number. The

phone rang out. 'Sounds like something happened with Jasmine and Alejandro but the line went dead before she could tell me.'

'Is that your Love Alchemist lady?' Natalie said.

'Yeah.'

'I hope she finds love,' Natalie added. 'She deserves it after she brought you two together.'

'Definitely,' Colton nodded.

'So.' Natalie turned to Max. 'Have you given any more thought to the offer?'

'I have,' Max said as we filed out of the stadium and onto the street.

'And?' Colton said as we headed towards the exit.

Natalie and Colton had put Max forward to coach the girls' football team at Betty's school. Of course the head teacher had loved the idea and offered Max the voluntary role straight away and they were waiting to hear his response.

'*And* I'll do it!' he beamed.

'Yes!' Natalie cheered.

'That's great news!' Colton patted Max on the back.

I was so proud when he told me earlier.

Seeing him bring football back into his life brought me so much joy and now knowing he was going to help a future generation of footballers made me so happy too.

'I'm so proud of you.' I leant forward and kissed Max on the lips.

'Thanks. I'm proud of you too,' he said. 'We make a great team.'

'We do.'

'Say cheese.' Max held up his phone and took a selfie, which I knew we'd print and add to our growing memory book. 'Here's to creating many, many more happy memories, *together*.'

ACKNOWLEDGEMENTS

Yay! It's time for one of my favourite parts of the book-writing process. Please put your hands together for the amazing people who helped me to bring *The One That Got Away* to life.

First up, huge thanks to my wonderful husband for your constant support, epic hugs and for introducing me to so many beautiful locations in Spain which gave me loads of inspiration for this book. *Te quiero.*

To my fantastic friend, Jas. Thanks for your unwavering belief in me and for visiting the Caminito del Rey then sending me pics and videos so that I didn't have to do the terrifying walk myself!

To Mum, thank you for always encouraging me, reading my first drafts, giving helpful feedback and your greeting card worthy words of wisdom.

To my smart, sassy and beautiful first-born niece: I don't know how you do it but your eagle eyes always spot things that would've been missed, so thanks for meticulously reading over my novels and for being so brilliant!

To Dad, thanks for your constant support and sharing your football expertise for this novel. If you'd like to see the sections you helped with, I'll send them separately, because this book is *way* too spicy for you to read, lol!

To Emma Gibbs: thank you for championing my books and shouting about them on social media. Your enthusiasm for my characters is infectious. I truly appreciate all that you do.

To my lovely editor Megan Haslam, thanks for your enthusiasm for this book and for the fantastic suggestions that helped my words sparkle.

Huge thanks to the brilliant Boldwood team for giving me such a warm welcome and working so hard to bring my novel to a wider audience.

Shout-out to my talented cover designer Rachel Lawston. You knocked it out of the park with this cover! Thanks for making my book look so pretty!

Thanks to my copyeditor Cecily Blench and proofreader Rachel Sargeant for helping to polish this novel.

I'm endlessly grateful for the brilliant bloggers, Bookstagrammers, ARC readers and BookTokers who read and wrote lovely reviews for this book. I really appreciate you helping to spread the word about my novel. You rock!

And last, but by no means least, to *you*, my lovely reader I send a HUGE, heartfelt thank-you, with a cherry on top for buying and reading *The One That Got Away*. It's because of you that I have my dream career. I appreciate you SO much!

Right, I better get back to writing Jasmine and Alejandro's love story. Until next time...

Lots of love,

Olivia x

ABOUT THE AUTHOR

Olivia Spring is a bestselling author of contemporary women's fiction and romantic comedies, now writing spicy romance for Boldwood.

Sign up to Olivia's mailing list for news, competitions and updates on future books.

Visit Olivia's website: www.oliviaspring.com

Follow Olivia on social media here:

facebook.com/ospringauthor

x.com/ospringauthor

instagram.com/ospringauthor

bookbub.com/authors/olivia-spring

tiktok.com/@oliviaspringauthor

LOVE NOTES

LOVE IN EVERY CHAPTER

WHERE ALL YOUR ROMANCE
DREAMS COME TRUE!

THE HOME OF BESTSELLING
ROMANCE AND WOMEN'S
FICTION

 WARNING:
MAY CONTAIN SPICE

SIGN UP TO OUR
NEWSLETTER

https://bit.ly/Lovenotesnews

Boldwood

Boldwood Books is an award-winning fiction publishing company seeking out the best stories from around the world.

Find out more at www.boldwoodbooks.com

Join our reader community for brilliant books, competitions and offers!

Follow us
@BoldwoodBooks
@TheBoldBookClub

Sign up to our weekly
deals newsletter

https://bit.ly/BoldwoodBNewsletter

Printed in Great Britain
by Amazon